...nnot pretend what happened did not occur.'

'We cannot change it

Lord Brentmore relea

'Perhaps it is best tha

'Leave?' Her voic

daggers at him. 'Leave your children.

use me as an excuse to neglect them. If you

have no wish to help them, then, indeed, go

back to the pleasures of London. Forget them

as you have done before—'

'Enough!' He closed the distance between them
again. 'You forget your place, Governess!'

He sounded just like the old Marquess. She
did not back down, none the less. Instead
she looked directly into his eyes. 'Last night
you lamented the damage done your children
by your absence. Now you seize upon the
slimmest excuse to leave them again.'

His gaze was entrapped by her blue eyes—
so clear, so forthright and brave. Before he
realised it his hands had rested on her
shoulders, drawing her even closer to him.
A memory, foggy and blurred, returned. He
remembered kissing her...

He stepped back, jarred at how easily his own
behaviour turned scandalous. 'See, Anna—
Miss Hill—how easily I might compromise
you a

AUTHOR NOTE

BORN TO SCANDAL is my homage to Charlotte Brontë's *Jane Eyre*—a story of secrets and betrayals, with a governess at the centre of it. Charlotte Brontë had been a governess in Yorkshire in the late 1830s, and well knew the loneliness of the position, later drawing on her experiences in writing her timeless classic.

A governess in the nineteenth century was often a pitiable creature. Neither servant nor family, she lived a lonely life between the two, working long hours caring for children, receiving little pay and no protection from those who might abuse her. Worst of all, she had little recourse for anything better.

Jane Austen, that astute social observer of her time, certainly shared the perception of the governess as a sad creature. In *Emma*, Austen even likens the prospect to slavery. Her character Jane Fairfax, who feels fated to become a governess, remarks that the governess trade is '...widely different certainly as to the guilt of those who carry it on; but as to the greater misery of the victims, I do not know where it lies.'

Never was there a Regency character more in need of a happy ending!

I wondered... What if I created a governess with a past even more scandalous than Jane Eyre's and an aristocratic hero who, like Mr Rochester, is desperate to overcome the scandal in his own life? How could I give these two their happy ending?

BORN TO SCANDAL is the result.

I love to hear from readers. Visit me on Facebook and Twitter, or come to my website at http://dianegaston.com

BORN TO SCANDAL

Diane Gaston

MILLS & BOON

First published in Great Britain 2012
by Mills & Boon, an imprint of Harlequin (UK) Limited.
Harlequin (UK) Limited, Eton House, 18-24 Paradise Road,
Richmond, Surrey TW9 1SR

© Diane Perkins 2012

ISBN: 978 0 263 89283 3

As a psychiatric social worker, **Diane Gaston** spent years helping others create real-life happy endings. Now Diane crafts fictional ones, writing the kind of historical romance she's always loved to read. The youngest of three daughters of a US Army Colonel, Diane moved frequently during her childhood, even living for a year in Japan. It continues to amaze her that her own son and daughter grew up in one house in Northern Virginia. Diane still lives in that house, with her husband and three very ordinary housecats. Visit Diane's website at http://dianegaston.com

Previous novels by the same author:

THE MYSTERIOUS MISS M
THE WAGERING WIDOW
A REPUTABLE RAKE
INNOCENCE AND IMPROPRIETY
A TWELFTH NIGHT TALE
  (in *A Regency Christmas* anthology)
THE VANISHING VISCOUNTESS
SCANDALISING THE TON
JUSTINE AND THE NOBLE VISCOUNT
  (in *Regency Summer Scandals*)
GALLANT OFFICER, FORBIDDEN LADY*
CHIVALROUS CAPTAIN, REBEL MISTRESS*
VALIANT SOLDIER, BEAUTIFUL ENEMY*
A NOT SO RESPECTABLE GENTLEMAN?†

*Three Soldiers mini-series
†linked by character

And in Mills & Boon® Historical *Undone!* eBooks:

THE UNLACING OF MISS LEIGH
THE LIBERATION OF MISS FINCH

Chapter One

Mayfair—May 1816

The Marquess of Brentmore walked out of the library of his London town house and wandered into the drawing room.

He'd agreed to consider his cousin's scheme. What the devil had he been thinking?

He strode to the window and gave a fierce tug at the brocade curtains. Why hang heavy curtains when London offered precious little sunlight as it was? One of many English follies. What he would give for one fine Irish day.

At times like this, when restlessness plagued him, his thoughts always turned to Ireland. He could never entirely banish his early years from his mind, no matter how hard his English grandfather, the old marquess, had tried to have it beat out of him.

He stared out the window, forcing his mind back to the weather. The sky looked more grey than usual. More rain coming, no doubt.

A young woman paced in Cavendish Square across the street. Something about her caught his eye and captured his attention.

He could not look away.

She brimmed with emotion and seemed to be struggling to contain it. He felt it as acutely as if those emotions also resonated inside him, as if he again waged a battle with a fiery temperament. The Irish inside him, the old marquess always told him.

Were his thoughts to always travel back to those days?

Better to attend to the pretty miss in the square.

What was she doing there all alone, looking as unsettled as he felt? She stirred him in a way the countless *ton*'s daughters who attended the Season's balls and musicales failed to do. Foolish girls, who gazed at him hopefully until their mamas steered them away, whispering about his *reputation*.

Was it his disastrous first marriage those mothers objected to? he wondered. Or was it the taint of his Irish blood? The title of marquess did not make up for either one.

He did not want any of it. Not the Season. Not

the marriage mart, certainly, no matter what his cousin said. He'd done that once and look where it had led him. No, he had no wish to be stirred by any woman, not even a glimpse of one, pacing across the street. He had work to do.

He pushed away from the window, but, at that same moment, she turned and the expression of anxious anticipation on her face cut straight to his heart.

He could see her eyes were large and wide, even from this distance. Her lips looked as if kissed by roses. Dark auburn hair peeked from her trim bonnet and the blue muslin of her skirt fluttered in the rising winds, showing a glimpse of her slim ankles.

He took in a quick breath.

She gleamed with expectation. Passion. Hope. Fear. She roused him straight from his heart to his loins, something not easily done, certainly not since Eunice soured all women for him.

Was she waiting for someone? A man? Was this to be some forbidden tryst?

Brent bit down on a stab of envy. Once he would have yearned to have such a young lady flouting respectability…to meet him.

He spun away from the window, dropping the brocade curtain again to block out the tempting sight of her.

What foolishness. Having endured a marriage

from hell, he well knew how easily passion could lead to misery.

Brent marched back to the library and the piles of paper on his desk. He riffled through his correspondence. With one hand he lifted a letter and re-read the news from Brentmore. Parker, his man of business, was there taking matters well in hand.

The children's elderly governess had died suddenly. Parker had been there and was able to attend to her affairs. He'd seen to her funeral and burial, but, damnation—how much were two young children supposed to endure?

First their mother's death…now their governess?

Brent rubbed his face.

His children had suffered too much in their young lives. Perhaps his cousin was right. Perhaps it was time for him to consider marrying again. Eunice had been dead a year and the children needed a mother to watch over their care, to handle matters about governesses and such, to make certain their lives were worry-free.

Brent knew nothing of children. Eunice had taken charge of them and resented his interference. He'd been a virtual stranger to them. His brief visits to the children since Eunice's death had been almost a formality. The governess always assured him she had the children under excellent control. Who was Brent to question her years of experience? When he'd been a boy, the old marquess had left him in the care of rather harsh tutors and then sent him off to school. He hardly saw the man until he'd returned from his Grand Tour. From what he could tell, other peers were similarly uninvolved in the care of their children.

Brent pressed his fingers against the smooth dark wood of his desk. He always felt sick inside when thinking of his children and how they would suffer for the sins of their parents. Better to go back to the drawing-room window and pine over a passionate young woman awaiting her paramour, than agonise over what he could not change.

There was a knock. Davies, his butler, opened the door a crack. 'Pardon, your lordship. A Miss Hill to see you. Says she has an appointment.'

His mind went blank. An appointment?

Ah, yes. Sometimes luck actually shone on him. At White's last night, he'd overheard someone saying he had a governess to fob off on someone. No longer needed her and wanted to settle her elsewhere as soon as possible. Brent told the fellow—who had it been?—to send the woman to him today. He wanted this problem of the children quickly solved, even if he had no clue what to look for in a prospective governess.

'Send her in.' Brent put down the letter and sat behind his desk.

'Miss Hill, m'lord,' Davies announced.

A soft feminine voice murmured, 'My lord.'

Brent raised his eyes and every sensation in his body flared.

Standing before him was the passionate young lady he'd spied in the square. She took two steps towards him, close enough for him to catch the faint scent of lavender and to see that her large, wide eyes were startlingly blue and even more vibrant than the blue of her most un-governess-like dress. Fringed with long curling dark lashes, those eyes gazed at him with the same hope and fear he'd witnessed from the window.

Up close she did not disappoint. With skin as smooth and flawless as a Canova statue, she bloomed with youth. Her rose-coloured lips were endearingly moist. Worst of all, her obvious nervousness piqued tender feelings inside him, a much greater danger to him than his body's baser response.

'Anna Hill, sir.' She made a small curtsy.

His gaze seemed unable to break away from how gracefully she moved, the expectant brightness in her eyes, the rise and fall of her chest.

She was no governess. That was apparent with a glance. She was quality, some society daughter all dressed up to impress.

She lifted her chin in a show of bravado and he broke his gaze, lowering it to the papers on his desk.

'This will not do at all, miss.' Whatever her game—attempting to compromise him into marriage or some other foolish idea—he was not playing. 'You may leave.'

She did not move.

He glanced at her again and waved her away with his fingers. 'I said you may leave.'

Two spots of red tinted her cheeks.

Damnation. He did not want to care about upsetting her.

She lifted herself to a dignified height and walked haughtily to the door. Yes, she was definitely quality.

As she turned the latch and opened the door a crack, he spoke again. 'Let this be a lesson to you, Miss Hill.'

She whirled around, arching one brow. 'A lesson, sir?'

Brent rose and impulsively walked towards her, closing the distance in a few long strides. She stood her ground, fixing her eyes on his approaching form. He put his hand on the door, whether to close it or force it open, he did not know. It brought him inches from her.

But she suddenly seemed small and vulnerable.

'You would not have gained entry, but for the fact that I was expecting a woman applying for the position of governess.' He deliberately flicked his gaze down to her breast, to intimidate her and teach her how dangerous being alone with a man could be. 'You are no governess.'

She, however, did not flinch. 'How would you know, sir, when you are not civil enough to hear my qualifications?'

Qualifications? Ha!

He touched her shoulder, rubbing his finger lightly over the cloth of her pelisse. 'You do not dress like a governess.'

She pulled her shoulder away. 'I do not know who you think I am, sir, but I have come to enquire about the position of governess. I concede I do not yet have the wardrobe of a governess.' Her lovely blue eyes flashed with fleeting pain. 'My clothes are provided by Lady Charlotte, for whom I act as companion.'

He shook his head in confusion. 'Lady Charlotte?'

She lowered her gaze. 'Earl Lawton's daughter.'

That's who it was! Brent felt like slapping his forehead. Lord Lawton had set up this interview. Good God. *This* was the governess.

It was her turn to look confused. 'Did Lord Lawton not explain my situation?'

Brent had consumed a lot of brandy that night. He did not remember much of what Lawton explained, only that there was a governess when he needed one.

'You tell me, Miss Hill.' He pushed the door

shut and stepped back a more respectable distance.

She averted her gaze. 'I have been Lady Charlotte's companion. Now that she is launched in society, my services are no longer needed.'

He turned sceptical again. 'Companion, Miss Hill? You look as if you just stepped out of the schoolroom and are in need of a chaperone yourself.'

Her chin rose. 'I was Lady Charlotte's *companion*, not her chaperone. I—I've been her companion since we were children. The situation was...' she paused as if searching for the right words '...unusual.'

He folded his arms across his chest. 'Explain it to me.'

Her eyes sparked with annoyance, but she also looked on her guard. 'I was raised with Lady Charlotte. She was an only child and extremely timid. She needed a companion. To take the place of an older sister, so to speak.' She locked her gaze with his. 'I also must tell you that I was— am—the daughter of Lord Lawton's servants. My mother is a laundress and my father a groom.'

Brent shrugged. His lineage was nearly as undesirable. His mother had been as poor as an Irish woman could be. Brent had spent his early years on his Irish grandfather's tenant farm in Culleen.

Until his English grandfather took him away. An uncle he'd not known existed died and suddenly Brent was heir to a title he'd known nothing of and sent to a land he'd considered the enemy's.

'I was raised as a lady,' Miss Hill went on. 'I studied the same lessons as Lady Charlotte. Learned everything she learned.' She reached in the pocket of her pelisse and withdrew a paper. She handed it to him. 'I have written it out.'

His fingers grazed hers as he took the paper. He noticed that her glove was carefully mended.

He pretended to read, then glanced back at her. His bare fingers still registered the soft texture of her glove. 'My apologies, Miss Hill.'

She straightened her spine, as imperious as a lady patroness of Almack's.

Her neck, so erect and slim, begged for his fingers to measure its length. In fact, his fingers wished to continue lower to the swell of her breasts—

'Why do you regard me so?' Her voice quivered slightly.

Good God, he'd been contemplating seduction.

Why did this beauty wish to bury herself in the thankless job of governess? Surely she knew the perils that befell a young woman in the employ of the wealthy and privileged. A governess had neither the protection of the other servants, nor that of society. She would be prey for any man who wished to seduce her.

He shut his eyes and turned to the bookshelves, fingering the bindings. 'My apologies once more, Miss Hill. I fail to understand how a young woman of your—' he turned back to her, involuntarily flicking another full-length gaze '—particular disposition would seek the position of governess.'

Her eyebrows rose in a look of superiority. 'Do you doubt my ability to perform the task?'

He admired her bravery much more than was prudent. 'You are very young.'

Seating himself on a chair by the library window, he stretched out his legs and crossed them at the ankle.

Her chin lifted again. 'My youth is an asset, Lord Brentmore.'

He frowned. 'Precisely how old are you?'

She pursed her lips. 'I am twenty.'

'So old as that.' He spoke with sarcasm.

She took a step towards him. 'My youth shall lend energy to the education of my charges.'

He tapped on the arm of the chair. The previous governess had been ancient. Retaining her had been a terrible error. Would hiring one so young also be a mistake?

'I shall understand the children better,' she went on. 'I well recall the mischief of young children.'

He narrowed his eyes. 'I do not need a governess who would join them in mischief.'

'I would not!' His insinuation obviously irritated her. 'I am a most sober young lady.'

He stood and moved close to her again, close enough for his skin to warm from the proximity.

'Tell me more, Miss Hill.' His voice turned low.

She backed away, her hand fluttering to her hair, trying to brush a tendril off her cheek. 'I know I am not a lady, precisely, but I was trained in the same way. I received every advantage....' Her voice trailed off.

Curse him. He needed to keep his distance.

She took another breath. 'There is another reason to engage me, sir.'

'Pray tell,' he said.

She looked him in the eye. 'I have an acute appreciation of learning, my lord. My unique situation—that of one who would never otherwise be so educated—makes me appreciate the advantage. It has opened the world to me.' She swept her arm towards the walls covered with leather-bound books. 'I would show your children the world.'

For the first time, her face filled with sincere pleasure. It touched something deep within him, something he needed to keep buried. 'You would create a bluestocking.'

'Indeed not,' she snapped. 'I would create a lady.' She pointed to the paper she'd handed him. 'I learned all the feminine arts. Stitchery, watercolours, the pianoforte. Manners and comportment and dancing, as well.' She jabbed her finger at her list. 'I also have skills in mathematics and Latin, so I am well able to help prepare a boy for Eton…' Her voice trailed off as if she feared she'd said too much. Her eyes pleaded. 'I would please you, my lord. I am certain I would.'

He forced his gaze downwards, as hungry as a starving man for some of that youthful passion. Lawd. He was only thirty-three, but, at this moment, he felt like Methuselah.

The children deserved a proper education. A proper upbringing. He tapped a finger against his leg.

More than that, his children deserved some joy. The children were innocents, even if they embodied all his failures and mistakes. Let this governess—this breath of spring air—be a gift to them.

What's more, she would be in a household where no man would take advantage of her. It was not as if he would be tempted. He hated Brentmore Hall and spent as little time there as possible.

He allowed his gaze to wander along the bookshelves, less dangerous than looking again into those hopeful eyes.

'You need not attire yourself in drab greys,' he finally said. It would be a shame to conceal all that loveliness under high necklines and long sleeves. 'Your present wardrobe should suffice.'

'I do not understand.' Her voice turned breathy. 'Do you mean—I have the position?'

He swallowed. 'Yes, Miss Hill. You have the position.'

She gasped. 'My lord! You will not regret this, I assure you.'

Her relief was palpable and the smile that broke out on her face made his insides clench.

He cleared his throat. 'You will make yourself ready to assume your duties within the week.'

Her eyes glittered with sudden tears, and his arms flinched with an impulse to hold her and reassure her that all would be well, that she had nothing to worry about.

'I will be ready, sir.' Even her voice rasped with emotion.

He had to glance away. 'I will send word to Lord Lawton that I have hired you.'

Anna blinked away relieved tears furious at herself for allowing her emotions to overrun her at this important moment. She wanted— needed—to remain strong or risk the chance that this marquess would again change his mind.

She'd not imagined him to be so formidable, nor so tall. And young. She'd thought he'd be like the gentlemen who called upon Lord and Lady Lawton, shorter than herself, with rounded bellies, and at least ten years older than the marquess. His eyes, as dark as the hair that curled at the nape of his neck and framed his face, unnerved her. Her legs trembled each time he looked at her with those disquieting eyes. Especially when he dismissed her without even allowing her to speak. At that moment she'd been sure all was lost.

What would she have done? Lord Lawton had made it clear there were limits to the assistance he'd render to help her find employment. And there was no one else she could turn to in London. Her parents and all the other people she knew were back at Lawton.

But the marquess had hired her! Even after she'd lost her temper with him. Even after that speech of hers about her esteem of learning.

Hopefully her love of learning would be enough to make her a governess, because she possessed no other qualifications for the job.

'Well.' She struggled for what to say next. 'Excellent.'

His brows lowered again.

Oh, my. What if he changed his mind?

She cleared her throat, groping for an idea of what a governess ought to ask. 'May I ask about the children? How many will be in my charge and—and to whom do I answer regarding their care?'

That sounded sufficiently like a governess.

He frowned, as if her question vexed him. 'Two, only.'

She tried a smile. 'Their ages?'

He averted his gaze. 'My son is about seven. My…daughter, five.'

'Lovely ages.' Two children did not sound terribly daunting, especially two so young. 'And are they at Brentmore Hall?'

She and Charlotte had looked in the *Topography of Great Britain* and an old volume of *Debrett's* in the Lawtons' library to learn about this marquess. They knew the marquess's wife died a little over a year ago, but all else they discovered was that the marquess's manor house, Brentmore Hall, was in Essex.

'Of course they are at Brentmore,' he snapped. 'Where else would they be?'

Did that question offend him? Conversing with him was like walking on eggs.

He paced like a panther, a huge wild cat she and Charlotte saw once at the Tower of London. That black cat had prowled its cage, back and forth, back and forth, lethally dangerous and yearning to escape.

This marquess's hair was as dark as a panther's. As were his eyes. When he moved, it was as if he, too, wished to break free.

In any event, there was no call for him to growl at her.

'I do not know where the children *should* be,' she said in her haughty voice. 'That was the point of my asking. I also wish to know where I am to live.'

He waved a hand. 'Forgive me once more, Miss Hill. I am unaccustomed to interviewing governesses.'

She lifted a brow.

He pressed his lips together before speaking. 'The previous governess passed away suddenly.'

She gasped. 'Passed away? Your poor children!' First their mother, then their governess? She felt a wave of tenderness for them. It seemed a lot for two little children to bear.

He stared at her again and some emotion flitted through those black eyes. Precisely what emotion, she could not tell.

'How are they managing?' she asked.

'Managing?' He seemed surprised at her question. 'Tolerably well, Parker says.'

'Parker?'

'My man of business,' he explained. 'Fortunately he happened to be at Brentmore and has taken care of everything.'

'You have not seen the children?' How appalling.

His eyes narrowed. 'Not since this happened. Not for a few months.'

She clamped her mouth shut. It seemed the only way to control it. Charlotte's governess used to tell Anna to mind her tongue and never forget her station. It had always confused her, because she was also supposed to show Charlotte how to speak up and be bold.

She changed the subject. 'Will I answer to your man of business, then?'

Oh, dear. Did he hear the disapproval in her tone?

'You will answer to me.' He fixed his panther eyes on her again. 'In daily matters you will be in total charge of the children. You will decide their needs and their care. The other servants will defer to you in matters regarding them.'

Her eyes widened.

His expression turned stern. 'If you are not up to the task, tell me now, Miss Hill.'

She could still lose this position.

She took a breath. 'I am up to the task, my lord. I merely felt it wise to know the extent of my responsibility.'

He held her captive with his eyes, which turned unexpectedly sad. 'Provide my children what they need. Make them happy.'

For a moment it was as if a mask dropped from his face and she glimpsed a man in agony.

This glimpse shook her more than the pacing panther.

'I shall try my best,' she whispered.

'We are done, Miss Hill. I will send word to you when you are to leave for Brentmore.' He turned away and prowled to the door.

She remembered to curtsy, but he did not see her. He left the room and a moment later the butler appeared to escort her to the hall. Once in the hall, the butler walked her to the door and opened it.

She was about to step across the threshold when the marquess's voice stopped her. 'Do not leave.' He stood on the marble staircase, looking down on her.

Her anxiety returned. Perhaps he had reconsidered.

'It is raining,' he said.

The rain was pouring in sheets outside.

'I do not mind the rain,' she assured him.

'You will be soaked within minutes.' He descended the stairs and walked directly towards her.

Her fingers fluttered. 'It is of no consequence.'

'I will call my carriage for you.' The marquess gestured towards the open door.

Her hand flew to her throat. 'That is much too much trouble, sir. If you insist, I will borrow an umbrella—'

He cut her off. 'An umbrella will be useless.' Again he stared at her and did not speak right away. 'I must go out. Very soon.'

The butler made a surprised sound.

The marquess shot him a sharp glance and turned his panther gaze back to Anna. 'Wait a few moments. I will drop you off on my way.'

Ride with him in the carriage? Enter the panther cage? She could not refuse. He all but demanded it.

She curtsied again. 'Thank you, sir. It is beyond generous of you.'

'Shall the young lady wait in the drawing
room, my lord?' the butler asked, closing the door.

'Yes.' Lord Brentmore turned back to the
stairs.

'Very good, sir.' The butler bowed curtly.

He led Anna to a beautifully furnished drawing
room on the same level as the hall. Its brocade-
upholstered sofas and crystal and porcelain spoke
of opulence. One wall held a huge family portrait
from a generation ago. A Gainsborough? It certainly appeared to be. She and Charlotte had seen
engravings of Gainsborough's portraits.

There was even a fire lit in the room, taking
away the early spring chill.

'Do sit, Miss Hill,' the butler intoned.

She lowered herself into a chair by the fire
and listened to the ticking of the mantel clock as
she waited.

Twenty minutes later Brent was informed that
the carriage waited outside. He donned his top-
coat and hat, and had Davies collect Miss Hill.

He was putting on his gloves when Davies led
Miss Hill back to the hall. Brent nodded to her
and Davies escorted her to the door where footmen waited with umbrellas. One walked her to
the carriage and helped her inside.

When Brent climbed in, she had taken the

backward-facing seat, which meant he could not avoid watching her the whole trip.

She sat with graceful poise, her hands folded in her lap.

The carriage started moving.

He ought to engage her in polite conversation but, in such intimate quarters, he could not trust what might escape his mouth.

Finally it was she who spoke. 'This is kind of you, sir. I am certain it takes you out of your way.'

He shrugged. 'Not too far out of the way.'

Lord Lawton's town house was on Mount Street, not more than a mile from Cavendish Square.

While the carriage crossed the distance, she looked out the window, but glanced his way occasionally. He could not keep his eyes off her, although he tried. When she caught him gazing at her, she smiled politely. He pined to see that genuine smile, the one that burst from her when she realised he had hired her.

The carriage reached Mount Street and stopped at the Lawton town house. One of the marquess's footmen put the stairs down and opened the door, his umbrella ready to shelter her. The footman assisted her from the carriage.

She turned back to Brent. 'Thank you again, my lord. I will await word from you when I should leave for Essex.'

He inclined his head. 'I will see you are informed as soon as possible.'

'I shall be ready.' She smiled again, a hint of her sunshine in this one. 'Good day, sir.'

He watched as the footman escorted Miss Hill to the door of the Lawtons' town house. Even hurrying through the rain, she made an alluring picture. He watched until she disappeared behind the town house door.

He groaned.

It was a good thing she'd be on her way to Brentmore in a few days.

The coachman knocked at the window. Brent leaned forwards to open it.

'Where to next, sir?' the man asked.

'Home,' Brent said.

'Home?' His coachman probably thought Brent was addled.

And the man would be dead accurate if he did.

Brent had ordered his carriage, his coachman, footmen and horses out in the pouring rain. All to carry a governess one mile.

He was addled all right.

'Home,' he repeated and leaned back against the leather seat.

Anna glimpsed Lord Brentmore's carriage pulling away through the crack of the town house door.

Rogers, the Lawton footman attending the hall, bent forwards to see as well. 'Fancy carriage.'

'Indeed.' Anna's emotions could not be more in a muddle. 'Imagine riding in it with a marquess.'

'So, what happened with your interview?' Rogers asked.

She tried to smile. 'He hired me. I am going to be a governess.'

Rogers closed the door. 'Do I congratulate you?'

The position of governess was not an enviable one. A governess existed somewhere between servant and family, but was a part of neither. It was a rank to which Anna was very accustomed, though. Her unique situation as Charlotte's companion made her too educated and refined to fit in with the servants, but she never, ever, could be considered family. She belonged…nowhere.

She took a breath. 'Congratulate me.'

At least she would not wind up alone and penniless on the London streets.

Tears threatened suddenly, so Anna rushed up the stairs to her room, which once had been a maid's room attached to Charlotte's bedchamber. Charlotte and her mother would still be out making calls. Anna had time to compose herself.

She removed her gloves, hat and pelisse and tossed them on a chair. She flopped down on the small cot that was her bed and covered her face with her hands.

It had been only two days ago that Lord Lawton informed her it was no longer desirable to have her act as Charlotte's companion. She was uncertain why. Perhaps it was because she had danced with some young gentlemen at a recent party? She'd thought it would have been rude to refuse. That was, however, the last social engagement she'd attended. Charlotte had henceforth gone on her own with only the company of one or both of her parents.

She'd not frozen or become mute as everyone feared. Charlotte had conquered her timidity, as Anna always knew she could.

Anna's days as companion had always been numbered. Charlotte was expected to make an excellent match and marry well. When that time came, Anna's place in Charlotte's life would have been lost. Anna had always assumed she'd return to Lawton House when Charlotte no longer needed her. She thought some useful role would be found for her. Lord Lawton, however, made it very clear he and Lady Lawton were terminating her services altogether.

What had she done to displease them so?

She'd never expected nor aspired to their affection, but she'd expected to be treated as a loyal servant.

At least Lord Lawton had troubled himself enough to arrange the interview with Lord Brentmore. For that she should be grateful.

Instead her emotions were consumed with the idea of losing the only home she'd ever known and being separated from all she knew and cared about. Her mother. Her father.

Charlotte.

Especially Charlotte. She was closer to Charlotte than to anyone else, even her mother.

Her chin trembled.

She put her fist to her mouth and fought for control of her emotions.

This was not a banishment, even though that was precisely how it felt. It was a natural progression of change, nothing more. It had been her folly not to anticipate its possibility. She must remain strong and fearless. Being strong and fearless were precisely the qualities that had led to her becoming Charlotte's companion in the first place, a circumstance she could never regret.

She'd told Lord Brentmore the truth when she'd said her education opened up the world for her. She could not imagine not knowing about geography, philosophy, mathematics. She'd learned Latin and French. Painting. Dancing. Needlework. There was no end to all the wonderful things she'd learned at Charlotte's side. No matter what happened to her, no one could ever take away all she'd learned.

She sat up and thrust her unhappiness aside. How bad could it be to become a governess to two small children in a country house that was very likely similar to Lawton House? And as a governess, she would have an excuse to continue to study and read.

The door to Charlotte's bedchamber opened. 'Anna?'

Anna rose from her bed and walked to the doorway that separated her little room from Charlotte's. 'I am here.' She smiled at this young woman with whom she felt as close as a sister. 'How were your calls?'

Charlotte grinned, showing the pretty dimple in her cheek. 'Very tolerable. I made myself join the conversation and soon I was not even thinking about it.'

Anna crossed the room and gave her a hug. 'That is marvellous. Did you also enjoy yourself?'

Charlotte nodded, her blonde curls bobbing. 'I did! Very much.' She pulled Anna over to the chairs by the window. 'But you must tell me about your interview!'

Anna sobered. 'I am hired. I start within a week.'

Charlotte jumped out of her chair, looking stricken. 'No!'

'It is true.' Anna watched Charlotte sit again. 'But it is a good thing, Charlotte.'

Lines of worry creased Charlotte's brow. 'Maybe you should not take the first position offered you. I've heard things. People talk as if there is something wrong about Lord Brentmore. Something about his past.'

'It does not matter.' Anna took her hands. 'I cannot afford to refuse. I have nothing to recommend me. I am very fortunate the marquess agreed to hire me.'

'Why did he hire you, then?' Her tone turned petulant. 'If you have nothing to recommend you?'

'I believe he was in urgent need of a governess.' She squeezed her friend's hands.

Charlotte lips pursed. 'You sound as if you met the man.'

'It was he who interviewed me.'

Charlotte's eyes grew wide. 'What was he like? Was he as grand as a marquess should be?'

The image of the panther, restless and dangerous, returned. 'He was formidable, but I doubt I shall have to encounter him much. I will be at Brentmore Hall with his children.'

'So far away?' Charlotte cried.

Far away from all she knew.

Charlotte's lip trembled. 'I am telling Mama I will refuse all invitations. I'm going to spend every second of this week with you. It is all we have left!'

The prospect of being separated from Charlotte tore Anna apart inside. This bond between the two of them, borne of sharing a childhood together, was about to be shattered. They could never again be together like they had been before.

Not even for this last week.

Chapter Two

⚬⚭⚬

Only three days later Anna was again riding in Lord Brentmore's carriage, this time travelling alone to Essex, a long day's ride from London.

The countryside and villages passed before her eyes, becoming indistinguishable as the day wore on. From one blink of an eye to the next, her life had changed and each mile brought her closer to something new and unknown. With each bump in the road, she fought a rabble of butterflies in her stomach.

'This is an adventure,' she said out loud. 'An adventure.'

Such an adventure would test her mettle, certainly. She'd often acted braver than she felt, because that was what was expected of her as Charlotte's companion. She must do so again here. At Charlotte's side she'd tackled each new lesson, mastered each new skill. This should be no different. Except this time she had no instructor guiding her, no friend looking up to her. This time she was alone.

The sun dipped low in the sky when the carriage approached an arched gate of red brick. Atop the gate was a huge clock upon which were written the words *Audaces Fortuna Juvat.*

'Fortune favours the bold,' she murmured.

She laughed. Fortune certainly put her in a position to be bold.

She girded herself as the carriage passed through the gate and a huge Tudor manor house came into view. Also made of red brick, it rose three storeys and had a multitude of chimneys and windows reflecting the setting sun. Two large wings flanked a centre court with a circular drive that led to a huge wooden door where the carriage stopped.

The coachman opened the window beneath his seat. 'Brentmore Hall, miss.'

Her nerves fluttered anew. 'Thank you, sir.'

She gathered up her reticule and the basket she'd carried with her. A footman appeared at the carriage door to help her out. As she stepped on to the gravel, the huge wooden door opened and a man and woman emerged.

The man, dressed as a gentleman and of about forty years of age, strode towards her. 'Miss Hill?'

He extended his hand. 'Welcome to Brentmore Hall. I am Mr Parker, Lord Brentmore's man of business.'

She shook his hand and summoned the training in comportment she'd received at Charlotte's side. 'A pleasure to meet you, sir.'

A gust of wind blew her skirts. She held her hat on her head.

Mr Parker turned to the woman, who was more simply dressed. 'Allow me to present Mrs Tippen, the housekeeper here.'

The woman perfectly looked the part of housekeeper with grey hair peeking out from a pristinely white cap and quick assessing eyes.

Anna extended her hand. 'A pleasure, Mrs Tippen. How kind of you to greet me.'

The woman's face was devoid of expression. She hesitated before shaking Anna's hand. 'You are young.'

She stiffened at the housekeeper's clear disapproval, but summoned a smile. 'I assure you, Mrs Tippen. I am old enough.'

The housekeeper frowned.

Mr Parker stepped forwards. 'The previous governess was of a more advanced age.' He gestured towards the door. 'Shall we go inside? The footmen will see to your trunk and boxes.'

The trunk and boxes contained all her worldly belongings, sent from Lawton to London so that she could carry them with her.

Anna entered a large hall with grey marble floors and wainscoted walls. A line of flags hung high above her head. A larger-than-life portrait of a man with long, curly, blond locks, dressed in gold brocade, filled one wall and one of a woman in a voluminous silk dress faced it on the other wall. The hall smelled of beeswax from the burning branches of candles and the polish of the wood.

Intended to be majestic, Anna supposed, the hall seemed oppressive. Too dark. Too ancient.

So unlike Lawton House, full of light and colour.

Another man crossed the floor and Mr Parker spoke. 'Ah, here is Mr Tippen, Lord Brentmore's butler.'

This butler was as stern-faced as the housekeeper. His wife?

'Mr Tippen,' Mr Parker went on, 'this is Miss Hill, the new governess.'

The butler nodded. 'We have been expecting you.'

Mrs Tippen spoke, her face still devoid of expression. 'You'll be weary. Come with me to your room and then dinner.'

'What about meeting the children?' Her whole reason to be here.

'Asleep. Or nearly so,' Mrs Tippen said.

'Did they not expect to see me?' She would hate to fail them on her first day.

'We did not tell them,' Mr Parker said.

'You did not tell them I was coming today?' Should the children not have a warning that their new governess was arriving?

'We thought it best not to tell them anything at all.' Mr Parker inclined his head in an ingratiating manner. 'Go ahead and refresh yourself. I will see you for dinner.'

Anna had no choice but to follow Mrs Tippen up the winding mahogany staircase.

Was she to be another surprise to the children, then? Had they not received too many surprises already, with the death of their mother a year ago and now the death of their governess?

She followed the housekeeper up two flights of stairs. 'Your room is this way.' She turned down one of the wings, stopping at a door and stepping aside for Anna to enter.

The room was panelled in the same dark wood as the entrance hall and stairway. It was furnished with a four-poster bed, a chest of drawers, chairs and a small table by the window, and a dressing table. Compared to Charlotte's bedchamber, it was modest, but would be comfortable if it were not so dark. Even the fire in the fireplace and an oil lamp burning did not banish an aura of gloom.

Had this been the previous governess's room? Anna wondered. Had the woman died here?

She decided she'd rather not know. 'This is a nice room.'

Mrs Tippen seemed unmoved by her compliment. 'There is fresh water in the pitcher and towels for you. Your trunk will be brought up forthwith.'

'Where are the children's rooms?' Anna asked.

'Down the hallway,' a young woman answered as she entered the room. 'This whole wing is the children's wing.'

The housekeeper walked out without bothering to introduce Anna to this new person. The newcomer was a servant, obviously, from the white apron she wore and the cap covering her red hair. She appeared to be only a few years older than Anna and had the sturdy good looks of so many of the country women of Lawton.

Anna felt a wave of homesickness.

The servant strode towards her with a smile on her face. 'I'm Eppy, the children's nurse. Well, I'm really a maid, but since I take care of the children, I call myself a nurse.'

'I am pleased to meet you.' Anna extended her hand. 'I am Anna Hill.'

'I'm sure I'm more pleased than you are.' The nurse laughed. 'I am also to act as *your* maid, so what can I do to assist you?' She turned towards a sound in the hallway. 'Oh, that will be your trunk now. You must be eager to change out of your travel clothes.'

Two footmen carried in her belongings, nodded to her and left.

Anna removed the key of her trunk from her reticule. 'I must change. I am expected for dinner.'

The maid took the key and unlocked the trunk. While Anna removed her travelling dress and washed the dirt of the road off her skin, the maid chattered on about how lovely the clothing was that she unpacked for Anna, the gowns which once were Charlotte's. Eventually Eppy found one gown without too many wrinkles that would be suitable for dinner.

Anna always felt a sense of irony about having a servant attend her, the daughter of servants, but she'd been accustomed to the assistance of a Charlotte's maid. As Charlotte's companion, she'd received nearly the same services as Charlotte herself, to show the timid girl that there was nothing to fear. That had been her main task—showing Charlotte there was nothing to fear.

Eppy helped Anna into her dress.

'Are the children really sleeping?' Anna asked. It was nearing eight in the evening according to the clock in the room.

'Last I checked,' Eppy replied good-naturedly. At least the maid was cheerful, unlike Mr and Mrs Tippen.

'Have the children truly not been told I was coming?' Anna straightened the front of her dress.

The maid tied her laces. 'That was Mr Parker's idea. Goodness knows what he was thinkin'.'

Indeed. The children should have been told. Charlotte always adjusted better when warned of something new.

Anna herself would have preferred to be warned in advance that the future she'd expected for herself would be snatched away from her.

After Charlotte married, she'd thought she'd return to Lawton House and eventually also would encounter someone who wanted to marry her. A scholarly man, perhaps, a man who would value an educated wife. They'd have children, she'd hoped, to whom she could pass on all that she'd learned.

Now she did not dare to look into her future. She did not dare dream. She knew now that nothing could ever be certain.

She sat down at the dressing table and pulled pins from her hair. 'Can you tell me about the children?' she asked the maid. 'I know nothing. Not even their names, actually.' Lord Brentmore had never mentioned their names.

'Well—' Eppy continued to unpack her trunk '—the boy is Cal—Earl of Calmount, if you want to get fancy. Given name is John, in case you need it. He is the older at seven years and a quiet little thing. Next is little Dory—Lady Dorothea, that is. Not quiet at all.'

'And she is five years old?' Anna remembered.

'That she is, miss.' Eppy placed some folded articles of clothing in a bureau drawer.

Anna repinned her hair. 'It must have been difficult for them to lose their governess.'

The maid shrugged. 'Mrs Sykes was sickly for a while. You'll be a nice change for the little ones.'

She hoped so.

She stood and smoothed out the skirt of her dress. 'I am supposed to dine with Mr Parker. Will there be someone downstairs to show me the way?'

Eppy closed the drawer. 'One of the footmen will be attending the hall. I expect you'll eat in the dining room. That is where Mr Parker is served.'

The maid accompanied her out in the hall. She pointed down the long hallway of the wing. 'I have been sleeping in the room at the very end of the hall. The children are two doors down from you here. Come knock on my door if you need help before you retire.'

Anna walked down the stairs to the entrance hall. As Eppy had said, a footman was there to escort her to the dining room.

Mr Parker stood when she walked in the room. 'Ah, there you are. I hope everything was to your liking.'

As if she were free to complain. 'It was.'

Two places were set at the end of a long table, across from each other, leaving the head of the table, with its larger chair, empty. Lord Brentmore's seat, obviously.

Mr Parker helped her into her seat and signalled to another waiting footman. 'We shall be served in a moment. May I pour you some wine?'

'Certainly.' She glanced about the room, as wainscoted as the rest of the house she'd seen. Were there any rooms with plastered walls and colourful wall coverings? The only attempt at brightness in this room was a huge tapestry that covered the wall behind the table's head. Its faded colours told the story of a hunt that must have taken place at least two centuries ago. The sideboard held gleaming silver serving dishes, which, she suspected, would not be used to serve a man of business and a governess.

Mr Parker raised his glass. 'Here is to Brentmore, your new home.'

It was hard to imagine this place, both grand and dismal, ever feeling like home. Home was Lawton House. And the small cottage she sometimes shared with her parents.

'To Brentmore,' she murmured.

A footman brought in a tureen of soup and served them.

Mr Parker tasted the soup and nodded his approval. Anna ought to be starving after her day of travel with only quick meals at posting inns, but sipping the soup was more formality than famish.

'Tomorrow before I leave I will make certain

Mrs Tippen knows you need a tour of the house and grounds.' He took another spoonful.

She looked up at him. 'Before you leave? You are leaving tomorrow?'

He nodded. 'Lord Brentmore wishes me to return to town as soon as possible.'

Did Lord Brentmore not feel the children needed some transition? Even if Mr Parker did not involve himself in their care, he must be a familiar figure to them.

She pursed her lips. 'I suppose the marquess's needs are greater than the children's.'

His spoon stopped in mid-air. 'The children? The children do not need me here. Oh, no, no, no. All I've done is see to the former governess's burial. She had no family to speak of, so it was entirely up to me. The nurse takes care of the children.' He cocked his head. 'You met her, I hope. She was to have presented herself to you.'

'She did.' She frowned. 'Have you had nothing to do with the children at all? Did you not speak with them and tell them that you were attending to the burial?'

His brows rose. 'Their nurse took care of that. I thought it best not to disrupt their routine.'

Disrupt their routine? Their governess died, for goodness' sake. That was a disruption. She'd better say no more about that, lest she really lose her temper.

The footman brought turbot for the next course.

'What can you tell me about the children?' Anna asked.

'Not a great deal.' Mr Parker dug his fork into the fish. 'I understand they are easy to manage.'

She needed to learn something about them. 'Their mother died, did she not?'

He glanced down at his plate. 'Yes. A little over a year ago. It happened here. A riding accident.'

'Here?' She swallowed. 'The children must have been very affected.'

He took a bite. 'I suppose they were.'

Anna expelled an exasperated breath. This man knew nothing of the children. 'Tell me about their mother. Did you know her?'

He froze, then put down his fork. 'I cannot say I knew her. She was…' He paused. 'Very beautiful.'

That told her nothing.

His voice stiffened. 'You should ask Lord Brentmore about his wife. It is not my place to discuss such matters.'

She thought she was discussing Lady Brentmore and her children. Not the lady's husband.

'Was Lord Brentmore here when his wife died?' She hoped so for the children's sake.

'He was abroad.' Mr Parker took another bite.

'Finishing up his diplomatic mission.' He followed with a sip of wine. 'He did travel back as soon as he could.'

That was something, at least. 'I did not realise he was involved in diplomacy.'

'During the war and Napoleon's first exile.' Mr Parker relaxed. 'Very hush-hush, you know.'

She had a sudden vision of the marquess moving through dark alleys, meeting dangerous men. 'He was away a great deal?'

'For very long periods. I managed his affairs for him and the estate business while he was absent.' He said this with a great deal of pride.

She supposed that the marquess's absence from his children might be forgiven while he performed the King's service. Perhaps she could not expect that every father show the same sort of devotion Lord Lawton lavished on Charlotte. Anna's father certainly never showed her much affection. He'd always resented her living with Charlotte in the House, she'd supposed.

But surely the marquess must see how painful it would be for his children to lose their mother and their governess. Why had the man not come to comfort them? Why had he sent his man of business instead?

She only hoped her woeful lack of experience would not cause the poor little ones more trouble and sadness.

For the rest of the meal, Anna fell back on the conversational skills she and Charlotte had practised to prepare for Charlotte's come out. Making pleasant conversation when one's nerves were all in disorder was an achievement, indeed.

By the last course, however, all she desired was solitude. 'Mr Parker, I wonder if you would excuse me. I am suddenly very fatigued. I believe I shall retire for the night.'

His expression turned solicitous. 'Of course you are fatigued. A day's carriage ride is vastly tiring.'

She rose from her chair and he stood, as well.

'In fact,' he went on, 'I will bid farewell to you now. I am leaving as soon as the sun rises.'

She extended her hand to shake his. 'I wish you a safe trip.'

She returned to her room and readied herself for bed without summoning Eppy to assist her. After washing up and changing into her nightdress, she extinguished the candles and sat for a long time in a chair, staring out the window overlooking extensive gardens, landscaped so naturally she wondered if they had been designed by Inigo Jones.

Beautiful, but unfamiliar.

She took a deep breath and forced her emotions to calm. She must accept what she could not change.

* * *

The next morning Anna woke to the sun shining in her window. She rose, stretched her arms and gazed out her window. The sky was clear blue and cloudless and the country air smelled every bit as wonderful as at home—at Lawton, she meant. This was home now.

When a maid entered to feed the fire in her fireplace, Anna introduced herself and asked the girl to have Eppy attend her when it was convenient.

A quarter-hour later, Eppy knocked on her door. 'Good morning, miss,' she said cheerfully. 'Are you ready for me?'

Anna had already washed and donned a gown. 'I just need a little assistance with the laces.'

'Certainly!' Eppy tightened her laces.

Anna looked over her shoulder. 'Are the children awake?'

'They are indeed, miss. Eating their breakfast in the nursery.' She tied a bow.

'I am anxious to make their acquaintance.' Best to jump in right away.

Eppy frowned. 'You are supposed to tour the house. Mrs Tippen was very clear about that.'

'Do the children know I am here?' she asked.

Eppy lowered her head. 'I told them. I could not keep it secret any more.'

'You did right, Eppy,' Anna told her. 'But I'll

not keep them wondering another minute. The tour of the house can wait.'

She followed Eppy to the nursery.

'I've brought someone to meet you,' Eppy called out as she entered the room. She turned to the doorway. 'Your new governess.'

Anna put on a brave smile. 'Good morning! I am Miss Hill.'

All she saw at first were two small faces with wide eyes. Both sat ramrod straight in their chairs. The little boy was dark like his father; the girl so fair she looked like a pixie.

Anna approached slowly. 'I'll wager you did not expect a new governess today.'

The girl relaxed a bit, smiling tentatively.

Anna turned to Eppy. 'Will you do the introductions, Eppy? I should like to know these children.'

Eppy hurried over.

'Miss Hill, may I present Lord Calmount.' She squeezed his shoulder fondly. 'We call him Cal.'

'You call him Lord Cal,' the girl corrected.

Eppy grinned. 'That I do, because I'm your nurse.'

'Do you know what you wish me to call you?' Anna asked the boy.

His eyes remained fixed on her.

His sister answered. 'He likes Cal or Lord Cal.'

Anna smiled at both of them. 'Very well.'

Eppy put her hands on the girl's shoulders

and shook her fondly. 'This little imp is Lady Dorothea—'

'Dory,' the little girl piped up.

'Dory,' Anna repeated. She looked at each one in turn. 'And Lord Cal. I am delighted to make your acquaintance.'

Lord Cal remained as stiff as before, but little Dory now squirmed in her chair.

'What plans did you have today,' Anna asked, 'if I had not arrived so suddenly?'

'Cal said you came last night,' Dory said. 'He peeked out the door and he said you were our new governess, but how he knew we were to have a new governess, I cannot say.' Her expression turned solemn. 'Our other one died.'

Anna matched her seriousness. 'I know that. That must have been dreadful for you.'

The girl nodded.

Anna sat in a chair opposite them. 'Lord Cal was very clever to learn of my arrival and to figure out who I was.'

A look of anxiety flashed through the boy's eyes.

She faced him directly. 'I greatly admire cleverness.'

She thought she saw surprise replace the anxiety in his eyes. Eppy had not been exaggerating about him being very quiet. Up close he appeared to be a miniature version of his father. The same eyes that bore into you. The sensitive mouth. The nearly imperceptible cleft in his chin.

The same austere expression.

She smiled at him. 'Lord Cal. You look a great deal like your father.'

He glanced away.

'Do you know our father?' Dory asked, eyes wide again. She acted as if her father was some mysterious legend she'd only heard about.

Anna turned to her. 'It was your father who decided that I should be your governess.'

The girl's eyes grew even wider. 'He did?'

'He did,' Anna said firmly. She pointed to their breakfast plates with remnants of bread crusts and jam. 'I see you are finishing your breakfast. I have not yet eaten my breakfast. I wanted to come meet you right away.' She also needed a tour of the house and grounds. 'I will leave you for a little while, but I have an idea, if you both should like it.'

Dory leaned forwards, all curiosity. Cal at least turned his gaze back to her.

'I must have a tour of the house and grounds and I wondered if you would come with me. I would love to see this lovely place with you.'

Dory popped up. 'We would!' She thought to check with her brother. 'Wouldn't we, Cal?'

The boy apparently gave his sister his approval, although its communication was imperceptible to Anna.

Proud of herself for thinking of bringing the children on the tour with her, Anna left them to go in search of her breakfast and the waiting Mrs Tippen.

The footman in the hall directed her to a parlour with a sideboard filled with food. Although the parlour had the same wainscoted walls as the rest of the house she had seen, it had a large window facing east. The room was aglow with sunshine. She selected an egg and bread and cheese, and poured herself a cup of tea.

No sooner had she started eating when a scowling Mrs Tippen entered the room. 'I expected you earlier.'

Mrs Tippen's disapproval continued, apparently. What could be the source of such antipathy? The woman did not even know her.

Anna understood the servant hierarchy in country houses, having grown up in one. She knew a housekeeper would consider herself second only to the butler in overseeing the servants, but a governess would not be under her control. Was that what Mrs Tippen resented?

Anna lifted her chin. 'Good morning, Mrs Tippen,' she said in as mild a tone as she could manage. 'If there was an urgency about touring the house, I was not informed of it. In any event, my duties are to the children. I needed to meet them right away.'

The woman sniffed. 'I have many responsibilities. I will not be kept waiting by a governess.'

Anna gave her a steady gaze. 'I grew up in a house much like this one and I am well aware of the housekeeper's responsibilities. I did not ask you to wait for me, however. It matters not to me when I see the house and grounds. Name me a time convenient to you—'

'A half-hour ago was convenient for me,' Mrs Tippen snapped.

Anna held up a hand. 'You will address me respectfully, Mrs Tippen. As I will address you.' Goodness. She sounded exactly like Lady Lawton reprimanding a servant. 'I will be ready in an hour for the house tour. If that will not do, name a time and I will accommodate you. We are done discussing this, however.'

Mrs Tippen turned on her heel and left the room.

Anna took a sip of tea and fought to dampen her anger. The last thing she desired was to be engaged in a battle. She was no threat to a housekeeper. She was no threat to anyone.

An hour later Anna and the children waited in the entrance hall. Anna half-hoped Mrs Tippen would not show. In that event, Anna had already decided she'd ask the children to show her the house. She wished she'd thought of that earlier.

It would certainly be more enjoyable than enduring Mrs Tippen's company.

It was Mr Tippen, the butler, who presented himself, which was hardly better than his wife. Mr Tippen reminded Anna of an engraving she had once seen of Matthew Hopkins, the witch-hunter. Mr Tippen resembled him, with his long, narrow face and pointed chin. Put him in a capotain hat, cover his chin with a beard and the picture would be complete.

He frowned down on the children.

Anna spoke up in their defence. 'The children will accompany me on the tour, Mr Tippen.'

His nose rose higher. 'The marchioness preferred the children to stay in their wing.'

'The marchioness?' Anna was confused.

'Lady Brentmore.'

But Lady Brentmore was dead. How insensitive of him to mention her in front of the children.

Anna straightened. 'I am in complete charge of the children now, am I not?'

One corner of his mouth twitched. 'So Mr Parker informed us.'

'Well, then.' She smiled. 'Shall we get started?'

Lord Cal stared at the floor, looking as if he wished it would open up and swallow him.

Dory took Anna's hand and pulled her down to whisper in her ear. 'You were *insolent* to Mr Tippen!'

She whispered back, 'Not insolent.' What a big

word for a five-year-old. 'I am in charge of you. Your father said so.'

Cal's head snapped up.

The little girl's eyes grew wide. 'He did?'

'He did,' Anna repeated.

Mr Tippen began the tour in the formal parlour where hung a portrait of the late marchioness, fair like her daughter, and beautiful, as Mr Parker had said. She looked regal and aloof, and also as if she could step out of the canvas and give them all a noble dressing down.

The children, poor dears, barely looked at the portrait.

Anna directed their attention to a portrait of their father on the opposite wall.

'This looks very like your father!' she exclaimed, mostly because their late mother's image obviously upset them. Lord Brentmore's portrait, though of him younger and leaner, perfectly conveyed his sternness, but there was also a sad yearning in his eyes that tugged at her heart. His son's eyes carried that same sadness, she realised, but the boy looked as if he'd given up yearning for anything. Anna's heart bled for the child. How could she help him? she wondered.

Lord Brentmore's voice came back to her. *Provide my children what they need. Make them happy.*

How could she make them happy?

As the tour continued Mr Tippen turned out

to be a competent guide, able to explain the family connections in the myriad of portraits and other paintings all through the house. He proved knowledgeable about the furnishings and about the house's history, when parts of it were built and by which Lord Brentmore.

The children remained extraordinarily quiet, gaping at everything as if seeing it for the first time. How often had the children seen these rooms? Surely they had not been always confined to the nursery.

Mr Tippen, opening a door that led to the garden, seemed to read her mind. 'As you have seen, these rooms are filled with priceless family treasures, Miss Hill. They are not play areas. The children are not allowed in them—'

Anna stood her ground. 'If you are attempting to tell me how to manage the children, Mr Tippen, you would do better to be silent.'

Dory was holding Anna's hand. The little girl squeezed it and grinned up at her.

Anna grinned back. She was being *insolent* again.

She only hoped it did not make matters worse for all of them.

Chapter Three

❧⟐❧

Brent walked with his cousin up Bond Street, heading towards Somerset Street, where Baron Rolfe had taken rooms for the Season.

'I do not know why I let you talk me into this, Peter.'

Peter's grandfather had been the old marquess's younger brother, making Peter and Brent second cousins. The two of them were all that was left of the Caine family.

Besides Brent's children, that was.

'All I am asking of you is to meet her,' Peter responded.

They were to dine with Lord and Lady Rolfe, and, more importantly, Miss Susan Rolfe, their daughter.

Almost a month had gone by before Peter again broached the topic of Brent marrying again.

Peter considered Miss Rolfe the perfect match for Brent.

The Rolfe estate bordered Peter's property and Peter had known this family his whole life, had practically lived in their pockets since his own parents passed away. Brent was slightly acquainted with Baron Rolfe, but he could not recall if he had ever met the man's wife or the daughter.

'You could not find a finer woman,' Peter insisted.

Yes. Yes. So Peter had said. Many times.

His cousin went on. 'You need marriage to a respectable woman. It will counteract the unfortunate scandal that surrounds you.'

Brent averted his gaze. This was exactly what Brent had told himself before his first marriage. Eunice, he'd thought, had been the epitome of a good match.

In the end she'd only compounded the scandal.

Peter glanced around, as if a passer-by might overhear him. 'There are those who still believe your blood is tainted because of your poor Irish mother. Some claim that is why Eunice was unfaithful.'

Brent's gaze snapped back.

His grandfather had hammered it into him that his blood was tainted by his mother, the daughter of a poor Irish tenant farmer. Brent could still hear Eunice's diatribe on the subject, which had indeed been her justification for blatant infidelity.

Brent remembered only a smiling face, warm arms encircling him and a sweet voice singing a lullaby. He felt the ache of a loss that was over a quarter-century old.

'Take care, Peter,' he shot back, his voice turning dark and dangerous.

His cousin merely returned a sympathetic look. 'You know I do not credit such things, but your children are bound to hear this same gossip some day, as well as stories of their mother. These will be heavy burdens for them to bear. You need to do something to counter them or they will grow up suffering the same taunts and cuts that you have suffered.'

Peter rarely talked so plainly.

Brent held his cousin's gaze. 'My one marriage certainly did nothing to increase my respectability.'

He'd stayed away from Eunice as much as possible for the children's sake. There was no reason the poor babes should hear them constantly shouting at each other.

He'd been completely besotted by Eunice from their first meeting. She'd been the Diamond of the Season, the daughter of a peer, the perfect match for a new marquess, and she'd accepted his suit.

After marriage, however, Brent learned it was his title and wealth that had value to her. The day he'd held their newborn son in his arms, thinking himself the most fortunate man in the world,

Eunice had told him how happy she was that her duty was done. Now they were free to pursue other *interests*. After that her *interests*—her infidelities, that is—kept tongues wagging.

At least the war offered him ample opportunity to stay away from her.

Unfortunately, it had also kept him away from his son.

Brent consoled himself that most aristocrats had little to do with their children, instead hiring nurses, governesses and tutors, sending them away to schools and seeing them only at brief intervals until the children were old enough to be civilised, the way the old marquess had reared him. How he had spent his early years was considered strange—suckled by his own mother, cared for by his Irish grandfather in a one-room, windowless mud cabin.

Brent and Peter reached Oxford Street, a lifetime away from the land of Brent's birth.

He turned his attention back to the present. 'Peter, what makes you think another marriage would not make matters worse?'

In no way would Brent allow his heart to again become engaged as it had done with Eunice. It had cut to the core that she'd married the title and scorned the man.

Peter responded once they were on the other side of Oxford Street. 'Marry a woman of high moral character this time. A woman whose own reputation is unblemished and who can be trusted to be a faithful wife and attentive mother.' He glanced away and back. 'Miss Rolfe is all these things.'

Brent kept his eyes fixed on the pavement ahead. 'What makes you think Miss Rolfe will accept me?'

'Because you are a good man,' Peter said simply.

Brent rolled his eyes. 'You may be alone in believing that.'

'And because you could be such a help to her family.' The young man's tone was earnest.

At least it was out in the open this time. Miss Rolfe needed to marry into wealth. Her father was only a hair's breadth away from the River Tick, and the man had a huge family to support—two sons and two more daughters, all younger than Miss Rolfe. Brent's money was needed to save Rolfe from complete ruin.

'Ah, yes.' Brent nodded. 'My wealth is greatly desired.'

'By a worthy man,' Peter emphasised. 'The most important thing is Miss Rolfe will make a good mother to your children.'

His children. The only reason he'd consider this idea of marriage. Brent might not see his children frequently. He might not keep them at his side like his Irish grandfather kept him, but he wanted the best for them.

'Speaking of your children, how is the new governess working out?' Peter asked.

Brent welcomed the change in subject, although it pricked at his guilt even more. She'd sent him one letter shortly after her arrival at Brentmore, but he'd not written back to enquire further.

'Fairly well, last I heard.' Was the passionate Miss Hill making the children happy? He certainly hoped so.

Perhaps he would write to her tomorrow to ask if the children needed anything that he could provide. He had no clue as to what his children might need or desire. He'd tried to keep their lives as quiet and comfortable and unchanged as he could, knowing firsthand how jarring too much change could be. That was why he'd left them at Brentmore Hall, to disrupt their peace as little as possible with his presence.

Who could have guessed their old governess would die? He'd not protected them at all from that trauma. How difficult for them that the woman's death to come so soon after their mother's accident.

If a second marriage could accomplish all Peter said, how could Brent refuse? If Miss Rolfe was indeed the paragon Peter vowed she was, perhaps she could give the children a better life.

He and Peter turned on to Somerset Street and knocked upon Lord Rolfe's door. A footman opened the door and a few minutes later led them to the drawing room and announced them to the Rolfes.

Baron Rolfe immediately crossed the room to greet them. 'Lord Brentmore, it is a delight to have your company.' He shook Brent's hand. 'Peter, it is always good to see you.' He turned to two ladies who stood behind him. 'Allow me to present you to my wife and daughter.'

The wife was a pleasant-looking woman, the sort whose face just naturally smiled. She was soft spoken and gracious.

The daughter had a quiet sort of beauty. Her hair was a nondescript brown, her eyes a pale blue, her features even. There was nothing to object to in her. Brent gave her credit for being remarkably composed in the face of being looked over by a marquess as if she were a bauble in some shop.

'I am pleased to meet you, my lord.' She had a pleasant voice, not musical, perhaps, but not grating. 'Peter has told me so much about you.'

He hoped Peter had told her everything. He'd learned the hard way it did not pay to assume she already knew. He'd assumed Eunice had known of his early life. After their marriage when she'd learned of it, she'd been shocked and appalled.

'I am pleased to meet you as well, Miss Rolfe.' He bowed.

He ought to say something witty or charming,

but he was not trying to impress. If this idea of Peter's was to work, Miss Rolfe must know him as he was. There should be no illusions.

They sipped sherry as they waited for dinner to be served. Conversation was pleasant and amiable. Brent liked that these people were very fond of his cousin and were as comfortable as they were in his presence. He was supposed to be the family's salvation, after all, but they refrained from fawning over him and labouring to earn his regard.

The dinner proceeded in like manner. He was seated next to Miss Rolfe, which gave him an opportunity to share conversation with her alone. She, too, retained her poise, although she did shoot occasional glances to Peter, for his encouragement or approval, Brent supposed.

When dinner was done, Brent broke with the convention of the gentlemen remaining at the table for brandy and the ladies retiring to the drawing room.

'May I speak with Miss Rolfe alone?' he asked instead.

'Of course,' Lord Rolfe said.

Miss Rolfe glanced at Peter before saying, 'I would be delighted.'

Brent and Miss Rolfe returned to the drawing room.

She went to a cabinet and took out a decanter.

'My lord, would you like a glass of brandy as we speak?'

He was grateful. 'I would indeed.'

She poured his glass and settled herself on the sofa.

He chose a chair facing her. 'It is clear that Peter discussed this matter with you and your parents, as he did with me.'

She lowered her eyes. 'He did.'

'I need to know your thoughts on this.' She had to be fully on board with the scheme or he would not proceed.

She raised her head and gave him a direct look. 'It is a reality that I must marry well...' She paused. 'It is also a reality that my prospects to marry well are very slim. My dowry is very modest—'

He put up a hand. 'Money means nothing to me.'

She smiled. 'Actually, money means nothing to me, either. It is far more important to me to marry a good man.' Her gaze faltered. 'Peter— Peter assures me you are such a man.'

He glanced away. 'It is important to me that you realise precisely what you are agreeing to.'

'Peter was quite forthright.' Her expression turned serious. 'I know about your Irish parentage and your wife's infidelities. I also know that you keep your word and pay your creditors and fulfil your responsibilities to your tenants, your servants, and your country.'

He felt his cheeks warming. 'That is high praise.'

She lowered her lashes. 'It is what Peter told me.'

All Brent truly did was what any decent man should do. It seemed no great thing to him.

He changed the subject. 'What of children?'

Her cheeks turned pink. 'Our children?'

Lawd. He had not thought that far.

'You shall, of course, have children, if you wish it.' He could not contemplate bedding her, not at the moment. There was nothing about her to repulse, however. He could imagine becoming fond of her in time. 'What I meant was your feelings about my children. Are you willing to take charge of them and rear them as your own?'

Her hands fidgeted, twisting the fabric of her skirts. 'If you think they would accept me in that role.'

He had no idea. Sadly, his children were strangers to him.

She spoke more confidently. 'I am the eldest of five. I am certainly well used to the company of children. I would try my best for yours.'

The words of his new governess came back to him—*I would please you, my lord. I am certain I would*—spoken with a passion Miss Rolfe lacked.

Perhaps that was fortunate. Passion must not be a part of this decision.

'Do you have any questions for me?' he asked her.

She tilted her head in thought. 'I need your assurance that you will help my family, that you will help launch my brothers and sisters if my father is unable to do so. My father will repay you if he can—'

He waved a hand. 'I do not require repayment.'

'He will desire to, none the less.'

Brent had made enquiries about Lord Rolfe. His debts appeared to be honest ones—crop failures and such. His needs were a far cry from Eunice's father's incessant demands that Brent pay his gambling debts.

Brent shrugged. 'I am well able to assist your family in whatever way they require.'

'That is all I need,' she said, her voice low.

He stood. 'What I suggest, then, is that we see more of each other. To be certain this will suit us both. If you are free tomorrow, I will take you for a turn in Hyde Park.'

She rose as well. 'That would give me pleasure.'

Brent ignored the sick feeling inside him and tried to sound cheerful. 'Shall we seek out your parents? And let Peter know his scheme might very well bear fruit?'

She blinked rapidly and he wondered if she was as comfortable with this idea as she let on.

'Yes,' she murmured. 'Let us tell my parents… and Peter.'

'We do not need a physician!' Anna was beyond furious.

Three weeks in her new position had also meant three weeks of battling Mrs Tippen, who seemed intent on keeping things exactly as her late marchioness had wanted them.

'I have sent for him and that is that.' Mrs Tippen gave her a triumphant glare. 'We cannot have you endangering the children like this.'

'Endangering!' Anna glared back. 'The boy was running. He fell and cut his chin on a rock. He has a cut, that is all!'

'That is all *you* think,' the housekeeper retorted. 'You are not a physician.'

'And you are not in charge of the children!' Anna retorted.

From all she'd heard this woman had never expressed concern when the children were kept virtual prisoners in the nursery, rarely going out of doors.

Anna glared at her. 'If you have something to say about them, you will say it to me. Is that clear?'

Mrs Tippen remained unrepentant. 'You may bet Lord Brentmore will hear about this.'

Anna leaned into the woman's face. '*You* may be assured Lord Brentmore will hear about this! He gave me the charge of the children, not you.'

Mrs Tippen smirked and made a mocking curtsy before striding away.

Anna bit her lip as she watched the woman. Would Lord Brentmore believe the housekeeper over her? What would he think if Mrs Tippen reported that the new governess behaved in a careless fashion and allowed his son to fall and injure himself?

She and the children had been playing a game of tag on the lawn when Lord Cal tripped and fell. It had frightened him more than anything. A small cut right on his chin produced enough blood to thoroughly alarm his sister. Dory wailed loudly enough to be heard in the next county.

Anna had to admit she'd been alarmed herself. She'd scooped him up and carried him back to the house, but a closer examination showed the injury to be quite minor. She wrapped him in bandages and told the children about men in India who wore turbans for hats. Soon he and Dory were looking in a book with engravings of India and calm had been restored.

Until two hours later when Mrs Tippen informed her that the physician had arrived.

Trying to damp down her anger, Anna strode to the drawing room where the doctor waited.

She entered the room. 'Doctor Stoke, I am Miss Hill. The children's new governess.'

He stood and nodded curtly. 'Miss Hill.' The man was shorter than Anna, stick-thin, with pinched features and a haughty air. 'Inform me of the injury, please.'

'I fear you've made an unnecessary trip.' She smiled apologetically. 'Lord Calmount fell outside and suffered a tiny cut to his chin.'

'A head injury?' The doctor's brows rose. 'Did the boy become insensible?'

'No, not at all,' she assured him. 'It was not a head injury. Just a minor mishap, needing no more than a bandage—'

He broke in. 'Are you certain he did not pass out? Were you watching? A blow to the head can have dire consequences. Dire consequences.'

What had Tippen told him?

She gave the doctor a direct look. 'He did not pass out and he did not suffer a blow to his head. I was right there beside him. He fell and cut his chin on a rock.'

He responded with a sceptical expression. 'I must examine the boy immediately.'

'Certainly.'

She led Dr. Stoke up the stairs to the nursery wing.

'How old is the boy?' he asked as they walked.

He'd not asked the child's name, she noticed. 'Lord Calmount is seven years old.'

She led him to the schoolroom where she'd left the children with Eppy to draw pictures of Indian men in turbans in their sketch books.

Anna made certain she entered the room first. She approached Cal and spoke in a soft, calm voice. 'Lord Cal, here is Doctor Stoke. Mrs Tippen sent for him to examine your head so we may be certain it is only a very little cut.'

Cal gripped his pencil and glanced warily at the doctor.

'Hello, young man!' Doctor Stoke spoke with false cheer. 'Let me see that head of yours.'

The doctor reached for his head and Cal shrank back.

'None of that now,' the doctor said sharply, pulling off the bandages.

Cal panicked and pushed the man and soon was flailing with both fists and feet.

'No!' Dory caught her brother's fear and pulled on the doctor's coat to get him off. 'Don't take his turban! He wants to keep it!'

'Lord Cal! Dory! Stop it this instant!' She'd never seen them this way. She turned to Eppy. 'Take Dory out of here!'

Eppy carried a screaming Dory from the room.

Anna pulled the physician away and placed herself between him and Lord Cal. 'Cal, it is all right. The doctor will not hurt you. He wants to look at your cut and then we will make a new turban.'

Cal shook his head.

'Are you in pain?' Doctor Stoke demanded of the boy.

Cal, of course, did not answer. He pressed his hands against his chin.

It took a great deal of coaxing on Anna's part, but finally Cal allowed her to coax his fingers away and show the physician the cut. It had stopped bleeding and looked all right to Anna. She doubted it would even leave a scar.

The doctor then tried other examinations, like having the boy follow his finger as it moved side to side and up and down. Lord Cal refused. Cal also refused to answer any questions put to him, even those that could be answered with a nod of his head.

Doctor Stoke made no secret of his impatience with the boy. He finally gestured for Anna to leave the room with him.

'Come to the drawing room,' Anna said. 'We can speak more comfortably there.'

He was grim-faced as they walked to the drawing room, a room nearly as gloomy as the man himself.

Doctor Stoke stood stiffly as he faced Anna. 'How long has the boy been this way?'

'I think he was frightened,' she explained. 'It was a surprise to him that you came and he is not used to strangers.'

The physician pursed his lips disapprovingly. 'It was a mania.'

'A mania?' How ridiculous. 'It was a temper tantrum.'

He held up a halting hand. 'No. No. Definitely a disorder of the mind.'

'Nonsense!'

He steepled his fingers and tapped them against his mouth. 'I feel it my obligation to inform Lord Brentmore that his son is lapsing into lunacy. I've seen this happen before—'

'Lord Cal is not a lunatic!' she cried.

He tilted his head condescendingly. 'Ah, but you cannot deny the boy is prone to fits and is mute—'

'He is not mute!' she responded. 'He merely doesn't talk.'

The doctor smirked again. 'The very definition of mutism. I will write to the marquess this very day and inform him of this unfortunate circumstance. I will, of course, recommend the very best asylums. I know just the place. The child needs expert care.'

Anna's anxiety shot up. 'You will not write to Lord Brentmore!'

The doctor's mouth twisted in defiance.

She had to stop this! Who knew what Lord Brentmore would think if such a letter came his way?

She changed tactics. 'I mean, this is not

something for a father to read in a letter. Lord Brentmore…Lord Brentmore is…is due to arrive here very soon. You should speak to him in person. Surely there is no harm for the boy to remain a few more days at home. We…we will watch him carefully.'

Doctor Stoke averted his gaze as if thinking.

'I—I am certain it would be a good thing to meet the marquess in person. He is bound to have questions only you can answer.'

The doctor turned back to her. 'Very well. I will wait. Two weeks, no more. After two weeks I will summon the marquess myself.'

No sooner had the doctor left than Anna hurried to the library for pen and paper. She must write to Lord Brentmore immediately and convince him to come to Brentmore Hall.

Lord Cal was no lunatic! He was merely a frightened and timid boy who needed time to emerge from his shell. He was like Charlotte had been, although Lord Cal had no doting parents to support him. Lord Cal's parents had been anything but doting.

This time Lord Brentmore must not neglect his parental duty. He must come! Anna would show him his son was a normal little boy, albeit an unhappy one. He would see for himself his son was no lunatic.

She laboured to word her letter carefully.

After three tries, she composed the letter as

well as she could. She ended it with: *You must come, Lord Brentmore. You must. Your son needs you.*

Four days passed, too soon to hear back from Lord Brentmore. If he answered her right away, his letter could arrive tomorrow. Meanwhile she would do what she'd been doing since the doctor's ridiculous call. Keep the children busy.

Today they were outside again, taking advantage of glorious blue skies and bright sunshine. The weather had been cool for early June, but today the sun felt deliciously warm.

Anna dressed the children in old clothes, old gloves and perched wide-brimmed straw hats on them. She marched them outside to a small square near the kitchen garden that the gardener had prepared for planting at her request.

She and Charlotte had loved planting seeds and watching them grow into beautiful flowers, so why would Lord Cal and Dory not like such an activity as well? Besides, they had been so confined, it would be lovely for them to get a little dirty.

She made the whole enterprise a school lesson. In the school room they had read books about how plants grew from seeds. She'd discussed with the gardener what they might plant. He had suggested vegetables instead of flowers. Boys, he said, would value vegetables over flowers.

An excellent idea! Much more appealing to the practical Lord Cal, she was sure. Plus, eventually they could eat what they planted.

'We're going to plant peas and radishes and we are going to care for the plants until they are ready for eating,' Anna told the children as they walked towards the small plot of tilled earth.

As they reached the garden plot, a man stepped forwards. 'Good morning, miss.'

Anna smiled at him. 'This is your gardener, Mr Willis.' Mr Willis, a kindly man with children of his own, had proved a willing participant. 'Mr Willis, Lord Calmount and Lady Dory.'

Mr Willis had told her that he'd rarely even glimpsed the children up to now, even though he'd worked on the estate their whole lives.

Anna's anger burned at the thought of these children living as recluses. They'd been sheltered, clothed and fed, but not much more from what she could tell.

She had a theory about why Lord Cal had ceased speaking. It was not out of lunacy—he'd stopped speaking because no one but his sister had been there to listen to him.

'Are you ready for planting, then?' Mr Willis said.

'We are, sir,' Dory replied.

The gardener handed each of the children a small shovel. He showed them two wooden bowls.

Pointing to one, he said, 'These are the radish

seeds.' He put one seed in each of their hands. 'See? It is brown and it looks a little like a pebble, does it not?'

'It does look like a tiny pebble!' Dory cried.

Cal placed his seed between his fingers and examined it up close.

Mr Willis put his hand out to collect the seeds, replacing them with two other ones. 'Now these seeds look a little different. Can you tell what they are?'

Cal looked at his seed and quickly put a smug expression on his face.

'They look like old peas!' Dory said.

The gardener stooped down to her level. 'That is because that is what they are. The peas you eat are really seeds.'

Soon Mr Willis had them digging troughs in the dirt with their shovels. Next he showed them how to plant the seeds, starting with one row of peas, alternating with one row of radishes.

Soon they were happily placing the seeds in the trough and carefully covering them with soil. Anna was pleased that Cal participated in the activity with enthusiasm. She gazed at him, so absorbed in his planting and looking for all the world like a normal boy.

He needed time, she was convinced. Would his father give him time or would he lock him away in an asylum? Who was she to know better what a boy needed than a trained physician?

But she did know.

Would Lord Brentmore see his son as she did? Would he trust her to bring the boy out of his bashfulness? She could do it, she knew. She'd done it for Charlotte.

Charlotte.

Sometimes she missed Charlotte so much it hurt. She missed talking to her, confiding in her, laughing with her. There was no one here at Brentmore to talk to. Sometimes at night she wanted to weep out of loneliness.

And yet worse than the loneliness was the worry that Lord Brentmore would discharge her for being so brazen as to tell him and a physician what they should do. What would she do if she lost this lonely job?

Suddenly a shadow fell over her and a man's voice broke into her thoughts. 'Why are my children digging in the dirt?'

Mr Willis snapped to attention and the children froze.

Anna turned and faced an enraged Lord Brentmore.

'My lord.' She made her voice calm, though her legs trembled. 'We are engaged in a botany lesson. We are planting peas and radishes.'

The children dropped their seeds and scampered behind her skirts.

'My children will not dig in dirt.' His voice

shook with an anger that mystified her. What was wrong with planting a garden?

'Let me explain,' she began in a mollifying tone. 'We would not wish to frighten the children, would we?'

His eyes flashed.

She must take care. 'This is a botany lesson. Your children are learning how plants grow. We've read about it in books and now we are going to see how seeds grow into food we can eat.'

He looked no less displeased.

Her own temper rose. 'Your children are engaged in a useful occupation out of doors, in the fresh air, and are wearing old clothes which can be laundered. How is it you object to this, my lord?'

From behind her she heard Dory gasp. She felt Cal's grip on her skirt.

Lord Brentmore's eyes held hers for a long moment and she half-feared he was going to strike her.

Still, she refused to look away. It was imperative that the children not feel that enjoying themselves in useful activity was wrong.

His eyes still glittered, but he took a step back. 'Carry on your lesson, then.' He continued to hold her gaze. 'Attend me when you are done, Miss Hill.'

Before she could reply, he turned on his heel and strode back into the house.

None of them moved until he was out of sight.

'Why is Papa angry?' Dory cried.

Anna crouched down and gave the little girl a hug. 'Oh, I think we surprised him, didn't we? He probably thought Mr Willis and I were making you and Cal work like field labourers!' She said this as if it were the funniest joke in the world. 'Come on, let us finish. Mr Willis has the rest of the gardens to tend to.'

Luckily they had almost completed the task. Only two lines required seeding. The joy that had been palpable a few minutes ago had fled, however. Their father had made it vanish.

Anna put her hand to her stomach, trying to calm herself. Here she wanted Lord Brentmore to be her ally in helping Cal, and now she had offended him for planting a garden.

Would she lose her position over a botany lesson, over finding an excuse to take the poor reclusive children out in the fine June air?

Chapter Four

As soon as Brent entered the house, Mrs Tippen was waiting for him. He'd already had an earful from her when he arrived just a few minutes before.

'Do you see what I mean, sir?' the housekeeper said. 'She gives the children free rein over the house, the garden, everywhere! Allows them to get dirty—'

This he did not need. Tippen and her husband had come from Eunice's father's estate and had been Eunice's abettors. He'd never liked either of them.

He leaned down, bringing them face to face. 'Tend to the house, woman, and keep your nose out of what does not concern you!'

She gasped and backed away.

He pushed past her and made his way to the

hall where her husband was in attendance. 'Bring me some brandy!' he ordered. 'In the library.'

The library was about the only room in this house he could stomach. Eunice had possessed little desire to inhabit it, so the only ghost that lingered there was his grandfather's.

A footman soon appeared at the door with a bottle of brandy and a glass. Brent did not recognise him, but then he'd come to the house so rarely, he did not know half the servants. Eunice had replaced all his grandfather's old retainers.

Brent grabbed the bottle and glass from the man. 'Bring me another,' he ordered. 'Make that two. While I am here I want a bottle of brandy in the cabinet at all times.'

'Yes, m'lord,' the man said.

Brent poured himself a glassful and downed it in one gulp. He poured another.

An hour passed and still Miss Hill had not shown herself. Was the chit defying him? She would regret it if she were.

Brent paced the room, still attempting to calm himself. The sight of his son crouched down on the tilled soil had set him off.

He closed his eyes as memories washed over him. Digging hole after hole after hole, his stomach rumbling with hunger, his bare feet cold from the damp earth. He could still smell the soil, potatoes and manure. He rubbed his arms, his muscles again aching from the work.

By God, his son had looked exactly like him.

He poured another glass of brandy.

Where the devil was Miss Hill? He needed to have this out with her.

One more hour and two more glasses of brandy later, Miss Hill knocked at the door. 'My lord?'

He'd achieved a semblance of calm, but now his head swam from the drink.

She'd changed from the plain frock she'd worn in the garden to something soft and pink. Wisps of her auburn hair escaped from under a lace cap that framed her face and only made it appear more lovely.

By God, he did not want to be aroused by her! He was angry at her. What had he been thinking to come to this hated place?

He shook himself. His son. He'd come for his son.

'Come in, Miss Hill.' He straightened and hoped he would not sway.

She approached him, a wary smile on her face. 'Forgive my delay, sir. We finished the planting and a great deal of cleaning up was required.'

He narrowed his eyes. 'Because you allowed the children to wallow in dirt.'

Her chin rose. 'Getting dirty is all a part of planting, my lord.'

He closed the distance between them, coming so close the scent of her soap filled his nostrils. 'I know all about planting, Miss Hill.'

His first ten years of life had taught him.

She stepped back. 'Yes, well, perhaps then you can explain to me why planting peas and radishes in the kitchen garden made you so angry.'

She was questioning him? She needed to answer to him. 'Heed me, Miss Hill.' He glared at her. 'My son, my—children, are to be reared as a gentleman and lady, not as common serfs.'

She did not back down. 'It was a botany lesson.'

He held her gaze. 'It was demeaning.'

She looked incredulous. 'I do not think planting a garden and watching the plants grow could even remotely be demeaning.'

He slashed his hand through the air. 'My son does not need to know how to dig holes in order to become a gentleman.'

She countered, 'But as marquess some day, does he not need to know what effort goes into the crops his lands produce? What labour? What science? That was the intent of the lesson, my lord.'

He had no answer for that. He could only think of the back-breaking work of his childhood. 'He can read that in books.'

She bowed her head and fell silent, as if thinking how to proceed. He hoped she discovered it, because his brain felt too fuddled for conversation and his emotions too disordered to be trusted.

She walked over to the window and gazed out. The sun was near its brightest and it illuminated the air around her.

He swallowed.

She turned back to him, her arms crossed over her chest—her high, round breasts. 'We waste our time talking of this. I am so grateful you have come, and so quickly, too. You received my letter?'

'Yes.' He'd dropped everything to come to his son.

Her expression was earnest. 'Believe me, my lord, Lord Calmount is not demented. He is a normal little boy who is very timid and who has been very unhappy. He cannot be placed in an asylum. He cannot!'

No one would place his son in an asylum, of that Brent was resolved.

'He does not speak.' How could he, the boy's father, not know that the boy was mute? He knew the answer to that. He'd not been around long enough to notice. His brief visits had not included conversation.

'That is no reason for an asylum!' she cried. 'He is able to speak. He talks to his sister, but only to her. Doctor Stoke thinks this is some sort of insanity, but it is not, my lord. It is most assuredly not.'

It would be too cruel for the boy to suffer insanity on top of all the other strife he'd endured. From his mother. And his father. 'You contradict the expertise of the doctor, Miss Hill?'

'I do. I know Calmount can improve in time.' She leaned closer. 'I told you that I was Lady Charlotte's companion. When she was Calmount's age, she was not terribly unlike him. Charlotte was excessively timid. Starting when I was a child myself, I became her companion to help bring her out of her shell. I am convinced that your son is merely timid, as well. I know he can be helped.' She spoke earnestly. 'But not by sending him away!'

He glanced away. 'How am I to believe you?' God knew he wanted to believe her.

She lifted her chin and her blue eyes glittered with anger. 'Perhaps if you spent some time with your son, you would see for yourself. It has not helped him that neither of his parents troubled themselves very much about his welfare.'

His attention snapped back to her. 'I was compelled to be away.'

'Because of the war?' She shook her head. 'The war has been over a year.'

The truth of that stung. He'd stayed away as much as possible this last year.

But he refused to be scolded by a mere governess.

He rose to his fullest height and glared down at her. 'Do you presume to judge me, Miss Hill?'

A look of anxiety filled her eyes. She put a hand on her forehead. 'Forgive me, my lord. I spoke too plainly.'

He sank into a chair, feeling suddenly weary. 'Sit, Miss Hill. Tell me about my son.'

She lowered herself in a chair facing him. 'I have heard him talking to his sister, so there is no disorder of speech. But he will not speak to anyone else. In fact, Dory will speak for him every chance she gets. He hears well and is alert to everything. He is very clever, actually. He reads. He can write sentences, but he never writes to communicate. Instead, he nods or shakes his head or uses gestures.'

The poor boy. 'Why is this?'

What had happened to him, to cause him not to speak?

She hesitated. 'I must speak plainly again.'

He waved a hand. 'Proceed.'

She took a breath. 'The noise and commotion of children has been unwanted in this household. I am given to understand that your wife insisted the children remain in the nursery wing and later, after her death, the policy was unchanged and might have suited the governess because by then she was in ill health.' She paused. 'I do not know if that is precisely true. I only know for certain that…some…some members of the staff dislike having the children out and about.'

Mrs Tippen, no doubt.

She continued and her tone was accusatory, 'I do not believe that is healthy for children. That is why I plan as many activities outside as I can contrive. Like planting a garden.'

Undoubtedly she blamed him for not countering his wife's excesses, not realising the governess could no longer do her job, not paying enough attention to how his servants attended to his children's care and well-being.

His own conscience battered him for the same reasons.

'What would you have me do?' he snapped in defensiveness, even though there was no defense for his neglect.

'Do not allow Lord Calmount to be placed in an asylum!'

He averted his gaze.

Her voice quieted, but still trembled with emotion. 'I realise you are considering discharging me, but I beg you not to. Please give me a chance, for your children's sake. Do not listen to Dr Stoke. Give me a chance—' She broke off for a moment. 'Spend a little time with the children, at least? See for yourself. Observe your son for yourself. You will see what I see in him. I am certain of it.'

Her passionate defence of his son shook him to his depths. He was not considering discharging her. Quite the contrary. He thought her the children's salvation.

'How would I observe him?' he asked, his voice still sharper than he intended. 'I will not have him paraded before me.'

'I agree.' She leaned closer. 'Go to him. Join him in the nursery. Spend time with him. The children will be served dinner soon. Come share the meal with them.'

Share a meal with children? It was not something a marquess would do, at least not until children turned twelve or thirteen.

With the excess of brandy inside him, with his emotions so raw, could he even trust himself to sit with his children? It was hard enough to sit with Miss Hill.

But he'd dropped all his obligations in London to come to his son, to learn what had happened to the boy to make a physician declare him insane. To move heaven and earth to fix it.

He clenched his fist. 'Very well.'

She rose, walked to the door and waited for him.

He hoped he could cross the room without listing to one side or the other. When he managed to reach the doorway, the scent of lavender filled his nostrils and he remembered that first glimpse of her in the square outside his town house. She was no less beautiful now. No less passionate.

And he was no less aroused by her.

God help him.

Brent climbed the stairs behind Miss Hill. Her hips swayed seductively, while she kept up a discourse about the children, explaining the structure of their days. He hoped she would not ask him to recite the list back to her. At the moment there was not much staying in his brain beyond a reminder to keep his hands to himself.

When they approached the nursery door, Brent had a sudden attack of nerves. Ridiculous. These were children. They must respect and obey him.

Good God. Now he sounded like the old marquess, the English grandfather who'd despised him.

'Look who has come to eat dinner with us!' Miss Hill said brightly as she entered the room.

The two children were seated adjacent to each other at a small table upon which were four place settings.

'Papa!' Dory cried, jumping from her seat. 'Cal said it would be you. I said it would be Eppy.'

Cal stood as well, but, after sending an angry look at his sister, appeared as if he were facing the gallows.

'Oops!' The little girl covered her mouth with her hand. 'I must not speak unless spoken to.'

She was the image of Eunice, all bright blue

eyes and blonde curls. It pained him to look upon her.

He approached one of the chairs. 'Well, then I must speak and say good afternoon. And thank you for inviting me to dinner.'

Those blues eyes grew wider. 'But we did not invite you!'

He had an impulse to leave.

She giggled. 'I suspect Miss Hill invited you, did she not?'

He glanced at Miss Hill. 'She did indeed invite me.'

'I did.' She smiled, but tossed him an uncertain look.

He noticed an extra place was set at the table. She had apparently been confident he would accept.

Brent also noticed that Cal's forehead was furrowed as if he was not believing any of this conviviality.

Brent cleared his throat. 'We may be seated.'

He waited for Miss Hill to sit and noticed Cal waited as well. At least someone had taught him manners.

'Sit down, Miss Hill!' Dory commanded as she flopped into her seat.

Miss Hill lowered herself more gracefully. 'I do hope you children kept the covers on the dishes.'

Dory sent a very guilty look in Cal's direction. Cal, whose seat was directly across from Brent's, was too busy trying not to look at his father. He slipped into his chair, as if wishing he could disappear.

Brent remembered the agony of being in the old marquess's presence, the sure knowledge that sooner or later he would do something to raise the man's ire. It pained him that his son looked exactly as he had once felt.

He was not like his English grandfather, no matter how hard the marquess tried to make him so. Half of the old man's rages were on that very subject. How Brent failed to live up to the old man's expectations. How very Irish Brent was.

From a corner of the room, a maid stepped forwards to remove the covers from the dishes, starting with Brent's. His plate was filled with a generous slices of ham and cheese and one thick slice of buttered bread.

'Do you know our nurse, Eppy, Papa?' Dory glanced at the maid.

Another unfamiliar servant, Brent thought. 'I do not believe so. Good afternoon, Eppy.'

Eppy's face turned red. She bobbed a curtsy. 'M'lord.'

She uncovered Miss Hill's plate and then the children's. Their portions were smaller and the cheese on their plates showed definite signs of teeth marks.

So much for keeping the plates covered.

He glanced at Miss Hill, curious as to how she would rebuke them.

She merely returned an amused look. 'Who would like to say the blessing?'

Brent put down the fork he'd picked up.

Miss Hill's question was directed at Cal, who visibly shrank into himself.

Dory piped up. 'I will!'

Brent could not remember the last time he'd said a blessing before eating, but the brogue of his Irish grandfather returned to him—*Rath ón Rí a rinne an roinn...*

He no longer remembered what the words meant.

Little Dory straightened with great self-importance. 'Bless, O Lord, this food for thy use, and make us ever mindful of the wants and needs of others. Amen.' She spoke the words so fast they were nearly incomprehensible.

Miss Hill smiled at her. 'Very nicely done, Lady Dory.'

The little girl beamed.

She picked up her fork and stabbed down at a piece of ham. Cal merely moved his food from one side of his plate to the other.

Brent would learn nothing about his son if he did not address him. 'Calmount, Miss Hill tells me you can read.'

Cal's eyes rose and glanced at him.

'Cal likes reading,' Dory explained. 'He reads a lot.'

Brent turned back to Cal. 'What sorts of books do you like to read?'

The boy looked stricken.

'We read books about plants,' Dory piped up.

Miss Hill exchanged a knowing glance with Brent. Dory did indeed speak for her brother.

They ate in silence for a few moments, as if they'd all caught Calmount's inability to speak. It was unbearable. Worse still, Brent's head continued to swim and was starting to ache from too much brandy.

Miss Hill broke the silence. 'Shall we tell your father what we were planting in the garden today?' She pointedly looked at Calmount.

Dory rushed in to answer. 'We planted peas and radishes and Mr Willis told us just how to do it—' She launched into a detailed explanation of Mr Willis's instructions, glancing from time to time to her brother.

Brent tried to listen, but memories flooded him. His Irish grandfather's voice rang in his ears again, instructing him on how to plant the potatoes.

The man lived only four years after Brent was whisked away from him. Grandfather Byrne fought at the side of his kinsman, Billy Byrne, in the Irish Rebellion and was killed when Brent was fourteen. Brent read about it in a newspaper account.

The pain of that loss struck him anew and, for a moment, he could not breathe. Miss Hill kept up the conversation about the garden, but sent him a puzzled look. He blinked away the stinging in his eyes.

Had he stayed in Ireland, what would have been his fate? Would he have become an Irish rebel, too? Or would the others have shunned him because the blood of English nobility flowed through his veins? He'd long concluded he could belong in neither place. He belonged nowhere.

Dory's chatter filled the empty spaces. Brent tried watching his son, but that only intensified the boy's pain. And his own.

He wanted to spare his son pain. He wanted his son to be spared the suffering he'd endured. He wanted his son to feel he belonged wherever he was.

Clearly, he'd already failed.

'Papa? Papa?' Dory's tone mimicked her mother's.

'What is it?' he responded, trying not to sound vexed.

Dory gazed at him with her huge blue eyes. 'Why are you not angry at us now about the planting? You scolded us very severely when we were in the garden.'

Calmount looked alarmed and not very surreptitiously kicked his sister under the table. Dory kicked him back.

Brent took a bite of cheese and swallowed it, giving him time to compose himself. 'I was not angry at you.'

'At Miss Hill, then,' the child persisted. 'Why did you scold Miss Hill?'

He knew what the old marquess would have done had Brent spoken to him like that. Bitten his head off and spat it out.

He refused to respond in like manner. 'I—I was mistaken…'

Dory seemed even more emboldened. 'Miss Hill said you thought she had made us into field labourers.'

He glanced gratefully at Miss Hill. 'I did indeed.' It was an excuse a child would believe. 'I thought next she'd have you selling your wares at market.'

Miss Hill smiled and Dory burst into giggles. 'It was a *lesson*, silly! To teach us how things grow. She's been reading to us about it for days and days.'

He cut a piece of ham. 'So you are not to be planting my fields?'

Dory dissolved in more giggles. 'No!'

He could follow this tack. 'Has Miss Hill started reading to you about cleaning the stables? Will I see you raking out the hay and polishing the tack?'

Calmount looked very confused.

Dory turned to Miss Hill. 'May we read about stables? I like horses very much.'

Miss Hill laughed. 'Perhaps we can read about horses and visit the stables with your father's permission, but I have no plans to teach you to muck out a stable.'

'May we visit the stables and see the horses, Papa?' Dory fluttered her lashes, reminding him too much of her mother again.

'Not today.' His tone sounded sharper than he'd intended.

Calmount immediately stared down at his plate, looking stricken.

'Maybe tomorrow,' Brent added.

Maybe tomorrow he'd have more control over his emotions.

He stood. 'I must be going. I—I have some estate business to attend to.'

'Do not forget about tomorrow!' Dory said.

He nodded towards her and turned to Miss Hill. 'May I see you in the hallway for a moment?'

'Certainly.' She placed her napkin next to her plate and followed him from the room, closing the door behind her.

She immediately spoke. 'Do you see? It is as I described.'

He closed his eyes against the sight of her, so

close, before nodding. 'He seems so…so sad and so frightened.'

'Yes!' Her voice brightened.

He forgot what he wanted to say to her and his head was throbbing. 'I—I have much to do today.' This was a lie. All he needed to do was recover from too much brandy, too much emotion and too many memories. 'I will spend more time with Calmount tomorrow. I'll—I'll arrange a visit to the stables.'

'That will certainly make Dory happy.' Her lovely smile faded quickly. 'But what of Doctor Stoke? Will you see him?'

He might throttle the physician if he met the man in person. 'A letter should suffice.'

Anna had no idea when Lord Brentmore would send for them to see the stables, but she made certain the children were ready bright and early, having Eppy dress them in clothing suitable for the out of doors.

'Will Papa take us to the stables like he promised?' Dory asked as soon as Anna entered the nursery.

She swept a stray curl off Dory's forehead. 'If he said he would, I am sure he will.'

His prompt arrival so soon after she had posted the letter to him had been as astonishing as his burst of temper upon his arrival. Truth was, she did not know what to expect from him. In any event, she must believe his concern for Lord Cal was genuine. At least he'd believed her about Cal and would not even listen to Doctor Stoke. That seemed a miracle in itself.

For the moment her job seemed secure as well, which was a great relief. She was becoming very fond of the children and confident in her duties towards them, but she was lonely. She missed her home at Lawton House and especially missed Charlotte. She expected no correspondence from her parents, who could not write, but why had Charlotte not responded to her letters? Had she been so easily forgotten?

She shook these questions out of her head and faced the children. 'We will start our lessons, as always. Your father will come when it is convenient for him.' She handed a slate to each of the children. 'Dory, you may practise the alphabet. Lord Cal, I want you to write a sentence about planting radishes.'

Dory squirmed in her chair and made several pointed glances at the door while she laboured with her ABCs. Lord Cal quickly finished his sentence and put the slate down.

Anna picked it up and read aloud, 'Plant radish seeds three seeds to an inch in a trench that is one-half inch deep.' It was a verbatim quote from Mr Willis. 'Very good sentence, Cal.' She handed the slate back to him. 'Now write a sentence about planting peas.'

He wiped the slate with his cloth and bent over it with his piece of chalk.

Anna glanced at Dory's slate. The child was only on the letter D. Too busy watching the door.

A knock sounded and the door opened.

Lord Brentmore stepped inside. 'Good morning.'

The room seemed to fill with his presence and Anna's senses flashed into alert. She could not shake the image of a panther caged as she watched him move. The very air around him turned turbulent in a manner that she did not understand.

Cal had turned quickly back to his slate. Did the boy absorb the same impression of his father as Anna did?

Lady Dory, on the other hand, seemed oblivious.

'Papa!' The child jumped up from her chair and ran to him. 'Are we going to the stables now?'

Anna's heart beat faster. Would he be in a rage again? Or would he be kind?

His expression gave no sign. 'When Miss Hill says so.' He looked at Anna. 'I do not wish to interrupt your lessons.'

Dory's look was imploring.

Anna took a breath and made herself smile. 'Well, there is no sense doing lessons with this one.' She tweaked the girl's chin. 'She can think of nothing but horses.' Lord Cal was still riveted to his slate. 'Let me see if your son is near finishing his sentence about planting peas.'

Cal wrote hurriedly and handed her the slate, taking care not to look at anyone. Anna handed the slate to Lord Brentmore.

He read aloud, 'Plant peas every two inches in a trench two inches deep.'

Anna glanced at Lord Brentmore before putting her hand on Cal's shoulder. 'Another good sentence.'

Lord Brentmore looked at the slate again. 'Yes. A good sentence.'

Cal sat very still and stared at the table.

Dory skipped over. 'Cal is *excellent* at writing.'

'I can see that.' Lord Brentmore appeared uncomfortable and Anna had the strangest sense that it pained him to be in the presence of his children.

She clapped her hands. 'Let us get our hats and coats and gloves and we shall have our visit to the stables.'

Once they were outside, the children and Anna had to scamper quickly to keep up with Lord Brentmore's long-limbed stride. Did he not realise that children had short legs?

They crossed the lawn to a set of buildings made from the same stone as the house. The wide door of one of the buildings was open and the stable master awaited them.

'M'lord.' He pulled at his forelock.

'Good morning, Upsom,' Lord Brentmore said. 'We have come to see the stables.'

Anna waited to be introduced, but Lord Brentmore neglected that nicety.

She stepped forwards. 'I am Miss Hill, Upsom, the children's governess. We have not met before. And the children, of course, are Lord Calmount and Lady Dory.'

Upsom was almost as tall as Lord Brentmore and lanky, not at all like Anna's father, also a stableman, but shorter than herself and thick as a tree trunk. The smell of hay and horse, though, made her homesick for Lawton.

'Pleased to meet you, miss,' the man said. 'This stable is for the carriage horses and riding horses. The working horses are in a separate stable.'

They stepped inside. The stables were huge, more than double what Lawton possessed.

'But there are no horses!' cried Dory.

'The horses are not here, my lady,' Upsom said. 'They are all in the paddock.'

Dory looked crestfallen.

'We may go out to the paddock,' Lord Brentmore said.

'Yes!' Dory jumped up and down.

'Follow me, then.' Mr Upsom gestured towards the back of the stables.

In the paddock beyond the stables several horses grazed. Lord Brentmore whistled and a beautiful ink-black gelding trotted over to the fence.

'This is my horse.' Brentmore stroked the horse's muzzle.

'This is your horse?' Dory clambered up the fence for a closer look. 'Did you ride him here?'

'I did.'

'What is his name?' Dory asked.

'Luchar.'

Anna's brows rose. In an Irish myth she'd read, Luchar and his brothers killed their grandfather.

'May I pet him?' Dory begged.

Lord Brentmore hesitated a moment before lifting her up so she could reach the horse.

'Gently,' he said. 'Keep your hand away from his mouth.'

Anna glanced towards Cal, who held back. Cal's eyes were not looking at his father's horse, but at another horse on the far side of the paddock, a majestic white horse galloping restlessly, back and forth.

She crouched down to Cal's level. 'What horse is that?'

He crossed his arms over his chest and bowed his head.

Anna touched his shoulder and left him. Walking to Brentmore's side, she gestured to the white horse. 'Lord Cal was watching that horse.'

'That was Mama's horse,' Dory piped up.

Brentmore put her back on the ground and averted his gaze from the beautiful white horse.

Cal stood stiffly, clearly disturbed as well.

What was it about the horse that upset them all? Anna had half a mind to ask little Dory. She was the only one who talked.

Brentmore turned away from the horses. 'Do you children ride?'

Cal gave him a quick glance before withdrawing again.

Dory did not hesitate. 'No. We do not ride, but we would like to ride above all things.'

'Upsom!' Brentmore called. 'Have my horse saddled.' He turned to his son. 'Calmount, you are the oldest. You will be first.'

The boy's eyes widened, but he looked engaged. Whatever had happened inside him when he saw the white horse had disappeared.

Well done, Lord Brentmore, Anna thought.

When Luchar was saddled, Lord Brentmore lifted his son on to the horse's back and mounted behind him. He set a sedate pace, circling the paddock. Cal looked almost peaceful as he sat in front of his father.

When it was Dory's turn, she could barely contain her joy.

Anna smiled, liking Lord Brentmore very much at this moment.

His reaction to the white horse caused her

Chapter Five

Brent could not sleep. The morning at the stables had disturbed him all day.

He did not know what gave greater distress—Calmount's suffering, Miss Hill's allure, or the memories evoked by the white horse.

And little Dory.

She was so like Eunice. In her looks. Her charm. She possessed that gift of easy speech that so eluded Calmount—and Brent himself, if he were truthful. Eunice had always known precisely what to say to get what she wanted.

Except, perhaps, that fateful day when she was thrown from her white horse in her mad dash to catch up with her departing lover. She fell on to the hard rocks and broke her neck. When the news reached him in Vienna, his immediate reaction had been relief.

God help him.

But his next thought had been of how badly he'd failed her by not being the man she'd believed him to be. She'd been unfaithful, to be sure, but she'd also been made very unhappy by her marriage to a man with the blood of an Irish peasant flowing in his veins. Not even the birth of their son had made up for it.

As soon as Brent had heard of her death he'd hurried back to Brentmore for the children's sakes, but, once there, had not a clue how he could assist them. He still did not know.

Did the children enjoy riding in the paddock? He hoped so. Certainly Dory had seemed to, but he could not tell about Calmount.

Afterwards he'd taken Luchar for a proper run around the estate, checking on the tenants' welfare and on the planting. Luckily everything seemed well. The cottages looked in good repair. His tenants seemed content. His fields were verdant with crops.

At least his wealth did some good. It provided a comfortable livelihood to many people.

All his wealth, his huge house, his vast estate, had not prevented his children from living in a small set of rooms, their lives even more confined than his poverty-stricken early life in Ireland.

Awash with guilt, he paced the second floor in his shirt-sleeves and bare feet, surrounded by the trappings of his wealth.

It had been Miss Hill who had freed them from their prison, apparently defying Mrs Tippen in the process. He was beginning to see he owed her a great deal, not the least of which was saving his son from an insane asylum.

Now that he could not sleep, he pined for her company, her mettle, her passion. He yearned to talk to her, confide in her, rouse her from her bed—

He stopped himself. Thinking of Miss Hill in bed was not a good idea.

He'd be better off fetching another bottle of brandy. He picked up a candle to light his way and walked out of the bedchamber to the stairway.

A cry came from above.

From the children's wing?

He hurried up the flight of stairs and stopped at the top to listen.

He heard it again.

'Nooooo!' came the cry.

Brent rushed towards the sound, which grew louder and louder.

'Nooo! Do not hit me! Do not hit me!'

He flung open the door to the room that had once been his childhood bedchamber. Calmount was sitting straight up in bed, flailing his arms, a look of terror on his face.

'No!' he shrieked.

Brent ran to his side and seized his arms. He

tried to awaken him. 'Cal! It is a dream. Wake up! Wake up.'

Footsteps sounded in the hallway and Miss Hill rushed in, dressed in nightclothes, her auburn hair loose about her shoulders.

'What is it?' she cried.

'A nightmare. I cannot wake him.' Brent held the boy. 'Wake up, Cal. You are dreaming.'

Calmount's eyes suddenly focused on him. The child gasped and pulled away, scooting to the wall and cowering.

'Do not hit me!' he cried, awake this time.

And speaking!

'I will not hit you.' Brent reached for him. 'You've had a nightmare. That is all.'

The boy shrank away.

'I would never hurt you.' Brent wrapped the boy in his arms and held him close. 'It was only a dream.'

The boy stiffened. Brent felt his struggle, his terror, but finally Cal relaxed against him and his tears dampened Brent's shirt.

Miss Hill sat on the bed next to them, stroking the boy's hair and murmuring, 'There. There. It will be all right now. You are safe now.'

Brent rocked the boy as Miss Hill's warm voice assured him, over and over, that he'd only been dreaming. Eventually Cal fell asleep again, an exhausted sleep.

Brent laid him down on the bed and tucked the blankets around him.

He turned to Miss Hill. 'Good God. What was that all about?'

She whispered, 'This has not happened before.'

'Yes, it has.' A voice came from the doorway. Dory stood in the threshold in her nightdress. 'Cal has bad dreams a lot.'

Miss Hill picked Dory up and held her.

'Do you know what the dreams are about?' Brent asked the girl.

She nodded. 'They are about Mama. About that bad time.'

'What bad time?' Brent did not want to leave Cal, but did not wish to wake him either. He gestured for them to step further away from Cal's bed.

Dory snuggled against Miss Hill's chest. 'That bad time. I did it, though, so you should kill me and not Cal.'

Kill her?

Brent felt as if the child had pierced him with a dagger. 'I'm not going to kill anyone.'

'Why would you say such a thing?' Miss Hill asked.

'Because Mama said that Papa would kill us for breaking anything, especially the big vase, but I broke it. I ran in the hallway and knocked it down. Cal said he did it and told me to hush. So he got the beating and not me.'

'Beating?' Brent felt the dagger twist.

'Mama gave Cal a terrible beating. She said he was a terrible boy, but it was really me who was bad.' The child's voice rose. 'And then…then… she hugged Cal and said she was sorry. She was unhappy, she said. And…and that she was only trying to protect Cal. That it was you who would kill him if you found out about the vase.' A sob escaped her lips. She fell into a fit of weeping.

Brent could not breathe. He'd never imagined that Eunice's unhappiness had been that acute. She'd always vowed her children were more precious to her than any jewel and that she could not bear to be parted from them. But she beat her son. Because of her unhappiness?

How much responsibility of this belonged to him?

Dory's weeping quieted.

'Dory,' Brent asked. 'Did this sort of thing happen often? That your mother hit Calmount?'

'She hit me, too.' She turned to him, her eyes glistening with tears. 'And then she hugged us. Mrs Sykes told us we must be very good around Mama. Not be noisy or bother her. Mrs Sykes said we should stay in the nursery.'

Brent felt sick inside.

'We must get you back to bed,' Miss Hill told Dory.

She tightened her arms around Miss Hill's neck. 'I don't want to go. I want to stay with Cal.'

'Let her stay,' Brent said. 'I do not want Cal to be alone.'

Miss Hill carried her to the bed and tucked her in. 'You come to me if he has another bad dream.'

'He won't.' Dory yawned. 'They always stop if I stay with him.'

Brent fetched the candle and walked out of the room behind Miss Hill.

When they were in the hallway, he stopped her. 'Will you come with me? I am in great need of a drink.'

She hesitated for a moment, but nodded.

They walked side by side to the library, which still had coals glowing in the grate. He placed the candle on a table and added a few chunks of coal to the fire.

'Please sit, Miss Hill.' He gestured to one of the large comfortable chairs facing the fireplace. He retrieved a bottle from a cabinet nearby, glad he'd instructed the footman to keep it stocked. He lifted the bottle. 'It is brandy. Would you care for a glass?'

She nodded. 'Yes. I believe I am in great need of drink, too.'

He poured her glass first and handed it to her, his fingers grazing hers as she took it. He poured himself a glass, downed it and poured himself another before lowering himself in the chair adjacent to hers.

'What you must think of me.' He could not

face her. 'I must tell you that I knew nothing of Eunice's treatment of the children.'

She looked unconvinced.

He took a gulp from his glass. 'I thought she was devoted to them.'

She took a small sip from her glass.

He gave a dry laugh. 'I'm astonished you do not ring a peal over my head. Chastise me for not being around enough to know that my son and his sister were in the hands of a monster.'

She faced him. 'It is not my place—'

He lifted a finger. 'Ah, but you thought it, all the same.'

She looked away. 'It should not matter to you what a governess thinks.'

He fixed his gaze on her. 'It matters what you think.'

She looked as if she was considering whether to answer. She met his eye. 'I think it was convenient for you to stay away.'

He bowed his head.

She was right, of course. He didn't look too carefully at his children because he wanted to stay away. From them. From Eunice. From this house and its memories.

He took another gulp and refilled his glass. 'What do you know of me, Miss Hill?'

She blinked. 'Nothing.'

'I am surprised Lord Lawton did not warn

you.' The earl ought to have told her. 'I am half-Irish. Did you know that?'

She shook her head.

'My wife did not know it when I married her. She thought she was marrying an English marquess.' He rubbed his forehead. 'It never occurred to me that she did not know. Or perhaps I did not wish to consider that possibility. I was quite smitten…' He glanced at her. 'I did not wish to lose her, but I did that anyway.' He stared into his brandy. 'I knew she was unhappy. Her efforts to seek comfort elsewhere led to great scandal.' He downed his glass. 'And great conflict between the two of us. When I was with her there was turmoil. The opportunity offered itself to work for Lord Castlereagh on the Continent. I seized it. It seemed the perfect solution. I thought it would make her happy.'

The expression on her face gave him no idea of her reaction to this story.

He turned away again. 'Over the better part of three years, my visits to Brentmore were brief. I thought my wife's unhappiness was confined to the times I was present. I…I had no idea…'

She took a sip of her drink. 'You see the problems now, my lord. It is now you who must change.'

He rose from the chair and took out another bottle. 'What can I do? Except feel responsible for all the misery the children have endured?'

He could feel her eyes following him.

'If your neglect was responsible, as you say, then taking charge of making it better is what you must do.'

His gaze snapped back to her. 'Taking charge?' His head swam and his legs seemed unsteady, but he made it back to his chair. 'I must take charge.'

'Do not think of the past.' Her tone was soothing, as it had been when she murmured to his son. 'You cannot change what is past.'

Did she really believe he could atone for his past neglect? He would not know where to begin.

He gazed at her, at her long flowing hair, the thin layers of cloth that covered her naked body. He yearned for the comfort of her arms just like when she had held Dory.

He lifted his gaze. 'Will you help me, Anna Hill? I do not know what to do.'

The intensity of Lord Brentmore's gaze shook Anna. She'd watched him drink glass after glass of brandy, knowing he was trying to dull his pain. When he rose to fetch a second bottle, though, she could see he was quite inebriated.

'Anna,' he repeated. 'Such a pretty name. So much prettier than Miss Hill.'

Her face grew hot. No one had ever spoken her name like that before.

'Anna,' he repeated, then turned away, running a hand through his thick dark hair. He returned to his chair. 'Forgive me. We were talking about the children. You were going to tell me what to do.'

She sipped her drink, surprised that the brown liquid felt so warm in her chest. This had been her first taste of brandy.

She must say something quickly or he might speak her name in that deep, velvet voice again. 'I think you spend time with them. Let them become accustomed to you and you accustomed to them. Then you will know better what to do.'

That sounded wiser than she felt.

Since she arrived at Brentmore, she'd been sure that the children needed to be free of the nursery, free to run and shout and play. She knew that Lord Cal's muteness could improve, as Charlotte's bashfulness had improved. But what she did not know—and what she could not allow Lord Brentmore to guess—was if she was even a passable governess. Perhaps she'd helped only because the children's situation had been so dire anyone would have helped.

Now Lord Brentmore was relying on her to help him. The children's fate seemed squarely on her shoulders.

Not even for the children's sake should she be sitting in a dark room, so late at night, in her nightdress and robe, sipping brandy with a man who spoke her name in that disturbing way. She'd never been with any man like this, not even her

father, but then her father rarely spent more than
a few minutes in her company.

Something besides the children was vibrat-
ing between this powerful marquess and herself,
something that made her think of him as man,
not merely her employer.

He rubbed his hand back and forth on the arm
of his chair and she felt it as if he touched her
own bare skin.

'I must stay at Brentmore, then.' His words
slurred.

He stood. So suddenly she jumped in surprise.

He crouched down in front of the fireplace and
poked at the coals. Sparks scattered, brightening
the room momentarily. 'I despise this house and
have done since I was a child. Eunice wanted to
be here, but even living here did not make her
happy. There is nothing but unhappiness here.'
He threw down the poker and it clanged like a
bell against the stone hearth. 'From my grandfather to Eunice. Unhappy memories.'

He turned back and loomed over her, taut with
pain. 'I do not want to stay here.'

She felt small in the shadow of this man who'd
turned suddenly forbidding.

'Perhaps—' She swallowed. 'Perhaps this is a
time when you must not do what you want, but
what the children need.'

He dropped into his chair again and downed
yet another glass of brandy. 'The children. I

wanted to give them an easy life. Every advantage. Nothing like—' He broke off to pour more brandy.

She was afraid to speak.

Lord Brentmore buried his face in his hands. His shoulders shook and, in spite of her fear, Anna's heart went out to him. Without thinking, she left her chair and came to his side. She pulled his hands away from his face and made him look at her. 'Do not despair,' she said. 'It will come to rights, my lord. You will see.'

He rose and his arms went around her, pulling her flush against him. He buried his head in her shoulder. She felt the warmth of his skin through the thin fabric of his shirt, the steady beating of his heart, the prickly texture of his beard.

But his pain shook her most of all.

She held him close and murmured to him, trying to soothe him the way she had tried to soothe Lord Cal. Could she make everything turn out right, as she was promising?

He eventually relaxed, as Lord Cal had relaxed.

His hold on her loosened and she drew away. 'I think you should go to bed, my lord.'

His eyes darkened and he did not answer her. Another sensation flashed through her, one she could not identify. Not fear. Not pity. Something else. She felt as out of breath as if she'd run a mile.

He seized her hand and wrapped his fingers around hers.

She pulled her fingers from his grip and held his arm to steady him. Picking up the candle, she urged him to walk with her to the stairway. They climbed together, Lord Brentmore gripping the banister. He led her to his bedchamber, a room she'd only glimpsed during that first tour of the house. She intended to leave him at the door, but he pulled her in the room and took her in his arms again.

'Stay with me, Anna,' he whispered in her ear. 'Do not leave me. I have no wish to be alone.'

His hand slid down the length of her body and pressed her *derrière*. She felt the bulge of his manhood beneath his trousers.

She gasped, almost dropping the candle.

It was the drink causing him to behave so. And his unhappiness. He was not in control of his mind or his urges.

Her head was clear, however. So why did she not push him away? Why so wantonly allow his hands to move over her body, sparking sensations she'd never known possible?

Why was his invitation so difficult to resist?

'Of course I will stay,' she murmured. 'Let us get you to your bed.'

She placed the candle on a nearby table and let him lean on her as she walked him to his bed, its covers rumpled and disordered as if abandoned after a fitful sleep. He climbed into the bed and reached for her.

'In a moment, my lord,' she managed.

His fingers twisted locks of her hair, causing even more disturbing new sensations. He pulled her towards him and placed his lips upon hers.

Her first kiss from a man.

And such a kiss. Dizzying in its intensity. His lips were warm, firm. Wanting. Coaxing her to part her lips. His tongue touched hers, tasted her, savoured her as if she were some exotic delicacy. He tasted of brandy and heat and her body ached with new urges. Carnal urges.

With difficulty she broke off. 'Settle yourself under the covers, my lord.'

'Join me,' he rasped as he slid himself under the covers.

'I will.' She tucked the blankets around him the way she had done for the children. 'Close your eyes. I'll be only a moment or two. I must blow out the candle.'

'Candle,' he murmured, pulling on the sash of her robe.

She stepped away and her sash slipped off, but she did not dare pull it from his grip. Instead she waited, watching him by the light of the candle. He lay still, her sash in his hand. In a moment his breathing turned even.

She picked up the candle and backed towards the door. Still he did not move. She quietly crossed the threshold and pulled the door closed as she stepped into the hallway.

As quickly as she could, she returned to the stairway and made her way to the second floor. Before returning to her own bed, she peeked in at the children, snuggled together and sleeping peacefully.

She might have lain with Lord Brentmore as close, his strong arms encircling her, but nothing about lying with him would be peaceful. Her heart pounded in her chest as she returned to her room. Her senses still flared with the memory of his body against hers, his lips tasting hers.

But she climbed into her bed alone.

Brent woke to the sound of rain pattering the windows and a servant tending to the fire in his fireplace. He found a sash in his hand.

Miss Hill's sash.

The events of the previous night came back in a muddle. He remembered being unable to sleep. Remembered hearing Cal cry out in a nightmare. Remembered hearing of the abuse the children suffered out of Eunice's unhappiness.

The rest was confusion. He could recall drinking brandy in the library, confessing to Miss Hill his mistakes. His devastating mistakes.

Why was her sash in his hand?

He vaguely recalled the feel of her hair through

his fingers, her soft skin under his hands, the taste of the soft recesses of her mouth.

Lawd. Had he seduced her?

He quickly hid the sash under the covers so the servant would not see, not that this sort of thing could ever be kept secret in a country house. As a boy, he always knew which of the maids his grandfather took to his bed. Poor women. They'd hardly been in a position to refuse.

Had Miss Hill presumed the same? That she must do as he asked or be tossed out on her ear?

Even in his misery and his drink-soaked mind, he'd noticed how beautiful she'd looked with her hair loose about her and her robe tightly cinched at her waist. He remembered that.

He balled the sash into his hand. He also remembered calling her Anna.

Anna. She could no longer be Miss Hill to him, but he hoped it was not because he'd forced an intimacy upon her that was beyond all that was respectable.

The servant left the room and Brent shook the memory of Anna from his brain.

He climbed out of bed.

He was still in his shirt-sleeves and trousers, but that meant nothing, only that perhaps he'd not taken the time to undress before slaking his need. Lawd, was he truly to add seducing the children's governess to his many sins?

His head pounded like the very devil. In two

days' time he'd twice imbibed to the point of inebriation. It was not like him at all. It was this house. Brentmore Hall brought out the worst in him.

He quickly washed and shaved and dressed without summoning the footman who'd assumed duties as valet. He stuffed the sash into his pocket and made his way to the breakfast room where a pot of hot tea and a sideboard filled with food awaited him.

Mr Tippen stepped into the room. 'Do you require anything, m'lord?'

'No.' Brent's stomach roiled at the smell of kippers. He reached for the tea pot.

The butler turned to leave.

'Wait.' Brent stopped him. 'Do you know if the children are awake? Have they been served breakfast?' He did not dare ask if their governess had yet risen from her bed.

'I am sure I do not know, m'lord,' Tippen replied, acting as if the question was beneath him.

The prig.

'Find out for me,' Brent ordered. 'If they have not eaten breakfast, I want them to eat here. In this room. With their governess.'

He needed to see them, to assure himself that the night that had disturbed him so had not scarred them even more.

And he needed to see Anna.

Tippen gave him a disapproving look, but bowed. 'Very good, m'lord.'

A few minutes later a footman appeared with more place settings. 'Mr Tippen said I was to tell his lordship that the children will be eating with you as you desired.'

'Thank you—' He did not know the footman's name.

'Wyatt, m'lordship,' the footman offered.

'Wyatt.' Another task to forge for himself, Brent thought. Learn the servants' names.

Wyatt retreated to a corner of the room while Brent finished a second cup of tea. The door opened and Anna—Miss Hill—entered, the children behind her.

Brent stood. 'Good morning.' He caught her eye, but her expression revealed nothing.

'Are we being punished?' Dory asked, somewhat defiantly.

'Punished?' Had he done something last night to give the child that impression? 'No. I wanted your company, that is all.'

'Oh.' The little girl slid into a chair. The table top came up to her chin.

Anna turned to the footman. 'Wyatt, I believe Lady Dory could use a fat pillow to sit upon.'

'I'll attend to it, miss.' He left the room.

She did not look at Brent, but said, 'Please sit, my lord.' She addressed the children. 'Come see what is on the sideboard for you to eat.'

Dory scooted off the chair and decisively made her choices. Cal tentatively pointed to what he wanted.

By the time they settled back at the table, Dory had her pillow.

Anna again spoke to Brent. 'Shall I fix you a plate, my lord?'

Was her tone sharp? Wounded? He could not tell for certain. 'Some bread and butter, perhaps.' Definitely no kippers.

When she placed the plate in front of him, he finally caught her gaze. 'Do I owe you an apology, Miss Hill?'

Her face flushed. 'You are not obligated to me, my lord.'

What did that mean? He still did not know and could not ask for clarification in front of the children. He ought to have summoned her alone, perhaps. But he'd wanted to see the children, too.

She fixed her own plate last. When she finally seated herself and they all commenced eating, no one talked. Brent remembered countless mornings seated with his grandfather in this very room, with nothing but oppressive silence. With Eunice, the silence had been fraught with her undisguised disdain for everything about him.

He hated that his children were left to imagine what was unspoken.

He turned to Dory. 'Why did you think coming here was a punishment?'

Her blue eyes looked up at him over her jam and toasted bread. 'Because we woke you up. We *disturbed* your sleep.'

Brent could hear Eunice in those words. He glanced at Cal, who watched them both warily.

Brent leaned towards him. 'You had a nightmare last night. Do you remember waking up from it?'

The boy very slightly shook his head.

Brent was heartened. This was at least communication between them. Other than the boy's words during and after the nightmare, that was. 'Dory told us you dream about your mother. Do you remember dreaming about your mother last night?'

Cal paled and shook his head again.

Brent deliberately attended to his food, buttering his piece of bread. 'I've heard your mother said I would kill you children if you broke anything—a vase—anything.' He pretended to look absorbed in spreading the butter. 'She was very mistaken. I do not kill children for breaking things, nor do I hit them for it. I was a boy once, too, and boys and girls break things sometimes.'

He glanced at Anna, to see her assessment of this little speech.

She gave him an approving look.

It encouraged him. 'I do not kill children under any circumstance and I cannot think of one reason to hit children either. If I had not been busy with the war, I would have forbidden your mother from hitting, as well. She was wrong to do so. Apparently even she recognised that fact and re-gretted her actions.'

Dory's eyes were wide as saucers and colour returned to Cal's face.

Lawd, he hoped he chose the right thing to say.

Dory's brows lowered and she tilted her head. 'Are you going back to war?'

Cal rolled his eyes at her question. He knew about the war, Brent realised.

Brent winked at him, then took a bite of his bread, chewed and swallowed, trying to make this conversation as easy as possible for them. 'The war is over.'

He wanted to say to them that he would stay for a while at Brentmore, that he would give them more rides on his horse and share more meals with them. But he did not know if what he had done the night before might make his presence here impossible. He needed Anna to tell him.

There were countless reasons not to stay. Financial matters mostly, although his man of business could take charge of most of those. Parliament was still in session, but he could still work behind the scenes, if he wished. Miss Rolfe—

Good God. Had he betrayed Miss Rolfe, as well as seducing the governess? He was a betrothed man and he'd be no better than Eunice had been if he would bed one woman while committed to another.

But perhaps he had not dishonoured himself. He must find out. Even if he had not, his absence was bound to disturb the Rolfes. He ought to write his cousin and ask him to explain his abrupt absence to Miss Rolfe and her father. Brent was perfectly willing to immediately settle some money on Lord Rolfe if the man needed it right away, so there was no reason to set a quick date for the wedding. Peter ought to be able to reassure the Rolfes and inform Brent what they required.

Brent wanted to stay with the children and help them if he could. It all depended on Anna.

Dory blinked her long-lashed eyes at him. 'If you are not going back to war, will you take us for a ride on your horse?'

She reminded him of Eunice again. He tried not to frown, instead gesturing towards the window. 'Not in the rain, Dory.'

'You will have lessons today,' Anna broke in. She slid Brent what seemed to him a wary glance. 'Unless you have other plans for them, my lord.'

She was being cautious with him.

'Not at the moment.' He met her eye. 'I would speak with you first, Miss Hill.'

She lowered her gaze. 'As you wish.'

Brent took a sip of tea and stood. 'I will see you in the library when you have finished breakfast.'

Before he left the room he turned back and

saw his son staring at him with an expression of discomfort and confusion that mirrored precisely what Brent felt inside.

Chapter Six

Brent paced the library. It seemed he was always waiting on this governess. Were not those in his employ supposed to be at his beck and call?

He pressed his fingers against his temples. It did him no credit to be churlish, especially since her primary concern must be the children.

And he had very likely seduced her. She would be in no hurry to see him, certainly.

He paced and watched the clock for a good forty-five minutes before there was a light knock on the door.

She entered. 'I am sorry to keep you waiting, my lord.' Her voice sounded calm. 'The children needed to be started on their lessons.'

He strode straight for her and placed the sash in her hand. 'I need to know what happened last night.'

She lifted her gaze from her sash and responded quietly. 'Nothing happened, my lord.'

His irritation flashed. This would get them nowhere.

'Do not tell me that.' He gestured to the sash. 'Something happened.'

'*Nothing* happened,' she repeated more emphatically.

She stood her ground, but her gaze faltered, betraying her.

He leaned closer. 'Speak plainly, Anna. I need to know if I seduced you last night. If I compromised you. I need to know what is required of me.'

'Required of you?' She looked surprised.

'Do not play games with me,' he snapped, but immediately lifted an apologetic hand and lowered his voice. 'You must know I cannot marry you—'

A wounded look flashed across her face, so quickly he thought he might have imagined it. She lifted her chin. 'Of course you cannot *marry* me. I am a governess and base born, as well.'

He stiffened. That was not what he meant. He meant he was betrothed to Miss Rolfe, but somehow, with no date set and no banns read, it still seemed unreal. Until he knew for certain that Miss Rolfe wished their betrothal to be generally known, he spoke of it to no one. For him to break off the betrothal would be a serious breach of gentlemanly behaviour. Miss Rolfe might do so, however.

'I must marry without scandal,' he said instead.

Her posture stiffened. 'Of course you must, but why say this to me? What does it matter if you compromised a governess or not?'

Brent had no wish to explain that his behaviour towards her did matter a great deal, but that, if he'd indeed taken her to bed, he could not avoid wronging someone. Her or Miss Rolfe. He needed for her to tell him what he'd done to her and then he would know what impossible decision he must make.

He fixed her with a steady stare. 'Tell me what happened last night.'

She waved a dismissive hand. 'You embraced me. You kissed me. That is all. You had a great deal to drink…'

'That does not explain the sash in my bed,' he persisted.

She drew in a quick breath. 'I—I helped you into bed.'

He pressed on. 'And did you share the bed with me?'

'I did not.'

He drew close to her again. 'You are not telling all.'

Her eyes filled with pain. 'Very well, I will tell you.' She lowered her gaze. 'You asked me into your bed. I made an excuse to extinguish the candle. As I stepped away, you pulled off my sash. I knew you had consumed too much brandy. I knew you would easily fall asleep. I thought it prudent not to retrieve my sash. I waited until I was certain you were sleeping and I left the room.'

He closed his eyes and felt sick with self-loathing.

At least she'd had her wits about her.

She went on, 'So you see, nothing happened.'

'A great deal happened.' A few drinks of brandy and he acted upon the attraction to her that had been present from his first glimpse. 'I do not know how to apologise to you.'

Her cheeks flushed with colour. 'All I wish to know is if I still have employment.'

His brows rose. 'Of course you have employment.' Did she think he'd disrupt the children's lives again? Punish her for his transgression?

Her posture relaxed and her expression turned to one of relief.

She straightened again, as if recouping her dignity. 'Then we have nothing left to discuss. I will return to the children.'

She turned to leave.

'Wait.' He seized her arm. 'We cannot pretend what happened did not occur.'

'We cannot change it either,' she countered.

He released her and stepped away. 'Perhaps it is best that I return to London.'

'Leave?' Her voice rose and her eyes shot daggers at him. 'Leave your children? Do not use me as an excuse to neglect them. If you have no wish to help them, then, indeed, go back to the pleasures of London. Forget them as you have done before—'

'Enough!' He closed the distance between them again. 'You forget your place!' He sounded just like the old marquess.

She did not back down, none the less. Instead, she looked directly into his eyes. 'Last night you lamented the damage done your children by your absence. Now you seize upon the slimmest excuse to leave them again.'

His gaze was entrapped by her blue eyes, so clear, so forthright and brave. Before he realised it, his hands had rested on her shoulders, drawing her even closer to him. A memory, foggy and blurred, returned. He remembered kissing her...

He stepped back, jarred at how easily his own behaviour turned scandalous. 'See, Anna—Miss Hill—how easily I might compromise you again?'

Under the intensity of his gaze and her skin still tingling from his touch, Anna's limbs trembled. Ever since she first entered the library, she'd been a mass of quivering fear inside and now all her bravado was failing her.

She'd thought it her greatest talent, pretending to be calm and fearless even when shaking with fear inside. She'd honed the skill for Charlotte's sake, but with the marquess, she needed her pretence of courage for her own sake. She'd done well until he touched her and come so close she could feel his breath on her face.

She'd done so well she'd scolded the man who employed her. How foolhardy could that be? She needed this position. She had nothing else.

But she was correct that he needed to be here as well. His children needed him to stay. They needed to know there was someone who loved them, someone to whom their welfare was important. Someone who, unlike herself, was not paid to love them.

To not be loved by anyone was a terrible loneliness.

Perhaps that was why her senses begged for the marquess's touch, why her body wished so much that he would wrap her in his arms, why she had come so close to sharing his bed. She yearned for the illusion that someone loved her. She'd seemed of very little importance to her mother, none at all to her father and Charlotte seemed to have forgotten her.

Her heart pounded when she looked up in his eyes. She wanted to tell him to compromise her all he wished, anything to keep her from feeling so alone.

'That is why I need to return to London,' he murmured.

Anna forced herself to take a deep breath. She

tensed her muscles and gave him a steady look. 'No, my lord. We must see to your children's needs and behave as we ought.' She curled her fingers into a fist.

His expression was pained. 'I want to stay. I want to mend the damage of the past and give the children the life they deserve, but—'

'Then you must stay with them. Certainly you are able to exert self-control...about...about the other.' As she must do, as well, Anna ought to add.

'You are correct, as I suspect you often are, Miss Hill.' His jaw set. 'There will be no repeat of my improper behaviour, I promise. I will do nothing to bring scandal upon you or upon this house.'

'Then you will stay?'

He nodded. 'I will stay.'

Two weeks passed and Lord Brentmore spent part of every day in the company of his children. He started the day having breakfast with them. He spent time with them in the school room. He took them riding on his horse. He even helped them tend their peas and radishes. He never asked anything of them. Never raised his voice.

Anna's esteem for him grew, but that made it only more difficult to be in his presence. Luckily they were never alone together for more than a few moments. The children or the servants or other workers were always present or nearby.

What had passed between them that night did not disappear, however. Her senses heightened whenever he was near. She caught herself gazing at him far too often, but he also gazed at her. Sometimes their eyes caught and the colour rose in his face. She knew he was responding to her as a man responds to a woman. Everything about him captivated her. The easy way he sat upon his horse. His deep voice. His rare laugh.

Nights were often worse. The marquess now slept in a room near where the children slept, so he would be near if Cal had a nightmare. It meant he was also near to where Anna slept—or tried to sleep. Each night she tossed and turned and remembered the feel of his arms around her, the press of his lips against hers.

Her regard for him increased even more when he took another bold step.

He removed all visible reminders of his late wife.

The marchioness's portrait was crated and sent to the attic. Her stunning white horse was sold. Her belongings were removed from her bedchamber to be stored away. Most of her clothing was given away.

Most surprising of all, the marquess rid the house of Mr and Mrs Tippen. He pensioned them off and sent them away, presumably to return to the marchioness's home county from whence they had come. The gardener's sister, Mrs Willis, who'd been a senior housemaid in Brentmore Hall, became the new housekeeper. Wyatt, the footman, was promoted to butler.

A stunning number of changes in so brief a time.

One thing had not changed, though. Lord Cal still did not speak. But he was not totally unimproved. He smiled sometimes and was more free with his nods of the head or his hand gestures. Anna was very encouraged.

Lord Brentmore no longer shared dinner with Cal and Dory. Rather he insisted Anna dine with him so they had time to discuss the children and make plans for them. Dining together, with the footmen coming in the room and out, provided a safe place for them to be together without the temptation of those urges simmering beneath. Most of the time they talked about the children, but sometimes it became natural for them to converse on other topics. The social or political issues of the day. Their personal lives.

Anna shared a little about her growing up at Lawton House. Lord Brentmore told her of his activities during the war. He'd been a spy, slipping into France to receive messages from informants and passing on information to those working against Napoleon.

Dinner became Anna's favourite time of the day, a time for the sort of camaraderie she'd missed so desperately since losing Charlotte's company. It was all the more special because her companion was the marquess. The more he shared with her, the more Anna began to know the man and the more difficult he was to resist.

When she left the dinner table, however, Lord Brentmore remained behind. If he had once knocked upon her bedroom door, she did not know what choices she might make.

This morning he was not in the breakfast room when she and the children entered. Instead there was a folded piece of paper at Anna's seat.

'What does it say?' asked Dory before Anna even had a chance to read the words.

'A lady is not so rude as to ask what is in a letter that may not concern her at all,' Anna scolded in good humour. The spirit that was so appealing in the five-year-old would quickly be seen as ill mannered if Anna did not succeed in dampening it. 'It is addressed to all of us, so I will tell you. It is from your father.' She quickly read the note. 'He will not be joining us this morning, but expects to see us mid-day, when he will have a surprise.'

'A surprise!' Dory's eyes lit up.

As did Lord Cal's.

'What is the surprise?' Dory asked.

Anna laughed. 'It would not be a surprise if he told us what it was.'

Word came in the early afternoon, summoning them to the stables and telling them to be dressed for riding.

'Papa is taking us riding this afternoon,' Lady Dory guessed as they walked the pathway to the stables. 'That is why he wanted us dressed for it. That's the surprise, isn't it, Miss Hill?'

'I do not know.' Anna turned to her brother. 'Do you think that is the surprise, Lord Cal?' She and Lord Brentmore agreed to seize any opportunity to ask him to communicate.

The boy shrugged his shoulders, but clearly he was excited about what they would find. Anna's heart swelled. Cal was anticipating something good happening to him.

With the stables in sight, the children broke into a run.

'Slow down!' Anna called to them, but they were not listening.

When she reached the stable door, Mr Upsom was there, trying to fend off two excited children.

But he had a grin on his face. 'His lordship said to meet him in the paddock.'

She grabbed the children's hands to keep them in tow as they walked through the stable to the paddock on the other side.

Lord Brentmore stood inside the paddock. In his hands were the reins of a black pony and a brown one.

Dory let out a shriek and pulled away. *'Ponies!'*

Cal was right behind her, and Anna thought she heard him cry aloud.

Lord Brentmore flashed a smile.

'Ponies!' Dory cried again. 'You brought ponies!'

Both children climbed through the fence.

Anna stayed on the other side. 'My lord, what have you done here?'

He smiled directly at Anna. 'I conceived an idea.'

He handed the reins to a stable lad and stepped forwards to halt the children's mad dash. 'Not so hasty. An explanation is needed.'

'May we pet the ponies?' Dory took no heed of him and tried to scamper past him.

He caught her arm.

'Lady Dory!' Anna said sharply. 'Mind your father this instant!'

Her brother grabbed her and pulled her back, whispering something into her ear that made her stand still.

Lord Brentmore crouched down to their level. 'These ponies *might* be yours. You *might* learn to ride them—'

'They are our ponies?' Dory cried.

'*Might* be,' her father corrected. 'But there is a stipulation involved.'

Dory's brow furrowed. 'What is a *stipulation*?'

'A condition that must be satisfied,' Anna offered. 'Something you must do first.'

'That is correct.' Lord Brentmore took Dory's hand. 'You may pet the brown pony while I speak first with your brother, but heed Samuel here. He will hold the reins.'

She suddenly hesitated, looking back at Cal as if reluctant to leave his side, but the pony was too tempting. She approached it carefully, but finally stroked its neck.

Lord Brentmore took the reins of the black pony and walked it over to Cal.

He crouched down again to the boy's level. 'Would you like this pony, Cal? Would you like him to be yours to ride?'

Cal enthusiastically nodded his head.

'When I was a boy,' his father said, 'I was taught that I must perform a task in order to get something that I wanted, so I have a task I want you to perform.'

Cal looked a bit wary.

His father continued. 'It is time for you to get used to talking again—'

'Cal talks,' Dory broke in.

'Dory!' Anna scolded.

Her father turned to her. 'The task you must perform, Dory, is to stop speaking for your brother. I will explain about that in a minute.' He addressed his son again. 'Do not be concerned. You may get used to speaking a little at a time, but I must see you trying. Do you understand?'

The boy nodded again, solemnly this time.

'If you give me your word that you will practise talking again, this pony will be yours. You

may name him and I will teach you to ride him.'
Lord Brentmore looked directly in the boy's eyes.
'But you must give me your word. A gentleman
always keeps his word. Can you do this? Do you
wish to do this?'

Cal nodded again.

'Will you give me your word?'

Cal nodded.

'No.' Lord Brentmore lowered his voice. 'To
give your word, a gentleman must say it aloud. It
is a rule. Will you give me your word?'

Anna held her breath.

Barely audible, she heard Lord Cal whisper,
'Yes.'

Tears sprang to her eyes.

Lord Brentmore exchanged a glance with her
and she sensed that he shared her emotions. His
plan would work. Lord Cal would begin to talk
again.

Later when they were all walking back from
the stables, the children ran ahead.

'Did you see Cal?' she said to Lord Brentmore.
'He leaned forwards and spoke to the pony! This
is marvellous, my lord. Whatever gave you the
idea?'

He showed some pleasure at her compliment.
'I merely thought about what I wanted most at
his age.'

She smiled. 'And did you receive your pony?'

He shook his head, his expression sobering. 'No. My Irish grandfather could barely put food on the table. But I would have done anything to have had one.'

That day of the ponies was just the beginning of more enjoyable days passing quickly. The weather was a great deal cooler than a normal summer, but the children still spent much of their time out of doors, learning to ride, taking walks, tending the garden. They picked their first crop of radishes and put trellises up to support the growing pea vines.

Riding became the children's favourite activity and their skill on horseback quickly improved. It helped that their father had chosen two very mild-mannered, tolerant ponies. Lord Brentmore found a horse in the stable for Anna and sometimes the four of them would ride together, exploring the marquess's vast lands. The marquess often took Cal alone to ride over the estate while Anna and Dory made games of learning to serve tea or sew dresses for her dolls.

Lord Cal started talking again, bit by bit, although rarely without being spoken to first and always with as few words as possible. He was making the effort, though, and Anna believed it was because his father had made his home a comfortable place.

It seemed as if everything about Brentmore

Hall had changed. The dark wainscoting stopped looking so bleak and maids might be caught humming while they worked. The footmen and other workers performed their tasks cheerfully.

It felt as if someone had taken a bucket and washed away all the gloom that had been there before.

It was all due to Lord Brentmore, Anna knew. He made the summer as idyllic a one as Anna had ever experienced. The pain of being thrust out of the only home she knew and banished from the only people she'd cared about faded with the joys of a summer without stress, spent with a man whose companionship she relished and with children she'd grown to love as if they were her own.

She still battled the surge of excitement inside her when Brentmore was near, but she supposed he had mastered any attraction he might once have felt towards her. His manner with her was always gentlemanly, even convivial, as if he was more friend than employer.

And he'd moved back to his own bedchamber.

This morning promised to be another sunny day. She and Lord Brentmore sat in the breakfast room with the children, encouraging Cal to speak by discussing plans for the day.

'What would you like to do today?' Lord Brentmore asked him.

Cal hesitated, as he always did before speaking. 'Ride.'

'May we ride to the village?' Dory piped up. 'We should like to go to the village.' She clamped her hand over her mouth. 'I mean, *I* would like to go to the village.'

Anna lifted a finger. 'Lady Dory, your father was speaking to your brother. Wait until you are addressed.'

'Yes, Miss Hill.' The girl lowered her head.

Lord Brentmore's gaze passed quickly over Dory. He turned back to his son. 'Where would you like to ride, Cal?'

Cal glanced from his sister to his father, a hint of mischief on his face. 'To the village.'

No doubt he and his sister had discussed the matter ahead of time.

'Your sister is not ready to ride to the village yet,' their father replied. 'There is too much commotion. Too many people and wagons. So we must pick some other place to ride or some other way to go to the village. What say you?'

Cal appeared to mull this over. 'Both?' he asked in a hopeful tone.

His father laughed. 'Perhaps.' He turned to Anna. 'How does that suit you, Miss Hill?'

'I believe I will forgo the riding, if I might.' All this activity left her with little time to sort out the nursery, mend her clothes and plan lessons. 'But a trip to the village—'

The butler entered the room. 'Your newspaper and mail, m'lord.'

Lord Brentmore took them from the tray. 'Thank you, Wyatt.' He set the paper aside and looked through the mail, opening one envelope.

A letter fell from it. He picked it up. 'It is for you, Miss Hill. It must have been mailed to London by mistake.'

'For me?' Who would send her a letter besides Charlotte? Charlotte knew she was not in London.

'It is from Lawton House.' He handed it to her.

'From Lawton?' Her anxiety rose.

Anna quickly broke the seal. She felt the blood drain from her face as she read.

'What is it?' Lord Brentmore asked, sounding concerned.

The children grew very quiet.

'It—it is from our housekeeper at Lawton.' Her heart pounded in her chest. 'My—my mother is very ill. Very ill indeed.' A fever and an affliction of the lungs, she'd written. 'This was sent days ago.' She handed the letter to him.

'You must go to her,' he said.

She shook her head. 'How can I? The children. My duty here—'

He looked up from the letter and captured her gaze. 'You must go.' He turned to the children. 'We will manage without Miss Hill, will we not?'

Cal sat wide-eyed, staring from his father to Anna.

'No!' Dory's voice rose in panic. 'I do not want Miss Hill to leave us!'

Lord Brentmore gave her a dampening look. 'None of that, now. We must not be selfish. Miss Hill's mother is ill and she must tend to her.' His tone turned reassuring. 'Besides, Miss Hill will only be gone a few days. Until her mother is recovered.'

Dory blinked. 'She will come back?'

Anna left her chair to gather Dory into her arms and hold her close. 'Of course I will come back, my little pet. Do not fear.'

'Do you wish to leave today?' Lord Brentmore asked.

Things were moving so fast. 'I do not see how I can.' She gave Dory a kiss on the cheek and returned her to her chair. 'I must make arrangements. Check the coaching schedules—'

He raised a hand. 'Nonsense. You do not need a public coach. Not when I have a number of carriages to offer. Leave those arrangements to me. If you wish to be in Lawton before dark, it can be done.'

Her throat tightened. 'How can I ever thank you?'

His gaze held hers. 'It is the least I can do, when I owe you so much.'

Chapter Seven

Anna excused herself from the breakfast table and went in search of Mrs Willis to inform the housekeeper of her impending absence.

The housekeeper gave her a warm hug and admonished her against excessive worrying. 'It will help nothing, my dear. You must save your strength for the care of your mother.'

They discussed the menus for the children and other issues about their care.

'You are not to worry over the little ones, either, Miss Hill,' the woman said. 'They are doing splendidly under your care and their father's. We are all astonished at the change in them. I promise you, we will keep up your good work.'

'Thank you.' Anna thought she might weep at the kind words. 'I think Eppy can handle them. And Lord Brentmore, of course. I believe they could be placed entirely in his care, actually. He is so good with them.'

'That he is, my dear,' the woman agreed. 'He is changed, as well, thanks to you. He is like a new man.'

Thanks to her? Surely any governess with good sense would have acted as she had. Perhaps better.

Anna hurried to the nursery wing to find Eppy, who also enfolded her in her arms when hearing of her mother's illness.

'I am sorry to leave you with more work,' Anna said.

Eppy patted Anna's back. 'Now, now. You must go to your mother. Besides, the children are a pleasure now. Not ever so sad and skittish as before. It is an easy thing to take care of them.'

Anna was not so secure that the children would be no trouble. She would, after all, be one more person leaving them. The very idea of it was bound to upset them.

Eppy helped her pack and the two women discussed the children's care while they folded Anna's clothing and gathered the items she would need, placing them in her portmanteau.

She carried it down to the hall herself.

Mr Wyatt awaited her there. 'Cook packed a basket for you and his lordship sent all the instructions to Mr Upsom to have you driven in the chaise. It should be here directly.'

'Where are the children?' And Lord Brentmore?

He averted his gaze as he took the portmanteau from her and opened the door. 'With his lordship.'

Would she not have the chance to say goodbye to them?

She felt a stab of pain, disappointed in Lord Brentmore for the first time since he'd agreed to stay with the children. Did he not think it important that she say goodbye to them?

Did he not think it important for him to say goodbye to her?

She stepped outside and watched the chaise make its way towards the front entrance, one of the stable lads driving. Wyatt placed her portmanteau in a compartment behind the seat and helped her into the small carriage.

'I hope you mother recovers quickly,' Mr Wyatt said, handing her the basket. 'Come back to us soon.'

She squeezed the man's hand. 'Thank you, Mr Wyatt.'

But it was not the butler's good wishes she longed for.

She felt as bereft as when she'd left Lord Lawton's London town house. At least Charlotte had made a point to say goodbye to her. She blinked away tears as the chaise made its way down the drive towards the arched gate.

When it passed through the gate, the driver brought the horses to a stop. He jumped down.

'Why are we stopping?' she asked.

The man gestured with his thumb. 'You are getting a new driver.'

A man emerged from the shadows, followed by two children.

Anna climbed down from the carriage and the children ran into her arms.

She kissed them both. 'I thought I would have to leave you without saying goodbye.'

Dory grinned. 'It was Papa's idea!'

She glanced at Lord Brentmore. He was not dressed at all like a gentleman. In fact, her coachman was better dressed. 'Lord Brentmore?'

He climbed into the chaise. 'I am going to drive you to Lawton House.'

Her old driver was grinning. 'Do not fret, miss. I'll see the children back to the house, safe and sound.'

'Papa gave you a surprise!' Dory cried.

He certainly had. She could barely grasp it.

'Bid these children farewell!' He took the ribbons in his hands. 'We must be off.'

Anna kissed the children again and hugged them for good measure. 'I will return as soon as I am able. You mind Eppy, now. She will take care of you.'

'We'll be good!' Dory said.

Cal hugged her again. 'I—I hope your mother recovers.'

It was the longest sentence he'd spoken yet.

She held him tightly. 'Thank you, Lord Cal. I will miss you both so very much.'

She handed them over to the old driver and climbed back in the chaise.

Lord Brentmore flicked the ribbons and the horses started off again. He waved to the children, who enthusiastically waved back.

Anna leaned out the side of the chaise and called back to them, 'I'll return soon.'

When they reached the road, Anna turned to him. 'Lord Brentmore?'

He gave her a quick glance. 'The children will be well cared for. And I'll drive back tomorrow.'

'But look at you!' She took in his linen shirt, brown coat and trousers.

He shrugged. 'A costume that proved useful in the war.'

She was still not comprehending.

'If the Marquess of Brentmore drove the governess to an earl's estate, there might be gossip, but if Egan Byrne drives you, no one will credit it.'

'Egan Byrne?' Her brows rose.

'My name,' he explained. 'And my Irish grandfather's surname.'

'But someone might recognise you.' What if Lord Lawton saw him? 'What will they think?'

He dipped his chin like the lowest of servants. 'Don't you worry now, miss.' His accent turned to a lilt. 'No one will be noticing an Irish stable lad. I'll be quiet as a mouse and you'll be the only one knowin' the truth of it.'

She doubted such a man, even if dressed as a workman, could avoid notice.

He spoke in his own voice again. 'But you must remember to call me *Egan* and not *my lord*.'

She swallowed. 'But why would you do this?'

His expression turned solemn. 'I thought you might need the company of a friend.'

Tears stung her eyes.

This was a folly of the highest order.

Brent trained his eyes on the road, although that did not prevent him from being acutely aware of the woman seated beside him. He felt her tension. Her worry. And also the brushing of her arm against his when the road turned rough.

He must be mad to put himself in her company like this. His intense attraction to her had never abated. She was a constant allure, cause of a daily battle against an urge to lose himself in all that warmth and beauty. Knowing her better, seeing her kindness to his children, feeling her sadness, made it all the more difficult.

She never complained, but he caught snatches of how lonely life was for her, in how she spoke of her childhood, or in the fact that she never received letters even though she wrote them. The letter informing her of her mother's illness had been her first since coming to Brentmore Hall.

He'd had a bad feeling about that letter and could not send her off on the trip alone.

Her worry that someone would recognise him was unfounded. He'd learned as a boy how to make himself invisible—much like Cal had done. Or to make himself into someone else. He possessed a talent for mimicking accents, originally honed from a desire to rid himself of his Irish accent and avoid the taunting and teasing of his schoolmates. When he learned French, his French accent became nearly as flawless as his English one. During the war, no one in France had suspected an English marquess had been spying on them.

He'd slip in and out of Lawton as easily.

The chaise hit a rut and he reflexively threw an arm across Anna to keep her from falling.

'I beg your pardon.' He quickly removed his hand. Any time he touched her, it aroused his senses.

She glanced at him. 'I am not likely to complain about anything you do, my lord.'

God help him. If she only knew how many sleepless nights he'd suffered, thinking of marching into her bedchamber and slaking his need for her. It made it more difficult to know she would not refuse him. The idea that he could be the man to awaken her sensuality was more torture.

'Egan,' he said.

'What?' she looked puzzled.

'You called me *my lord* again. Practise saying *Egan*.'

If only he were Egan Byrne and not the Marquess of Brentmore. Then he would not be betrothed to a baron's daughter and no one would lend scandal to anything he did. No one would care.

'Egan,' she repeated. On her lips his name sounded as if murmured between bed linens.

This manner of thinking would not do at all. Better to change its direction. 'This is not the most comfortable of roads.' Perhaps inane small talk would help.

'Again, I shall not complain,' she assured him. 'If not for your kindness, I could be squeezed into a post-chaise with travellers who eat a great deal of garlic and transport cheese.'

'And bathe but once a year,' he added.

She almost smiled and his heart gladdened, relishing any moment of easy camaraderie between them.

'You have spared me such a fate,' she said, although her eyes quickly filled with pain and worry.

He wanted to ease it. 'Your mother could be recovered by the time we arrive, you know. Is she susceptible to inflammation of the lungs?' He feared worse, of course. Life was fragile.

'She is never sick.' She bit her lip. 'That is why I worry. Our housekeeper would not contact me if she thought this a trifling thing.'

Illness was never a trifling thing. Brent had a flash of memory of his mother, lying abed, the sound of her breathing as loud as a fireplace bellows.

A wave of grief washed over him.

He tightened his grip on the reins. 'Do not give up hope, Miss Hill.'

He rarely thought of his mother, but when he did, the yearning for her returned fullfold, even after twenty-five years. He never spoke of her. Whenever the old marquess had spoken of her, he'd called her *that Irish whore.*

Anna's voice pulled him out of his reverie. 'I was never close to my mother, you know. I was always with Charlotte. Weeks could go by and I would not even see her.' Her voice cracked. 'I want to see her again.'

He put his hand over hers.

As they rode towards Lawton, she talked about her life there, about growing up neither servant nor family, but something in between. She'd become close to the Lawton daughter, but separate from her as well, never truly accepted in her social circles.

Brent knew all about not being accepted. He'd

never been accepted, not by his grandfather, his schoolmates, his contemporaries.

Or his wife. How bitter a pill that had been. He'd believed she'd loved him.

At least when he married this next time, he'd know the woman did not love him.

Brent flicked the reins and drove as hard and fast as he dared.

They changed horses frequently at the coaching inns and did not pause for much more than a quick look at *Cary's Itinerary* or to pay at the toll gates. They ate from the basket Cook packed for them rather than wait for food at the inns.

By the time the light was waning in the sky, Brent's arms ached from holding the reins and from the bumps in the road. Anna looked more fatigued by the hour. Their fast pace had paid dividends, though. There was still plenty of daylight left when they finally passed a road sign indicating Lawton was near and soon a tall church spire rose in the sky.

'The village!' Anna cried.

Anna examined each building as they passed through the village. Committing it to memory, perhaps? Would he recognise any part of his Irish village? he wondered.

This village had nothing to distinguish itself from dozens of other English villages. Stone houses with steep slate roofs. A coaching inn. A smithy. Shops.

'Lawton House is not far,' she said as they left the village and the main road behind.

Brent felt her tension grow.

Suddenly a vista opened, revealing a majestic country house set in manicured lawns and flowering gardens. Constructed of the same grey stone as the village buildings, it was a hodgepodge of additions and wings, as if the various Earls of Lawton were seized with a compulsion to build every half-century or so.

This was the place Anna had spent nearly her whole life, the home she lost when Lord Lawton so abruptly terminated her services. She leaned forwards in the chaise as if in a hurry to be among familiar surroundings, familiar people.

Her mother.

The sight of Brentmore Hall always plummeted him into depression.

Brent turned the chaise on to the long gravel drive leading to the house. 'Do I leave you off at the house?'

'Yes. Our housekeeper said Mama was being cared for in the house.' Her brows knit. 'Unless you want me to go with you to the stables.'

He waved a hand and put on his Irish accent. 'Do not go concerning yourself about me, now. I'm not a marquess, a'tall. Just a simple stable lad who can find his way.'

He drove her to the servants' entrance and watched her enter quickly, hating to leave her alone.

He shook his head. What a ridiculous notion. She would not be alone. She'd be among people she'd known her whole life.

He drove the chaise towards the stables.

As he neared, a man stepped out into the stable yard. 'And who might you be?'

He touched the brim of his hat. 'From Brentmore Hall. I brought Miss Hill to visit her mother, you see.'

The man's face fell. 'She's come?'

'Miss Hill?' Brent pretended to be confused. 'Yes. Come to see her mother, she has.'

The man dropped his head in his hands for a moment, then seemed to recover. He gestured to Brent. 'Well, climb down. Do you stay?'

'The night at least,' he responded. 'I'm to await her instructions.'

The stableman called to some other grooms and tasked them with unhitching the horses and seeing to their care. Brent removed Anna's portmanteau and the kitchen basket. He was shown to a place to sit and given a draught of ale.

After a few moments the man who'd greeted him in the yard walked over to him again. 'Are you hungry? You can probably beg some food from Cook, if you've a mind to.'

He wanted to see what was happening to Anna.

'Food would be welcome, for sure.' He touched his stomach and tried not to look too eager.

The stableman gestured for him to follow. 'I'll show you the way.'

He knew the way, but a visiting worker would not argue with anyone who might be above him in station.

As they walked the man spoke, more to himself than to Brent. 'She should have come sooner.'

'Sooner?' Brent repeated.

The man stopped and gazed blankly into the distance. 'Her mother...' He paused and lowered his head. 'Her mother is dead. Buried yesterday.'

Brent's insides clenched. They were too late.

'Miss Hill will be grieved, indeed,' he said in a low voice.

The man's expression turned bleak. 'She was my wife.'

'You are Miss Hill's father, then?' Brent asked.

'In a manner of speaking,' the man replied.

Brent's brows rose. What the devil did that mean?

It was not a visiting stableman's place to ask questions, though.

He followed Mr Hill to the tradesman's entrance, which opened into a long corridor with doors to the other rooms. The sound of voices and clanging pots signalled that the kitchen was somewhere ahead.

Mr Hill escorted him to the servants' hall.

Anna was there, seated at the long table, surrounded by the housekeeper and maids, all trying to comfort her. Her expression was desolate and her eyes red from crying.

'I heard you'd come,' Anna's father said.

She looked up. 'Papa.'

The maids made way for him, but he did not approach her. 'They told you about your mother.'

That was obvious.

She caught sight of Brent, her silent communication of grief as clear as if she'd shouted aloud. To her father she said, 'How do you fare, Papa?'

He did not answer. 'Your room is ready at the cottage. Mrs Jordan expected you days ago.' He glanced at the housekeeper, who must be Mrs Jordan.

Mrs Jordan explained, 'The letter went astray.'

Mr Hill shrugged. He inclined his head towards Brent. 'Anna's coachman is hungry.'

Brent supposed that was an introduction. Or a changing of the subject.

Mrs Jordan turned her attention to Brent. 'I expect you would like some food, then?'

'His—his name is…Egan,' Anna volunteered.

'Egan.' Mrs Jordan patted the table. 'Sit down and we'll bring you a plate of food.' She snapped her fingers at one of the maids. 'Mary, find something for the man to eat.'

Brent took the nearest chair, trying not to

watch Anna too obviously. It pained him to see her so disconsolate.

Her father moved towards the door. 'Your things will be at the cottage.'

She nodded. 'Thank you, Papa.'

Brent frowned. Hill was so cold to her. He reminded Brent of the old marquess.

The girl brought food for Brent and tea for Anna. Servants drifted in and out of the room, completing their duties for the day or stopping to give Anna their condolences.

For a moment they were alone in the room. 'Anna?' he murmured, forgetting to address her formally.

She looked pale and desolate. 'I feel like I cannot breathe.'

He wanted to hold her in his arms and comfort her the way he comforted Cal after his nightmares. He moved to a chair across the table from her and reached over to squeeze her hand.

'Let yourself cry,' he murmured. 'It will help.'

Although, as a boy, he'd learned quickly never to cry.

She blinked rapidly and gripped his hand.

Someone approached and she quickly released him. 'Are you finished eating?' she asked.

'Yes.' His plate was nearly empty, but he'd tasted none of the food.

'We should go, then. We are in the way here.'

She stood. 'Wait a moment while I stop in the kitchen to tell them.'

When she returned and they left the house, he said, 'I'll walk you to your father's cottage.'

She did not refuse.

'I—I cannot believe she is gone,' she said after a time.

He steadied her with his arm.

When they reached the cottage, she rapped on the door before opening it. 'I am here, Papa.'

Inside the cottage, the room was dark, with only the glow of the fireplace for light. Brent caught a strong whiff of gin.

Her father rose from a chair by the hearth. 'Well, come in, then.' His tone was sharp and his words slurred.

Brent waited in the doorway, uneasy at leaving her.

'Come have a drink, you,' Hill called to Brent.

'Don't mind if I do,' he said in his coachman's voice. He'd stay as long as she needed him to.

Anna gave up any hope of sharing her grief with her father. She had never seen him drunk like this. It frightened her.

He gestured with his arm. 'You sit for a while, *daughter*.' This last word was bitterly said.

Anna sat.

He filled a glass for Lord Brentmore, some of

the liquid splashing over the sides from his un-steady hand.

'You should have come earlier.' Her father shook a finger at her.

'I waited for Egan to eat, Papa,' she explained.

He wiped the air with his hand. 'Don't mean that. Mean for your mother.'

'I could not.' That was the worst of it. Tears stung her eyes. She'd not arrived in time.

Her father stared into the fire. 'There was no one at her funeral, you know. No one to put her in the ground.' He turned his gaze on her. 'Why didn't you come? Too busy tending that lord's brats?'

Her gaze flashed over to Lord Brentmore.

He answered for her. 'She came as soon as she received the letter.' His Irish accent faded. 'Which was this morning.'

Her father made another dismissive gesture and took a swig directly from the bottle.

Anna glanced away and, her eyes now accus-tomed to the room's darkness, saw dishes left on tables, clothing scattered on the floor, bottles everywhere.

She stood. 'I'll just tidy a bit.'

She lit one of the lamps and moved around the room, picking up empty bottles.

Her father took no notice. 'Rankles me,' he said. 'After all her mother did. All those years.'

Anna only half-listened to him. She carried

the bottles to the bin by the sink, which was full of unwashed dishes.

Her father kept talking. 'She tolerated me. Nothing more. What chance did I have? A man who mucks out stables and comes home smelling of horse?' He swivelled around to Anna and pointed his finger at her. 'And the daughter. No better.'

All her life she'd wanted her father to love her. He never did.

Lord Brentmore rose and walked over to her. 'How can I help?'

His nearness was a comfort. She was grateful he'd remained. 'I would not ask you.'

'I know you would not ask,' he countered. 'I am offering.'

She picked up a bucket. 'Would you bring me some water? The pump is outside.'

He nodded.

She collected more plates, bowls and spoons from around the room and placed them in the basin. She could not properly wash the dishes without boiling some water on the hearth, but that meant crossing in front of her father. She did not wish to risk disturbing him. The dishes would keep until morning.

Lord Brentmore returned with the water bucket. She took it from him and poured water in the basin to soak the dishes.

'What is next?' he asked.

'That is more than enough, my lo— *Egan*.' She gave a grateful smile.

He did not return to his chair, but stood aside, his arms folded across his chest.

She moved through the room, picking up clothing and clutter from the floor. She paused near the chair where Lord Brentmore had been sitting. His glass was still full.

Her father, still rambling, reached for it and downed the gin as if it had been water. 'Cursed man,' he cried. 'You'd think *he* would come. After all those years—'

Anna's brow creased.

Her father went on, 'He owed it to her to come put her in the ground.'

Of whom was he speaking? 'Papa?'

He lifted his head to look at her. 'You know. Don't pretend you don't know what I'm talking about.'

She shook her head. 'Indeed I do not. Are you speaking of Mama?'

A bark of a laugh burst from him. 'Of course I am speaking of your cursed mother.' He jabbed his finger into his chest. '*My* wife!'

Brentmore walked up behind her, a silent support.

'Do not be profane when speaking of Mama,' she scolded.

The man half-rose from his chair. 'I'll speak

of her any way I like. She was *my* wife. Not his.'
He jabbed his chest again.

'Mr Hill.' Lord Brentmore spoke without accent in a low, firm voice. 'Heed what you say.
Your daughter is already overwrought with grief.'

Her father sprang to his feet. 'Heed what I say?
Ha!'

Lord Brentmore pulled her behind him, placing himself between her and her father. 'Enough,
sir!' he ordered.

A puzzled look crossed her father's face, but
that was the only indication he noticed the coach
driver now spoke like a marquess.

Her father sank back in his chair and covered
his face with his hands. 'He ought to have come.
He ought to have shown his respects.'

'Who, Papa?' Anna asked.

His bleary eyes caught hers. 'His lordship.'

'Lord Lawton?' She gaped at her father. 'You
are not making any sense. Why expect Lord
Lawton to come? Mama was only a laundress.'

Her father gave her a disgusted look. 'There
you go, pretending you do not know.'

Her anxiety rose. 'Know what?'

Lord Brentmore put a hand on her arm.

Her father lifted Lord Brentmore's empty glass
and peered into it as if it might be hiding more
gin. 'Why d'you think you were chosen to be the
companion?'

He was changing the subject.

Her father pointed to her. 'He could not have you reared to be a servant, could he?'

Lord Brentmore's grip on her arm tightened.

'Papa.' Her heart pounded. 'Speak plainly.'

'Papa,' he mocked her. 'I'm not your *papa*, girl, and I don't ever again have to say I am.'

She felt the blood drain from her face. 'Are you saying… Lord Lawton?'

He slapped the arm of the chair. 'See? You knew it all the time. His *lordship* sired you. Not me. Not me.'

Her head spun and inside she shouted, *No. No. No.*

Her father—the man she'd thought was her father—continued talking. 'She used to work in the house, y'know. An upstairs maid and the prettiest thing you ever did see. Caught *his* eye and every chance he got he tumbled between the sheets with her.' He stared into the fire. 'Then she was increasing. Made her ladyship furious when she found out. Sent her out of the house, but only far as the laundry because he wouldn't let her go. He had a plan, you see.' He sighed. 'His lordship came to me. How would I like a cottage? he says. More pay, he says. All I had to do was marry her.' He laughed, a dry mirthless sound. 'I was as young as she was. I thought she'd fancy me after a time, but it was always him.'

He glanced at her. 'She made him promise. Raise you to be a lady, not a servant. Wouldn't bed him 'til he agreed.' He rose from the chair and staggered to a corner where he rummaged until he found another bottle. 'Then his legitimate daughter turned out to be a mousy little thing and he sent you to teach her some backbone, not that her ladyship ever liked that.' He laughed again. 'You know all this. Everyone knows this.'

She'd never suspected.

No wonder this man had never loved her. No wonder Charlotte's mother had always been cold to her.

But Lord Lawton never showed her any favour. None at all.

'Does Charlotte know?' Was Anna the only one who didn't know?

He waved a hand again. 'The twit? Not at all.' He rose from his chair again, swaying as he tried to take a step. 'Thing is, he should have come. Should have come before she died. Should have come to put her in the ground!' He took a step and reached out to steady himself on the back of the chair.

He missed and collapsed to the floor.

'Papa!' she cried.

Lord Brentmore rushed over to examine him. He looked back at her. 'He's just passed out from the gin.'

She backed off. 'I—I can't believe—'

Lord Brentmore lifted him from under his

arms and managed to hoist him over his shoulder. 'Where's his bed?'

She led him into the room he'd shared with her mother, to the bed that her mother probably shared with Lord Lawton as well.

Lord Brentmore dropped him on to the bed like a sack of flour. He started immediately to snore.

What was she to call him now? Even in her head she could not say he was her father.

Brentmore took her arm. 'Come.'

As soon as he closed the door behind them, the enormity of her mother's death and her father's disclosure fell on her. It was like being pummelled with fists.

She clutched her stomach and closed her eyes.

Lord Brentmore enfolded her in his arms. He held her tight against him. The strength of his arms encircling her, the warmth of his body, the steady beating of his heart, held her together.

But the pain remained. 'I have nothing now,' she cried against his chest. 'Nothing.'

'Anna, you are exhausted,' he murmured. 'Go to bed. Tomorrow will be better.'

She shook her head. 'Nothing could be worse than today.'

'That is right.' He released her, but brushed her hair away from her face with his fingers. 'Nothing will be worse than today.'

He picked her up, surprising her so much she was speechless. 'Where is your bed?'

She pointed.

It soothed her to be absolved of the need to walk. He carried her into the little room she'd rarely slept in as a child and lowered her on to her bed.

'Goodnight, Anna.' He started to walk away.

She jumped off the bed and seized the cloth of his coat. 'Don't leave me, please. I—I don't want to be alone! I don't think I can stand to be alone.'

'I will stay right outside your door,' he assured her.

'No. I will still be alone.' She was sounding irrational, but she could not stop herself. 'Stay with me, my lord. Here. Hold me. Please.'

He stared down at her, his eyes darkening. 'Very well,' he murmured. 'I will stay.'

Brent held her all night. Both of them remained fully dressed, but he shared her tiny bed with her.

He could not say that no thought of making love to her crossed his mind, but she was in too much pain for him to take advantage of her and he cared about her too much.

He watched her sleep, savouring the sight of her pretty face, even though it was still pinched with pain. Sleep had not come easy for her.

Nor for him, but eventually he had dozed off and on until dawn illuminated the room.

* * *

Anna murmured something in her sleep and moved from her back to her side, cuddling against Brent.

He tried to remain very still.

The door suddenly burst open, banging against the wall with a report as loud as a musket.

Anna's eyes flew open and she sat up.

Brent vaulted from the bed.

Mr Hill stood in the doorway. 'Harlot!' he shouted. 'Just like your mother!' He advanced on her, rage and disgust on his face. 'Tumbling into bed with the likes of this.' He gestured to Brent. 'At least your mother bedded an earl. At least she got something for it.'

Brent blocked Hill's way and seized his arm. 'You, sir, are leaving.' He forced the man out of the room.

'How dare you put your hands on me! You scum!' Hill tried to break free of Brent's grasp, to no avail.

'Now you listen to me.' Brent forced the man against a wall. 'She's done nothing to deserve your words. You were cruel and drunk and I could not leave her alone with the likes of you. Her mother died, man! And all you cared to do was hurt her.'

Hill gaped at him. 'I thought you were Irish.'

Brent leaned into his face. 'I am more Irish than is safe for you.' He continued to glare at the man. 'Now tell me why you dared enter her room.'

Hill cowered. 'I—I wanted to see if she was there.'

He tightened his grip. 'Do you believe me when I say I am able to get you fired from your job?'

Hill's eyes widened and he nodded.

'Then say nothing of this. You created this situation. You will not make her pay for it by sullying her good name.' He shoved the man towards the door. 'Now go and make some use of yourself in the stable.'

Hill rushed out of the cottage. Brent turned away and saw Anna standing in the doorway of her room.

'He will tell them.' Her voice trembled. 'I will be the talk of the household.'

Brent raised his brows. 'Shall I have him fired, then?'

She shook her head. 'It does not matter. I will never come back here.' She glanced away. 'Would you take me home, my lord? To Brentmore, I mean. I do not want to stay here.'

He crossed the room, as drawn to her as he'd been that first glimpse of her. Only now he knew her. And cared for her.

He lifted his hand to touch her, but dropped it again. 'We can leave right away.'

Chapter Eight

❧

While Lord Brentmore stopped at the stables to have the horses hitched to the chaise, Anna walked over to the house to say goodbye.

'You mustn't go!' Mrs Jordan cried. 'It looks like rain outside.'

The maids chimed in, 'Stay longer, Anna. You just arrived.'

'I—I must get back to the children.' Anna explained. 'It is a very good position and I do not want to lose it.'

The maids nodded. They all knew the value of good employment.

Mrs Jordan sighed. 'Well, go if you must.' She turned and bellowed to one of the maids, 'Mary! Pack up some food for Anna and that nice coachman of hers.'

Would they gossip about her after she had left?

Her father—the man she knew as her father—
would certainly lose no time in passing the word
that he'd found her in bed with her coachman.
Blood will tell, they would likely say. *At least her
mother bedded an earl.*

Mary placed the box of food in her hands and
Mrs Jordan and the maids hugged her goodbye.
Anna knew she would never see any of them
again. Once they tired of the gossip, would they
ever think of her? She did not know.

She walked to the servants' door, past rooms
once familiar to her. She knew she would never
walk past them again.

She had an impulse to run up to Charlotte's
room. To see it once more. To see the schoolroom. The library. The music room. All the lovely
places she and Charlotte had passed their days.
She wanted to run in the gardens again where
they had picked flowers or played hide and seek.

She squared her shoulders and kept walking
to the outside door.

She'd had the privilege of growing up here because her mother bedded the earl. What she'd believed was a beautiful opportunity now seemed
soiled and tarnished.

When she stepped outside, Lord Brentmore
was there, waiting in the chaise. He'd secured her
portmanteau under the seat. She placed the food
into the basket she'd brought from Brentmore and

left the box by the door. No part of Lawton House would come with her.

Lord Brentmore helped her into her seat. 'How are you faring?'

She steeled herself against the grief of all she had lost. Her mother. Her home. Her very identity. 'I will fare well.'

His glance was sceptical before he signalled the horses to be on their way.

She made herself not look back. The life she'd missed so acutely had never truly existed. When they passed through the village, she kept her eyes resolutely on the road. Once the village was behind them, all that was once familiar to her was behind her. Lost to her for ever.

Anna's gaze was captured by a leaf caught in a whirlwind ahead of them. The leaf rose and fell at the whim of the wind. She felt like its kin.

After they passed through a tollgate, the road was nearly empty of traffic. Lord Brentmore gave the horses their heads.

Without looking at her, he spoke. 'Did I ever tell you about Ireland?'

He was attempting to distract her from her grief. His kindness made tears prick her eyes.

She tried to keep her voice steady. 'You lived there once.'

'I was born there.' He turned his gaze back to the road. 'My father's regiment was stationed in

Ireland and somehow my father met my mother and married her. My mother was the daughter of a poor Irish tenant farmer and was as common as they come. The poorest of the poor. The old marquess—my father's father—disowned my father for marrying her. Cut him off without a penny and never spoke to him again.'

'Because he married a commoner.' She was a commoner who had aristocratic blood in her veins. How ironic was that?

'Yes.' He looked away. 'My father died soon after and my mother and I lived with my Irish grandfather. I was barely out of leading strings when she, too, died.'

This distraction was only increasing her pain. Her heart ached at his loss.

He continued. 'Even as a small boy I worked the farm with my grandfather.' He glanced at her. 'Seeing you and the children in the kitchen garden that day brought that memory back.'

She could not look into his eyes.

He fell silent.

Keep talking, please! she wanted to beg. His voice seemed all that was keeping her together.

'How did you come to England?' she asked.

'An uncle I did not know existed—my father's older brother—died,' he said. 'The old marquess needed an heir and thus came looking for me. Up until that time, I thought I was Egan Byrne. I knew nothing of my real name, Egan Caine, and nothing of my father being English. I was suddenly the heir and the old marquess took me from Ireland and brought me to Brentmore Hall. I was ten.'

'Was that a good circumstance?' she asked.

He shrugged. 'At the time I did not think so, but it was good in that I had food to eat, clothing to wear and a fire to keep me warm.' He glanced at her. 'What I want you to know is that I remember that time in Ireland with a clarity that sometimes escapes me when I'm trying to recall what happened yesterday.' His Irish accent slipped into his speech. 'And I mostly remember the happy parts.'

She understood. 'So I will remember the happy times at Lawton?'

He gave the briefest of nods. 'The memories will be with you always.'

She wished she could believe she would some day remember Lawton without thinking of how her life was conceived and how the education she held so dear had been exacted. It seemed impossible.

'You have not spoken of happy times, though,' she accused. 'You tell of suffering and grief.'

'Only to show the contrast,' he explained. 'Those events are like shadows. What I remember most clearly is sitting near the fireplace in the cabin with my grandfather, while he told story after story of the fairies or silkies or pookas. Or walking at his side through the potato fields.' He shook his head. 'I know it rained a great deal, but I only remember the sunny days. Like one day when I worried my *daideó* by running all the way to the sea. Must have been three or four miles.'

'Your *daideó*?'

'My grandfather.'

'What happened to him?' she asked.

'He fought with Billy Byrne in the 1798 Rebellion and was killed at the Battle of Arklow.' His voice turned hard. 'I read of it in the newspapers when I was at school.'

She gasped and felt the pain of his memory as if it had been her own.

She stole a glance at him, needing now to distract him as he had tried to distract her. 'You should tell Dory and Cal your grandfather's Irish stories.'

'Never!' He looked appalled. 'The less they know about their Irish blood, the better.'

'You cannot mean that!'

'Indeed I do,' he said with emotion. 'I'll not have them suffer the taunts and cuts that were my lot. The less they know of their Irish blood, the better. They must think themselves the privileged children of a marquess. Nothing else.'

She'd merely pictured the children sitting on his lap listening to the stories, as she'd pictured he had sat on his grandfather's lap. It would be something she never had.

'Tell me the stories,' she said to him, lest she dwell on fathers who cared nothing for her. 'I want to hear about fairies and silkies and pookas.'

So he filled her ears with tales of mischievous little people, of fearsome horses with yellow eyes and fantastic creatures that shed their skins to become human.

As the day passed, the overcast sky turned grey and soon rain pattered the top of the chaise, getting thicker and thicker as the miles went by. When it started to pour as hard as it had done that first day she'd met the marquess, he pulled into an inn.

'We must wait out the rain,' he told her.

They left the horses and chaise to the care of the ostlers and ran through the rain to the door of the inn.

Inside it was noisy and crowded with other travellers taking shelter from the storm.

He found a space for her in a corner. 'Wait here. I'll speak to the innkeeper and see what is available.'

She watched him disappear behind the other people waiting out the rain and her anxiety rose, as if, without him, she might blow away like the leaf she'd watched on the road. The buzzing of all the voices filled her ears and mixed with the clatter of more carriages arriving.

There were all sorts of travellers stranded here.

Gentlemen. Tradesmen. Workmen of all types. She saw a woman holding a little girl's hand and she remembered how her mother's hand felt holding hers. Tears threatened again and she searched the crowd for Lord Brentmore.

It seemed an eternity until he came back.

'There are no private parlours and no rooms,' he said over the din. 'We can wait in the public room, though. I arranged for a bench near the fire. It is somewhat private.'

She nodded and took his arm. He led her through the people into the tavern, more crowded than the anteroom. The scent of ale and meat and unwashed people assaulted her nostrils. Their combined voices were like beating drums and every inch of the space seemed filled.

Except for a small bench and table near the fire. 'How did you manage this?'

'I told them you were my wife.' His gaze caught hers for a fleeting moment. 'And that you were not well.' He settled her in the seat. 'And, of course, I paid well for the men sitting here to move.'

She could not help but smile.

He sat next to her. 'They were happy with the coin and we have a warm place to sit and take away the damp from our clothes.'

A moment later a harried tavern maid brought hot cider and bowls of mutton stew. Lord Brentmore pressed a coin in the woman's hand

and her countenance brightened considerably. Anna ate and drank by rote, but soon she was warm inside and out and a lassitude washed over her.

'It has been a long time since I've spent more than a few minutes in a crowded tavern,' Lord Brentmore remarked. 'I fear we will be here for a while.'

'I am sorry, my lord.' If it were not for her, he would not have had to endure this discomfort.

He leaned to her ear. 'I am Egan Byrne here. Better we not command undue attention.'

She nodded.

'And I do not mind it,' he added. 'We are reasonably comfortable here.'

She was more than comfortable. She belonged nowhere and to no one, so there was some comfort in anonymity, in being the fictional Mrs Byrne.

She stole a glance at him and wondered why she'd ever felt he was formidable. Merely her employer, he'd extended himself as a friend.

But she could not think of him only as a friend. Her father—the man she'd thought was her father—had not been entirely incorrect. In her heart she was a harlot, as much as her mother had been. If she did not feel dead inside at this moment, she had no doubt that her desire for Lord Brentmore would be raging inside her.

Now it was even more crucial that she control

it. How long would she remain in his employ if she came to his bed? She could not depend upon him to keep her around as Lord Lawton had her mother.

Brentmore slipped his arm across her shoulders and nestled her against him. 'Rest, Anna,' he murmured.

His embrace felt more a shelter than the roof over her head, but it was as much an illusion as the rest of her life had been. She shuddered in pain and he held her tighter.

If only he really were Egan Byrne and she... his wife.

She felt wonderful in his arms. A peace came over Brent that made no sense at all in the midst of this simple tavern awash in all forms of humanity. No one cared who they were here. He could hold her without worry of censure or gossip.

Best of all, the sheer numbers of eyes prevented his more dangerous temptations from coming to the fore. Still, he would have forgone even the pleasure of holding her if he could have procured a comfortable room for her.

The last traveller who'd entered the tavern loudly declared it was 'raining stair rods' outside. A downpour, he meant, apparently.

In the crowd he spotted two gentlemen known to him. No matter. He blended so well with the rest of the ordinary people, those acquaintances would never notice him. They might gaze at Anna, though, whose beauty had turned melancholic from her shock and grief.

He pulled his cap down to shade more of his face, just in case.

Anna straightened. 'What is it?'

'Some men I know,' he replied. 'But do not fear. They've entered a private parlour.' He tipped his hat back again.

'You will not wish to be seen with me,' she commented.

He put his arm around her again. 'I merely wish to avoid explaining why I'm dressed as a coachman.'

'I wish you were a coachman,' she said, so quietly he barely heard her.

So did he. How free he might be. Free to look upon her not as the marquess who employed her, but as a man.

'I would make love to you, then,' she added.

Could she see into his mind? 'Anna—'

She hurried on. 'I want to. It has been hard not to.' She averted her gaze.

She was overwrought and how could she not be after the day she'd endured?

'You should not talk of this,' he said.

She lifted her chin defiantly, reminding him of that first interview with her. 'You want me, too, my lord. You would bed me if I permitted. That is a man's way, is it not? That is why daughters like Charlotte are chaperoned. If they were alone, they might permit men to bed them.'

There was truth in that. The daughters of earls were protected, but not so much from their own urges, but those of men who thought only of their own pleasure.

Lawton ought to have protected Anna. She was his daughter, as well. Damned man! He should have cared for her, not sent her off to fend for herself. He knew what could happen to unprotected governesses.

She took a deep breath. 'I thought there was something wrong with me, but now I see I am just like my mother.'

He turned so he could face her directly. 'Lawton seduced your mother, Anna.'

Her lovely brows rose. 'Or did she seduce him? She was given a cottage to live in and her daughter was educated. That was much more than other servants received.'

He shook his head. 'He should have given your mother an independent means. Set her up in a nice house.'

She placed her hand on his arm. 'She would not have known how to run her own house.'

'He should have acknowledged you at the very least,' he insisted.

Her voice turned low again. 'I expect he did not care.' She stared into flames licking a large log in the fireplace. 'It all makes sense now, though, does it not, why I want so much to bed you? I am like my mother.'

'Enough talking like this.' He gathered her in his arms again. 'You are upset and tired. Try to rest.'

If only he were not a marquess. He'd not have to worry about damage to the children because of him. He'd not be betrothed to a baron's daughter. It would not matter who he married. He'd be free…

He looked down into her face. Her eyes were closed and her expression was composed. She slept and he was free to relish the sight of her.

If he were indeed Egan Byrne he'd be free….

Chapter Nine

Anna had remained cosseted in the warmth of Lord Brentmore's arms the whole night. When morning dawned full of sunshine, the tavern began to empty of its travellers, but they tarried by silent agreement as if reluctant to return to the old routines, the old identities.

Over an unhurried breakfast, Anna searched the marquess's face for any hint he would address the loose words she'd spoken the night before. She felt her cheeks burn merely from thinking of what she'd said to him in her grief and despair.

Yet it was a reality she must accept within herself. She was her mother's daughter, yearning for carnal pleasure just as her mother must have done with Lord Lawton.

Her real father.

If only she could talk to her mother about such

yearning, discover why her mother chose to carry on a long affair with his lordship. Ask her why she'd hidden the truth from her daughter all these years.

Grief threatened to overwhelm her. She tried relentlessly to push it away. She was more fortunate than most women. She had employment. She had a lovely place to live. She had an education. And books. The library at Brentmore was filled with books.

She lifted her gaze to the man who sat across from her at the table.

She had a friend, as well as an employer, in Lord Brentmore. Likely back at Brentmore, they would return to their previous routine and the friendship would be as buried as her desire for him must be.

She pretended to eat with appetite and forced herself to talk of the trip ahead.

No more tears. No more feeling sorry for herself. Her mother was gone. Her life was what it was.

Her consolation must be the children for as long as they needed her.

After they'd eaten, Lord Brentmore asked, 'Are you ready to depart?'

She nodded.

Soon they were back in the chaise and on the road.

Anna confined her conversation with Lord

Brentmore to topics involving the children. Their needs. Their activities. Ways to make their lives secure and happy.

By early afternoon they reached the inn where Lord Brentmore's team of horses awaited him. His team was hitched to the chaise again, marking the last leg of the journey. Soon they reached the outskirts of the marquess's estate. When the house came into view, Anna felt relief.

'Lawd, I hate this place,' Brentmore said at the same time.

It disheartened her. 'Why? It is where your children are.'

He nodded. 'It is also where my unhappiest memories live.'

She squared her shoulders. 'Do not think of the past. Only the future. Only what is ahead.'

He covered her hand with his and his expression turned grim.

When they reached the arch, Lord Brentmore halted the chaise.

'Why are we stopping?' she asked.

He turned to her, and his eyes darkened. 'To say goodbye.'

'Are you getting off here?' She could not drive the chaise.

A ghost of a smile flitted across his face. 'No, but Egan Byrne is saying goodbye.'

He leaned over to her and kissed her cheek.

She gasped and turned her head, offering him

her lips and trembling with need to taste him again.

He indulged her, softly pressing his mouth to hers, but carefully holding back and enabling her to bank the passion that flared through her.

When he moved away again, she released a breath.

'Back to being the marquess and the governess,' he murmured.

She squeezed her hands together, to keep from clasping his. 'I cannot thank you enough, my lord, for coming with me.'

He bent down and kissed her cheek again, but said nothing. He flicked the ribbons and the horses passed under the arch.

They came closer and closer to the house and suddenly Anna's grief intensified. She'd just suffered another loss, the loss of a friend named Egan Byrne.

When they pulled up to the front door, it opened and two footmen emerged to attend to them. After they alighted, Cal and Dory burst through the doorway.

Dory vaulted into her father's arms. 'Papa! You are home!'

He hesitated before fully accepting Dory's embrace. Cal stopped a short distance away as if his shyness had grabbed hold of him and held him back.

'Miss Hill!' Dory cried and reached out for Anna.

Lord Brentmore handed the little girl into Anna's arms and Anna fussed over her while the marquess approached his son, drawing him into a huge hug. 'My boy, I missed you.'

Cal wound his arms around his father's neck. 'Me, too,' he said.

His father hugged the boy tighter.

'Cal talked to Eppy and to Wyatt, too, while you were gone,' Dory informed them.

'Isn't that fine!' Anna exclaimed, realising how genuinely she'd missed the children. 'And what mischief did you get into while we were gone?'

Dory giggled. 'Nothing.' Her brother actually smiled. She whispered to Anna. 'Cal caught a toad and put it in Eppy's pocket!'

'That is mischief, indeed!' And a marvellous change for him.

'Don't tell Papa!' Dory whispered loud enough for her father to hear.

Anna put Dory down and hugged Cal. 'What a prankster you are,' she said quietly.

One of the footmen retrieved her portmanteau and the basket, the other took the horses and chaise to the stables.

'Let us go inside,' Lord Brentmore said.

Dory reached up for him to carry her and Anna took Cal's hand.

As they entered the hall, Cal gestured for her

to bend down. He moved his mouth before finally forcing the words out. 'Is your mother better?'

A wave of grief engulfed her. 'No, Lord Cal. She was too sick. She died.'

The boy's expression turned solemn. 'Mine did, too.'

Anna crouched down and hugged him, tears pricking her eyes. 'I know.'

As the days went on, they returned to their previous routine and the children thrived. Cal spoke more and more, and Dory calmed down and became less vigilant and protective of her brother. Their former confinement made them hungry for new experiences. There was nothing they would not try and they soaked up information like sponges.

For Anna, though, everything seemed slightly askew. During the day she often felt as if she were standing beside herself, watching what she was doing, what she was saying, what she was hearing. She often declined riding with Lord Brentmore and the children and Lord Brentmore spent more time at his correspondence and estate business.

In the evening, she and Lord Brentmore still dined together and still discussed the children, but always Anna sensed the tension between them, borne of all they did not say.

Anna tried to convince herself that everything

was as it should be, that she would soon be content again, but at times a restlessness overtook her that was nearly as unbearable as her grief. Sleep was nearly impossible. When slumber finally came, she dreamed she was running and running until she reached the sea.

Just as he said he had done as a child in Ireland.

The happy memories he'd promised her never came and her desire for him never abated. At times she feared she would go mad if he did not touch her. If he did happen to touch her, she felt the touch in every part of her. That was enough to drive her insane.

Perhaps she should be locked away as a maniac in Doctor Stoke's asylum.

She was merely masquerading as sane, although she was reasonably certain no one could perceive her struggle. She could teach her lessons while her mind wandered back to Lawton or to the library below where Lord Brentmore wrote his letters. She could converse at dinner about the children, share anecdotes about them, make plans for them, while remembering the meals she and the marquess shared in the inn. She could bid him goodnight after dinner and confess to be sleepy when she knew she would stare at the ceiling for hours.

This night her thoughts turned to the future and all she could see was more bleakness and loss. He would not stay at Brentmore Hall for ever. Eventually he would return to London and take his place again in society. His visits here would become shorter and less frequent. She'd be alone.

Anna got out of bed and paced the room, hoping to tire herself.

It did not work.

She must train herself to think of him only as an employer, nothing more. She must distract herself. Fill her mind with something other than how he smiled, how he moved, how his lips had felt against hers.

This was ridiculous! She snatched a candle from the table and rushed out of the room, without bothering to put on her slippers or wrap a robe around her. She padded her way down the hallway to the stairs, headed for the library. Books had filled her imagination as a child—perhaps they could fill her mind now and crowd him out.

She wanted a book about some faraway place where people unlike herself lived lives totally different from her own. Perhaps the marquess's library had *Captain Cook's Voyages Around The World*, which would certainly fit the bill.

No. She had a better idea. She really did not wish to read. She wished to sleep. A glass of Lord Brentmore's brandy might bring her sleep. Perhaps he would not mind just one glassful missing. Perhaps he would not even notice.

Somewhere in the house a clock struck two,

its chime echoing in the silence and making her jump. The library door was ajar and inside the room the coals in the fireplace still glowed.

She crossed the room and placed her candle on the cabinet, which was kept stocked with brandy. She opened the cabinet door and took out a bottle and a glass. She poured a full glass and quickly drank it down, almost choking from its warmth.

'Anna?' A voice came from the sofa in front of the fire.

Lord Brentmore's voice.

She almost dropped the glass.

He sat up. He was in his shirt-sleeves. His coat, waistcoat, and neckcloth were tossed on a nearby chair. 'What are you doing?'

There was no sense lying. He'd caught her in her theft. 'Drinking brandy. I could not sleep and I thought brandy would help.' Servants were discharged for stealing spirits from their employers.

He rubbed his face. 'Brandy rarely helps.' He peered at her. 'I thought you said you were tired tonight.'

She was tired to the point of exhaustion. 'I was. I am. But I cannot sleep.'

He groaned. 'And I fell asleep on the sofa. We are like bookends, facing opposite ways.'

His analogy was apt, she thought. Together they held things in place, but were never meant to meet. To touch.

'I—I know this looks like theft.' Her hand

shook. He could end her employment. 'I was feeling quite desperate.'

With a dismissive wave of his hand, he stood. 'You are welcome to what I have.' He walked over to her. 'But what is amiss?'

'Nothing is amiss,' she replied. 'I cannot sleep.'

'It is not like you.' He felt her forehead. 'You are not warm.'

She was now. His touch enflamed her.

His gaze swept down her body and his hand slipped to her shoulder. 'What keeps you awake?'

Her limbs felt like melting candle wax under his fingers and his gaze. 'I—I do not know.'

'Or you will not say?' He put his arm around her. 'Come. Sit with me. Tell me. Pretend I am Egan Byrne. Tell me what makes it so difficult to sleep.'

He sat her down on the couch and leaned her against him. She could feel the heat of him through the thin fabric of her nightdress and his shirt. She wanted to discover what his bare skin felt like beneath his shirt.

'Talk to me, Anna,' he murmured.

What could she say that he would believe? She could not say the truth.

That she ached for him, although she'd confessed that very thing to him at the inn.

'At—at night thoughts consume me. About my mother. About Lawton. About all of it. About being alone now.' She did think about such things…and more.

He held her tighter. 'You are not alone.'

His words and his arms were meant to comfort, but they only tortured. She yearned for more and knew she could not have it.

She drew away. 'You could dismiss me for taking the brandy. That is how precarious my life is. What would happen to me then? I have nowhere to go. No one to help me.'

'I do not begrudge you the brandy.' His expression was sincere. 'You are safe here, Anna. You are wanted here.'

She wiped a loose lock of hair off her face. 'I do not mean to complain. Or to feel sorry for myself. Please do not pay me any mind.' She tried to rise, but he seized her hand and pulled her back on to the sofa.

'Anna.' He stroked her arm. 'What can I do to ease your worry?'

'Nothing, my lord,' she said, trying to remain composed. 'It is the lot of a governess.'

He turned her to face him. 'You know you are more than a governess.'

His lips were perilously close. His body was warm and hard-muscled. The scent of him filled her nostrils, so male, so pleasant, so unique to him alone. She yearned to join with him.

Wrenching herself away, she cried, 'I—I must go.'

She ran from the library.

Chapter Ten

'Anna!' Brent ran after her.

When she reached the second floor, he caught her by the arm and made her face him.

'What is wrong?' He gave her a shake.

She tried to pull away. 'Sometimes—sometimes I cannot forget all that I feel.'

He could not forget, as well. Travelling with her had changed something in him, made him wish to be a mere man, not a marquess. It had been a long time since he'd yearned to turn away the trappings of his title and strip himself down to mere flesh and bone.

He put his arms around her and held her close, wanting to comfort her, wanting her to comfort him. It was like a match to tinder. Her arms encircled his neck and through the thin fabric of her nightdress he felt the roundness of her breasts, the curve of her body, the special place that fired his senses. His hands travelled to her narrow waist and he pressed her pelvis against his, drowning in desire.

She tilted her face to his and he took possession of her lips, this time indulging in the full taste of her. Her tongue immediately sought his. She tasted like brandy.

He lifted her into his arms and carried her to his bedchamber, taking her to his bed. She was as willing as any woman could be, as lost in the passion as he was.

He tore his shirt off and lay with her on the bed, their legs tangling as his hands explored her and his mouth revelled in her kisses.

What harm could it do to make love with her? They both wanted it. And he would be good to her. He wanted to be a man with her, to join his body to hers, to bring them both to physical release.

What harm if they continued?

His hand slipped between her legs, to that place where pleasure could explode. She moved against his hand and his craving surged.

They could have many nights of pleasure until—

Until he married.

He stilled and moved away from her.

'No, do not stop,' she rasped. 'I want this.'

He took her face in his hands. 'I cannot.'

He ought to tell her that the Marquess of Brentmore was soon to make a respectable marriage, but this seemed the worst possible time and, when he was with her, he wanted to pretend his fiancée did not exist.

Her expression showed all the anguish he felt inside. 'Why?'

'You could have a child,' he managed.

Her eyes widened. 'Like my mother,' she whispered.

He climbed off the bed, found his shirt and put it back on.

He ran a hand through his hair. 'God knows I want to make love to you, Anna, but it would be wrong. It would change things between us.'

She pressed her fingers to her temples. 'What are we to do, then?'

'Not this.' He shook his head. 'We must take care. I promise, I will not do this again.'

'I am not certain that is what I want,' she said in a quiet tone.

He glanced at her. 'I know it is not what I want, but what I must do.'

'Things are changed between us anyway.' She gave him an intent look. 'I feel as if a door has opened that I cannot close, no matter how hard I try.'

He returned her gaze. 'I am sorry, Anna.'

She looked away and was silent.

If she were in society, he would be duty bound

to marry her for behaving in such an ungentle-manly manner. But she was not in society. And there was no one—no father who cared about her—to insist he wed her.

That thought made him ache for her, her vul-nerability, her aloneness.

If he made love to her, he would have to marry her—how could he live with himself otherwise? He could just imagine the scandal of it. Jilting Miss Rolfe to marry a governess with a back-ground as scandalous as his own.

His children would suffer the consequences if he behaved dishonourably.

'We must think of the children,' he said. 'I want what is best for them.'

She nodded and climbed off the bed, raising herself to her full height. 'I have behaved abomi-nably tonight. I hope you will forgive me for it.'

Before he could compose a response, she walked out of the room.

The next day they behaved as mere employer and governess, maintaining a distance between them that was as distressing as it was necessary. Having come so close to making love to her, Brent's desire surged stronger than ever, but she had been correct. Things had already changed between them.

If that were not enough, London beckoned. Parker had any number of matters to which Brent must attend. And he had letters from Members of Parliament who wished him to return. Even though it was August, they were still in session.

All these he could ignore, but today letters arrived from both Peter and Baron Rolfe, begging him to return to London and make final plans for the marriage. Matters were becoming urgent for Lord Rolfe.

He needed to return.

It seemed too soon to leave the children.

Or Anna.

Rain and chill kept them all indoors and the confinement did nothing to relieve Brent's unease. He wandered through the house, winding up in the gallery, gazing at portraits of ancestors stretching back to the sixteenth century. Men with pointed beards and embroidered jerkins. Women in lace ruffs. It was difficult for Brent to believe that their blood flowed in his veins. After all these years, he still felt as if he were in a foreign land.

Wyatt found him. 'Ah, there you are, m'lord.' The butler stood at the far end of the gallery and his voice echoed. 'Dinner is served.'

'Thank you, Wyatt,' Brent said.

By the time Brent reached the beginning of the gallery where Wyatt had stood, the butler had disappeared from the hallway. When he reached the dining room, Anna was already seated.

'I am sorry to keep you waiting,' he said. 'I lost track of time.'

She smiled politely. 'Mr Wyatt said he'd had difficulty finding you.'

Brent sat. 'I was in the gallery.'

'The gallery,' she repeated in a perfunctory tone.

'With my ancestors.'

The footman served the soup almost immediately and Brent asked about the children's lessons.

Anna responded in dutiful detail about what they had done on that rainy day. 'I hope we can go outside tomorrow,' she added. 'Both of them were very unsettled.'

'As was I,' he said, pained at how stilted their conversation was.

She dipped her spoon into the soup. 'If it continues to rain tomorrow, I will move to the music room and give them dancing lessons.'

He looked up from his bowl. 'If it rains tomorrow, I may join you.'

She caught his gaze. 'I would like that.'

Their gazes held.

She glanced away. 'And the children will love having you.'

When the second course came, he looked down at his plate. 'I tackled my pile of letters today.'

'Was there any news?' she asked, polite again.

'Parliament is still in session.'

'Is it?' she asked without real interest.

'Mr Parker has amassed a number of matters I must address.' He glanced over at her.

She stared at him.

He glanced away. 'I need to go to London.' When he returned his gaze to her, she'd gone pale.

'The children will miss you.'

He felt the emotions behind her words and reached over to her. He pulled back, remembering that touching made things worse for both of them. 'Will it do harm to leave, do you think? Is it too soon?'

She put down her fork and turned her face towards him. 'You must leave us some time, my lord.'

The inevitability of that statement depressed him. These weeks had given him more peace than any other time he could remember. With Anna he felt more himself than anywhere else.

The conversation between the two of them virtually ended at this point, even though Anna asked him dutiful questions about his need to go to London and he provided dutiful answers while they finished the meal.

He still did not tell her about his betrothal. When he was with her, it seemed too unreal to speak of. Besides, their emotions were still too raw after they'd nearly made love the night before.

'When will you leave?' she asked finally as the dishes were removed and his brandy was poured.

'In a couple of days, I suppose.' He stared into

the liquid in his glass and remembered her in the library. Nearly naked. Hair flowing about her shoulders.

She stood. 'Well. I will bid you goodnight, my lord.'

He stood as well. 'Goodnight, Anna.'

As she walked towards the door, he was seized with a desire to call her back. 'Anna, wait!'

She turned to him.

He walked towards her. 'Come with me.'

Her face coloured. 'My lord,' she whispered.

Without thinking he put his hand on her arm and spoke in a low voice. 'I meant you and the children should come with me to London.' Why had he not thought of this before? 'It will only be for a few weeks. There is much we can show Cal and Dory in London.'

She looked wary. 'I do not know.'

'We could take them places. Astley's, for one. Dory would love the horses at Astley's. We can have new clothes made for them. They need new clothes. It will be a good experience for them.' He held his breath, waiting for her response.

She regarded him with solemn eyes. 'Very well, my lord. We will go to London.'

A few days later they made the trip to London. Lord Brentmore rode his horse. Anna rode in his carriage with his children and Eppy.

It was a difficult trip. Cal and Dory had never

travelled further than the village. They were both giddy with excitement as well as unused to the rigours of riding in a coach all day. To break up the day, their father allowed them to take turns riding on Luchar with him, but that only temporarily amused them. By the time the carriage pulled up to Lord Brentmore's town house, the children—and Anna—were exhausted.

The door opened to the familiar hall where Anna took the first step into a new chapter of her life. Little did she know that day how thoroughly the previous chapters would be closed to her.

Brentmore entered first, but stood just inside the door waiting for Anna, who had taken the children by the hand.

Mr Parker stepped forwards. He'd obviously been awaiting their arrival. 'My lord.' He bowed to the marquess. 'Good to have you back. I've taken the liberty of having Cook prepare a meal for us. With your permission, we can discuss some of the more pressing matters that await your attention.'

Lord Brentwood shot a glance Anna's way and returned to his man of business with a stern glare. 'Have your manners gone begging, Parker?'

Mr Parker looked puzzled, then realised what his employer meant. 'Oh, I beg your pardon.' His apology was directed at Brentmore. He turned to Anna. 'Good day, Miss Hill.'

'Good day,' she replied, noting that he paid no

attention at all to the children who hid behind her skirts as soon as they'd seen him.

Lord Brentmore spoke again. 'I am not prepared to discuss business at dinner, Parker. Come back in the morning.'

Mr Parker looked as if he'd been slapped in the face. 'My lord, there are one or two things that I believe cannot wait, even for tomorrow.'

Lord Brentmore did not relent. 'Well, since you have invited yourself to dinner, we may talk about this afterwards, but I have no intention of boring Miss Hill with tedious business, not when she has spent the day riding in the carriage with two small children.'

'Miss Hill?' Mr Parker's brows rose into his forehead.

Clearly it had never occurred to Mr Parker that she would dine with the marquess.

And she was too weary to put up with not being welcome. 'My lord, if you do not mind, I would like to dine with the children. They are in a place that is new to them. I want to be certain they are comfortable.'

Lord Brentmore's brows knitted. 'Are you certain?'

'With your permission,' she responded.

He turned to Mr Parker. 'Very well, Parker. It will be as you wish.'

'May we see our rooms?' Anna asked.

'Certainly.' Lord Brentmore turned to his butler, who had just re-entered the house and closed the door behind him. 'Davies! Find someone to show Miss Hill and the children to their rooms.'

At that moment a grey-haired portly woman bustled in from the servants' entrance. 'My lord! I've this minute learned you'd arrived.'

'Ah, Mrs Jones.' The marquess nodded towards her. 'Allow me to present you to Miss Hill, the children's governess, and Eppy, the children's nurse. Mrs Jones is the housekeeper here. You did not meet her before, I believe.'

'That is correct,' Anna replied. 'How very glad I am to meet you now, Mrs Jones.'

The housekeeper's smile was friendly. She leaned down to peek behind Anna. 'And who is that hiding behind you?'

Anna brought the children forward. 'This is Lord Calmount and his sister, Lady Dory.'

The housekeeper put her hands on her hips. 'Well, what a treat to have you here. We've fixed up a set of rooms for you that I hope you will like.'

Lord Brentmore came over to the children. 'Go with Mrs Jones to see your rooms. We'll have your trunks and your dinner sent up to you.' He glanced at the butler. 'Is that not right, Davies?'

'The trunks are being carried up as we speak and Cook has planned a special meal for the young ones.'

'Excellent.' Brentmore turned to Anna. 'Is there anything we've forgotten?'

'Not that I can think of,' she replied, although she was really too fatigued to think at all.

'Then you children can be on your way.' He gave Cal a reassuring squeeze of the shoulder.

'I want Miss Hill and Eppy to come, too!' Dory whined.

Lord Brentmore crouched down to her. 'Of course they will come with you. And Miss Hill said she would eat dinner with you tonight. That will be a treat, will it not?'

'I want you to eat dinner with us, too, Papa,' Dory whimpered.

He patted her arm. 'I cannot, but I will come up later to say goodnight.'

She popped her thumb into her mouth and Anna did not bother to tell her to take it out.

She also did not trouble herself to say goodnight to Mr Parker.

They followed Mrs Jones up to the third floor.

'We've set up one room as the school room and another for the children to sleep in. There is a small room for Eppy and another for you, Miss Hill. I hope that sounds satisfactory.'

'I am certain it will do very nicely,' Anna replied. 'I think Lord Cal and Lady Dory will be happier in the same room. Everything will seem strange to them.'

Mrs Jones smiled. 'That is what his lordship told us.'

'His lordship?'

Mrs Jones nodded. 'The marquess wrote very specific instructions. You are also to have a maid attend you. I will send her to you after we settle you in.'

'How very kind of him.' Although his kindness made everything more difficult. How unfortunate he was not the stern, fearsome man she had first met in this house. It would be so much easier to dislike him.

She shook herself. Of course it was preferable for him to be kind, especially for the children. She was simply much too fatigued.

Their rooms were satisfactory, but the school room was sparse. Anna had packed the children's slates and chalk, their sketchpads and some books, but she doubted it would be enough to amuse them.

Their dinner consisted of roast beef and plum pudding, with wafers for dessert and a hot milk posset when the children were ready for sleeping.

As he had promised, Lord Brentmore came to wish the children a goodnight. He tucked the covers around them and kissed them each on the forehead. His tenderness made Anna's heart ache.

Making them promise to sleep well, he started to leave the room, but whispered to Anna, 'May I see you a moment?'

She nodded and hurriedly said her own goodnights to the children. 'You know which room is mine and which is Eppy's, so come fetch us if you need anything during the night.'

She walked out of the room to where Lord Brentmore waited. The hallway was narrow, placing her much closer to him than she would wish.

'How are they, do you think?' he asked her.

'Dory is much subdued and Cal has not said a word, not even to his sister,' she told him. 'But most likely that is from sheer weariness.'

He frowned. 'Did I make a mistake to have you come with me?'

Perhaps it would have been better to leave them all in the country. Perhaps accustoming herself to his absence was better done sooner than later.

But she could not speak to him of that. 'If I am able to keep the children occupied, it should be satisfactory, but there is nothing here in the house to occupy the children.'

His brows rose. 'I meant you—but, never mind. What do you mean, nothing in the house?'

'No toys. No blocks to build with. No games or puzzles. No dolls or toy soldiers.'

He rubbed his neck. 'Toys. How could I not think of that? We will remedy that first thing tomorrow.'

She nodded.

He gazed at her longer than was comfortable. 'But, Anna, how do you fare?' He extended his hand as if to touch her, but withdrew it again. 'Was the trip too much for you?'

She must look a fright. Not that it mattered so very much. She could not bear to see admiration in his eyes.

'I need rest, is all,' she managed.

He still looked concerned. 'I must return to Mr Parker. Will you be all right here? Will you ask the servants for anything you need?'

She nodded. 'Goodnight, my lord.' Her tone was more curt than she'd meant it to be.

She turned to leave, but he caught her arm. Instantly, her senses flared in response. She faced him and the yearning she'd worked so hard to conquer returned as strong as ever.

He must have felt it, too, because he held on to her arm and moved closer, but caught himself and released her.

'I wish to apologise for Mr Parker's rudeness to you,' he said. 'That was badly done of him.'

She touched her arm where he had held it. 'I am a governess. I did not expect more from him.'

'I do,' he responded hotly. 'In any event, you and I may dine together tomorrow.'

She inclined her head. 'As you wish.'

He searched her face. 'Anna,' he whispered, his tone aching.

She looked away. 'Goodnight, my lord,' she murmured and hurried into her room.

Chapter Eleven

The next morning after breakfast, Brent took Anna and the children to Noah's Ark, Mr Hamley's toy store on High Holborn Street.

When they stepped inside, Dory gasped. 'I have never seen anything so wonderful!'

Who could blame her? The toy store was a children's wonderland. From floor to ceiling toys filled the shelves. One whole wall honoured the store's name with its sets of Noah's Arks of various sizes and designs. Another shelf was filled with dolls. Another section held spinning tops and balls and other outdoor toys.

Cal was silent, but as wide-eyed as his sister. Even Brent was not indifferent to the sight. At Cal's age he would have been amazed that such toys existed. He remembered amusing himself for hours with the clay marbles his *daideó* made for him.

Where were they? he wondered. He'd hidden them from the old marquess and managed to bring them to England with him, but, over the years, he'd lost track of where he'd hidden them.

Brent glanced at Anna, but her expression was impossible to decipher. Was she thinking of the toys of her childhood as well? Surely Lord and Lady Lawton would have indulged their daughter with dolls and tea sets and all sorts of toys that little girls liked. Perhaps Anna only played with toys that were never to be hers.

Anna followed Dory over to the display of dolls, more than the child could count.

Some were made of painted wood. Others were made of wax and appeared so real Brent was certain they were about to open their mouths and demand to be fed. On the floor in front of the shelf was a huge doll's house, complete with miniature furniture so detailed one could imagine shrinking and living there in great comfort. Anna crouched down with Dory and pointed to the small doll family, the mother and father in the parlour, the children in the nursery with their governess.

He walked over to where Dory and Anna stood.

'Would you like a doll house, Dory?' he asked.

The little girl sighed. 'Oh, yes!'

'Should I purchase it for her?' he asked Anna. 'Is it suitable?'

She glanced at him. 'I believe she adores it.'

He would purchase it, if for no other reason than that Anna approved of it.

He turned. 'Shopkeeper!'

The gentleman behind the counter signalled for a clerk to assist the woman he'd been helping. He quickly approached Lord Brentmore. 'Your lordship? How may I serve you?'

It always surprised Brent how shopkeepers knew he was titled. Did the man spy the crest on his carriage through the shop window? Or was there some other clue?

'I want this doll house and everything in it,' he told the man. 'Packed up and delivered to me by this afternoon, if possible.'

The shopkeeper's face lit up. 'With pleasure, sir!' His expression turned shrewd. 'There are other sets of dolls that may be added. Would you like to see them?'

'What sorts of dolls?' Dory piped up.

'A set of servants, sir. A dog and cat.'

She looked beseechingly at her father and became the image of her mother.

Brent's enjoyment was shaken.

'Include all the dolls,' he said, turning away so Dory—and Anna—would not see his mood so abruptly change.

He turned to Cal, who seemed frozen in place,

looking from one display to another. The boy, like Brent at that age, had never seen such toys, Brent realised.

He put a hand on Cal's shoulder. 'What shall we find for you, Cal?' He glanced to the shop-keeper. 'What special toys do you have for my son?'

'Well.' The man wrung his hands in eager-ness. 'We've just received a set of tin soldiers from France. Made by Mignot. The finest I've ever seen. It is a Waterloo set, my lord.'

Brent felt Cal tremble with eagerness.

'Let us see it,' he said.

'It is still in boxes in the back, my lord. Give me a moment.' The man rushed off.

Brentmore looked at his son. 'Do you want to see the Waterloo soldiers, Cal?'

Cal nodded.

Brent crouched down to his level. 'Will you say it out loud for me?' he asked gently.

'Y-yes,' Cal uttered.

Brent squeezed his shoulder and glanced to-wards Anna, who stared at them both.

Once she would have smiled at Cal's effort.

'What else should we buy?' he asked her.

Anna looked around the shop. 'Puzzles? Spinning tops?'

'Choose whatever you like,' Brent would pur-chase whatever she liked, heedless of cost.

The woman who'd been passed on to the clerk

completed her purchases and left. They were the only customers in the shop.

The clerk approached them. 'May I assist, sir?'

'May we see that Noah's Ark, please?' Anna pointed to the largest wooden ark on one of the shelves.

'This is quite good quality,' the clerk said. 'Finest wood and paint.'

The ark was cleverly designed to act as a box for the pairs of animals in the set, about fifty in number and including Noah and his wife.

Dory skipped over. 'Oh, look at that Noah's Ark!'

The shopkeeper emerged from the back room. 'Here is a part of the Waterloo set, my lord.' He placed a box on the counter and brought out a replica of a French soldier and a British dragoon. Cal touched it with a finger.

'These are finely done. Very lifelike,' Brent remarked.

'Were you there, my lord?' the shopkeeper asked.

Brent placed the tin soldier back in the man's hand. 'Not as a soldier.' He'd been deep in clandestine work then, though, gathering information to send back to Wellington. He turned to Cal. 'Should we buy it for you?'

'Yes.' The boy responded without hesitation. 'Th-thank you.'

'Send it with the doll's house,' Brent told the shopkeeper.

They walked around the shop and added spellicans and dominoes, battledore and shuttlecocks, dissected puzzles and spinning tops, skittles and a fine set of marbles, small gems compared to the ones Brent had loved.

The shopkeeper appeared to be in ecstasy as he made a tally of all the purchases.

Dory pulled on Brent's coat. 'Papa, may I please have a doll?'

Her request was tentative so that, this time, she was very unlike her mother.

He felt a pang of tenderness towards her. 'Of course you may.'

Anna went with her to the doll shelf where Dory chose, not any of the finely made porcelain or wax dolls, but a simple wooden one, with hair painted yellow, eyes blue, and wearing a simple frock covered with an apron.

'Not one of the fancy ones, Dory?' Brent asked her.

Dory shook her head. 'This doll needs me.' She looked up at him. 'Please, Papa? This doll?'

He nodded, unable to speak. Perhaps she was not like Eunice at all.

Cal carried a toy sword over to Brent and asked just as tentatively as Dory had, 'Papa? May I?'

Brent's voice turned thick. 'Yes, Cal. You may.'

He swallowed the lump in his throat. 'What else do we need?'

Cal looked up at him. 'Blocks?'

The clerk added a fine set of blocks to the pile of purchases and Brent asked that everything be delivered to Cavendish Square that very day. He allowed Cal to carry his toy sword with him and Dory held on to her doll as if her life depended on it.

Anna glanced at him and he fancied she felt as he did: that these children deserved this indulgence. They'd been nearly as deprived as he until she came into their lives.

'Do you approve?' he asked her.

Her eyes were warm. 'Very much,' she said.

Brent felt that erotic pull between them, even in the middle of the toy store. Good God. He needed more distraction.

When they left the toy store and climbed into the carriage again, he instructed the coachman to take them to Berkeley Square.

'How would you like some ices?' he asked the children. 'I feel a great need for something sweet.'

Cal gave him a puzzled look.

'What are ices?' Dory asked.

These children had never tasted ices? Brent's guilt rushed back.

Anna explained, 'Ices are sweet and cold and delicious treats.'

Gunter's Confectionery on Berkeley Square

was one of the few places that a gentleman might properly escort an unmarried woman. A marquess, his children and their governess would raise no one's eyebrows.

Brent instructed the coachman to pick them up in a half-hour. Dory carried her doll and Cal his sword, both promising not to disturb anything with them.

As soon as they opened the door, the scent of sugar, spice and fruit enveloped them. The shop was filled with display cases of marzipan made in the shapes of colourful fruits.

'Oh, look!' cried Dory, peering into the cases. 'What are they?'

'They are sweets,' Anna explained.

Dory looked at her father. 'May we buy some? They are so pretty!'

'Yes, we may.' He gave her a serious look. 'But it is for a special treat. Not for all the time.'

She nodded solemnly.

He glanced at Anna and wondered how often she'd had sweets like this. Had Lord and Lady Lawton favoured her in even that small way or had she been forced to watch her half-sister eat them alone?

He ordered pistachio ices for all of them, including Anna, and a box of the marzipan.

As Dory and Cal quietly examined every confection in the cases, Brent leaned over to Anna. 'It pains me how much of childhood they've never seen. I want to make it up to them all at once.'

She looked up at him, her lovely blue eyes filled with understanding. 'You are doing very well, my lord.'

To his surprise she touched his arm, a light, fleeting touch, but one that he felt deep within him.

Lawd, he wanted to take away all her suffering, as well, but he had caused part of the sadness that now wrapped around her like a cloak.

The Gunter's waiter bowed and handed him the box of sweets. 'If your lordship wishes, you may wait in the Square and I will bring your ices as soon as they are ready.'

Anna took the box. 'I will carry it, my lord.'

Brent called to the children, 'Come. Let's wait outside.'

As they walked to the shop door, it opened and in walked the two people Brent most wished to delay encountering.

His cousin and Miss Rolfe.

'Brent!' His cousin Peter broke into a surprised grin. 'You are in town!'

'We arrived yesterday.' He intended to send word to Peter and Lord Rolfe later this afternoon. He nodded to Miss Rolfe. 'Good day, Miss Rolfe.'

'Good day, Lord Brentmore.' She appeared reticent and why should she not be? He'd left her abruptly and taxed his cousin to make his excuses.

Peter crouched down. 'Do not tell me this is Calmount and Dorothea! They are so grown.'

Dory appeared willing to accept the attention of this new person, but Cal stepped back.

'Yes.' Brent was glad to turn his attention away from Miss Rolfe. 'Children, this is my cousin, who last saw you when you were babies.'

'At their christenings!' Peter smiled at them.

Why had he not told Anna of Miss Rolfe?

He knew why. When he was with Anna, he wished to pretend Miss Rolfe did not exist.

'Say "How do you do," children,' Anna told them.

Brent felt sick inside.

Dory curtsied and parroted, 'How do you do.'

Cal nodded, but did not speak. Instead the boy looked as if he'd sensed his father's discomfort.

Brent had no choice but to continue the introductions. 'Peter. Miss Rolfe. May I present Miss Hill, the children's governess.' He turned to Anna. 'This is my cousin, Mr Caine, and Miss Rolfe...' he paused '...my fiancée.'

Anna felt as if she had no air to breathe, no control of her muscles.

She forced herself to curtsy. 'How do you do, Mr Cain. Miss Rolfe.' She quickly turned her attention to the children. 'Come, let us go to the Square. Give your father a chance to visit.'

The children did not hesitate to accompany her. She hoped that Lord Brentmore's…companions did not guess that she needed to flee.

From him.

They found a bench with a view of the teashop door and sat.

'What is a fiancée?' Dory asked, clutching her doll to her chest.

Anna should not be compelled to tell the children their father planned to remarry. 'Oh, a special friend. I am certain your father can explain it better.'

Cal gave her a searching look, as if he knew her suffering.

She picked at the string that tied the box closed. 'Shall we peek in the box and see what treats the waiter gave us?'

They complied, but Anna believed they were merely helping her to calm down.

Of course he should marry again. Widowed men remarried, especially if they carried a title and had only one son to inherit. He did not owe her any explanation of his private life. She was merely a governess, after all.

But could he not have told her of this fiancée before she showed him her heart and desire?

She glanced up and spied him crossing the

road. The waiter—and his cousin and fiancée—followed him. He looked directly at her.

She closed the box and tied its string. 'Your father is coming with the ices.'

'I'm not hungry now,' Dory said.

'Well—' Anna spoke in a firm voice '—your father has been very generous today and we will be very polite and eat what is offered to us. Can you agree?'

They both nodded.

Lord Brentmore's gaze remain fixed on her until he was within a few feet of them, then he seemed to force a smile for the children. 'Here are your ices.'

The children placed their toys on the bench and the waiter served them. They dutifully dipped their spoons in and had their first taste of ices.

'This is delicious!' Dory said too brightly.

Cal nodded.

Miss Rolfe and Mr Caine joined them, taking their own ices from the waiter's tray.

Anna stood. 'Miss Rolfe may sit here,' she said quietly to Lord Brentmore.

'Anna—' he began.

She did not give him a chance to say more. She walked behind the bench and stood by a tree as Miss Rolfe took her place.

A place that had never truly been Anna's.

It seemed an eternity before the carriage returned. Anna let Lord Brentmore gather the children to leave. She joined them at the carriage while the children were climbing in.

The marquess extended a hand to assist her. She avoided looking at him. He gripped her hand. 'Anna, I will not be accompanying you. My cousin wishes me to call upon Lord Rolfe.' He gave her an entreating look. 'I have been remiss...'

She finally looked at him directly, but she could not speak.

'Please tell Davies I expect to return in time for dinner.'

She climbed inside.

'Papa isn't coming with us,' Dory said.

Anna hugged her. 'Yes, he told me. He is going to visit more friends. We will see him later.'

She talked about all the toys that would be delivered and what enjoyment would come from playing with them and, by the time they pulled up to the town-house door on Cavendish Square, some of the children's excitement was restored.

Dory ran to show Eppy her doll and to tell her about all the toys her papa had purchased. Cal walked up the stairs with Anna, his sword gripped in his hand.

When they reached Anna's door, he pulled on her hand.

She leaned down. 'What is it, Cal?'

He lifted his sword. 'I can protect you with my sword.'

She threw her arms around him and held him close. 'Yes, you can, Cal.'

He looked so much like his father, it was as though his sword pierced her heart.

Lord Brentmore did not come home for dinner. He sent word of his absence at the last minute, when the table was already set. Rather than put the servants to more trouble, Anna dined alone at the big, unfamiliar table meant to seat at least a dozen people.

It merely made her mood more desolate.

All afternoon she had held her pain inside her and pretended nothing was amiss. Luckily the children had the toys to delight them. Anna tried to get caught up in their excitement as they unpacked the several crates that arrived. The crates stirred much curiosity. The footmen wished to see the Waterloo soldiers, and the maids were agog over the doll house.

Even in her misery, Anna realised this was a more relaxed and happy household than Brentmore Hall. Perhaps nothing would entirely erase the unhappiness of that place. She shuddered that she might spend years there.

Would the new marchioness be in residence there often? Or would she and the marquess spend most of their time in London? Would Lord Brentmore abandon the care of the children to his new wife? Would both she and the children lose him entirely?

How would Anna bear up under such changes? It was likely that she would be required to answer to the new marchioness and would lose her say over the children. Had she not lost enough already?

Most painful of all, how was Anna to endure the knowledge that Miss Rolfe would share Lord Brentmore's bed?

There was nothing to object to in Miss Rolfe, truth be told. Her eyes were kind and she'd tried to engage the children in conversation as they ate their ices. She'd been gentle with Cal. Her clothes were not extravagant. Her light brown hair was simply dressed and all but covered with her bonnet. She was shorter than Anna, about as tall as Charlotte, whose height the comportment tutor insisted gentlemen preferred.

By the time Anna had finished dinner, she'd erected walls around her pain. It had been her foolishness that had caused her to become infatuated with a marquess, the weakness like her mother's to wish to seduce him.

She was strong. She could overcome loneliness and need. She'd merely forgotten what her father—Mr Hill, she meant—always said to her. That she was not a lady, no matter how many ladylike airs she adopted, and that she should never expect to be treated as one.

'I had forgotten that, Papa,' she said aloud to the empty room. 'But I shan't forget it any more.'

After leaving the dining room, Anna checked on the children. Both were sound asleep in their beds. Dory still held her doll in her arms. Cal slept with his sword. She kissed their smooth, untroubled foreheads and tucked the covers around each of them.

Anna retreated to her room, and allowed the maid to assist her in readying herself for bed. She let the maid's chatter wash over her. The girl went on about all the toys his lordship purchased today and how delighted the children had been and how enjoyable it must have been to pick out whatever they wanted at the toy shop.

When the maid finally bid her goodnight, Anna stood in the centre of the room, her arms around herself in a vain attempt at self-comfort. Tears threatened, but she refused to give in to them. Instead she paced the room, scolding herself for romantic fantasies, forcing herself to return to the strong, sanguine person she'd once been as Charlotte's companion. Back then she'd never expected anything for the morrow, never made plans, just happily accepted what came her way.

She walked to the window that overlooked the street and faced Cavendish Square. The long summer day had finally given way to night and the silence and darkness was broken only by the occasional carriage, with its lamps lighting the way.

It was time for her to accept who she was and where she belonged—somewhere in between Charlotte's world and her mother's, but not part of either.

She would purge herself of that carnal awareness of Lord Brentmore and learn to regard him, not as a lover, not as a friend, but as her employer.

'I'll not weaken again,' she vowed.

Chapter Twelve

Brent and his cousin Peter climbed into Brent's carriage after spending an afternoon and evening with Baron Rolfe and his wife and daughter. It had not been Brent's plan. He'd planned to make a quick call on the baron, reassure him that all was well, make an appointment for a later time and return to his children—and Anna.

He'd forgotten how affable the Rolfes were and how dependent they were on him for the survival of the baron's estate and for the well-being of the baron's children. He'd forgotten how thoroughly duty to others ruled the time of a marquess.

So he'd stayed with the Rolfes the afternoon, remained for dinner, and for tea afterwards.

'It was good of you to spend the evening, Brent,' his cousin said as soon as he was settled in the rear-facing seat of the carriage. 'Lord and

Lady Rolfe were nearly at their wit's end when they had little word from you for so many weeks.'

'I'd not intended them to worry.' He'd actually given the Rolfes little thought when he was at Brentmore. 'The children were in great need of my attention.'

'The new governess summoned you, you said.' Peter leaned back on the seat, clearly wanting Brent to tell him more.

There was little detail Brent wished to provide, even to his cousin. That a physician declared his son insane? That the children had been like prisoners in their rooms? That he had formed this unusual and at times ungentlemanly attachment to their governess?

That he had treated her very shabbily this day?

He rubbed his face. 'It was fortunate that she summoned me. The children were more troubled over their mother's death and the death of the old governess than I had been led to believe. Parker, it turned out, was not a very good reporter on the children's welfare.'

'And the governess was?' Peter added.

'She made all the difference.' And look how he repaid her. Hurting her, over and over.

'She's quite stunning,' Peter said. 'I'd not expected that.'

Stunning was a good description. Not the perfection of feminine beauty, but none the less so lovely it was difficult to look away.

'Quite stunning,' Brent agreed, keeping his tone even.

'How is that for you?' Peter persisted.

'How is what for me?' Brent played dumb.

'That your governess is a beauty.'

Brent made himself shrug. 'That would be to no purpose if she were not excellent with the children.' Where would his children be without her?

Peter's expression turned sceptical.

Brent ignored it. Instead he launched a counter-attack. 'You said you would explain my continued absence to Baron Rolfe and his daughter. Did you not do that?'

'Of course I did!' Peter looked offended. 'But Rolfe is insecure. He needs funds quickly.'

'So I learned.' The baron had humbled himself, both in his recent letter and in his conversation with Brent this day, disclosing how desperate he was. 'I'll settle some money on him now. Parker can arrange it tomorrow.'

'That is good of you,' Peter murmured. 'I hope he accepts it.'

'Why wouldn't he?'

Peter glanced away. 'He's a proud man. He might think it is charity. You are not yet married to Susan—Miss Rolfe, I mean. You have not made an announcement or set a date.'

'I am not ready.' He frowned. 'The children are not ready.'

Brent knew Peter was right. He was being unfair to these good people to keep them in limbo, but he was not ready to marry.

Peter persisted. 'Do you not think it wise for the children to see Miss Rolfe as their mother as soon as possible?'

'No.' His tone was firm, but his reasons elusive. Why wait?

He wanted more time, like their time together during the summer. He wanted to help his son heal. He wanted to love Dory for herself.

And he wanted more time alone with Anna, as dangerous that was to them both.

Peter gave him a direct stare. 'Forgive me speaking my mind, Brent. But it is this attitude that creates the Rolfes' insecurity. I'll not have you trifle with these people. They are more than friends to me—'

Brent halted this speech with a raised hand. 'I have no wish to trifle with anyone. And certainly no wish to cause scandal. I've come to London to set everything straight, as you asked me to. Do not expect me to do so within a matter of hours.' He lowered his voice. 'Miss Rolfe must understand my children take precedence over everything. I intend to spend a great deal of time with them in London. I will make an announcement and set a date for the wedding when I feel it is right for the children. If she cannot accept that, then perhaps she ought to cry off.'

The carriage stopped and both men glanced out the windows. They had reached Peter's rooms.

Peter rose to leave. 'Very well, Brent. I suspect there are several who will think this attention to your children very odd, but I see much to commend in it. I will explain it to Miss Rolfe.'

He climbed out and the carriage moved again, heading back to Cavendish Square.

Brent's thoughts immediately turned to Anna.

He relived the shock on her face when he introduced her to Miss Rolfe and was filled with guilt and regret.

No one was more deserving of happiness than Anna. Brent despised those people in her life who had so callously caused her pain.

And he suffered from the knowledge that he was one of them.

As Anna stood at the window another carriage approached, but this carriage stopped in front of the town house and discharged its passenger.

Lord Brentmore.

His appearance was no more than a dark silhouette, but that familiar thrill erupted inside her. She was glad she was on the third floor, far away from him.

She walked over to her bed and stared at the pillows. She was too restless to climb in and burrow under the covers. The brief glimpse of him was enough to set her insides fluttering like butterflies. She pressed her palm against her stomach and tried to still them.

There was a knock on her door, causing her to jump.

She crossed the room and put her lips near the door, pausing before saying, 'Who is it?' She knew very well who it was.

'It is Brent.'

Why did he use a familiar address? She'd never called him Brent…although she had called him Egan.

'Will you open the door, Anna? I need to speak to you.' His tone was pleading.

She opened the door wide. No point in being tentative. She lifted her chin. 'Yes, my lord?'

'I owe you an apology—' he began.

She held up a hand. 'No, you do not, my lord.'

'I ought to have told you about my betrothal—'

She shook her head. 'I am governess to your children. I am in your employ. You do not owe me anything but wages.'

His cheek stiffened.

'I was surprised,' she went on. 'I admit that, but I quickly realised how inappropriate that was for someone of my station.' Oh, she was managing this so well!

'Stop it, Anna!' His stepped inside and closed the door behind him.

Anna's heart beat faster.

He stood inches from her. 'I ought to have told

you long ago about Miss Rolfe, because you know very well there is something more between us than governess and employer. I feel it now as I felt it the first day, when I spied you pacing back and forth in the square outside this house. It is what led us to overstep the proper bounds.' His breathing accelerated. 'It is what led us to almost make love.'

All she had to do was take one step forwards and she could be in his arms; she could feel his lips against hers. She wanted his hands to stroke her body. She wanted him to touch her, to arouse her and to show her at last what it meant to be a woman.

She forced herself to stand her ground.

He ran a hand through his hair and turned away. 'God help me, I want to make love to you right now—'

'Do not say so,' she rasped.

He raised a hand. 'I know we cannot. I will not. I will not dishonour you. I cannot dishonour her.'

She turned her cheek as if he had struck her.

He seized her arms. 'Do you not see, Anna? I cannot treat you as Lawton did your mother.'

She raised her eyes, full of pain and worry. 'What do you do then? Do you send me away?'

Lord Lawton—her father—had sent her away.

His brows knitted. 'Do you wish to leave?'

Her chest ached. 'If you wish me to, I have no choice.'

He dropped his hands and swung away. 'I want you to raise my children. I want them to know you will be there for them every day, but—but you are not trapped here, Anna. If you wish to leave I will help you in every way I can.'

She folded her arms around her. 'Who would hire me? You ought not to have hired me. I know nothing of being a governess.'

He gave her an intent look. 'You knew better than anyone what Cal needed. What both the children still need. You loved them. They feel secure with you. I want nothing to change that.'

She stared at him. 'Marrying Miss Rolfe will change things.'

He gave her no argument.

She straightened. 'So we are to ignore this—this passion between us for the sake of the children?'

'We must,' he said in a low voice.

She went on. 'There must be no pretence of a friendship between us. We must be governess and employer. Nothing more.'

He nodded and made a gesture of surrender. His face turned solemn. 'I agree, but you must know, Anna, that I am still your friend ready to help you in any way, at any time.'

Did he not know that his kindness was the sharpest dagger he plunged into her flesh?

He raised his hand and drew a finger lightly down her cheek. 'Goodnight, Anna.'

He slipped out of the room and Anna touched her cheek.

Would their bargain make matters better for her or worse?

The next morning Brent entered the dining room to find Parker seated there, sipping a cup of tea.

'What the devil are you doing here?' Brent barked.

Parker rose to his feet. 'I came early, my lord. There is much correspondence to pore through and since you were not available yesterday, I thought you might wish to get started as soon as possible.'

'I can give you an hour this morning, no more.' Brent poured his tea and sat. 'I am taking the children to see the menagerie at the Tower.' Not that he owed his man of business an explanation.

'The children?' Parker's brows rose. 'But you spent the day with them yesterday.'

'I will spend part of each day with them, not that it is any of your concern.' He lifted the teacup to his mouth and sipped. 'By the way, I should tell you that I eat breakfast with the children. The governess will bring them any time now. You may fix yourself a plate and wait for me in the library.'

'Wait for you?' Parker seemed shocked.

Brent nodded. 'There is something I want you

to arrange for me. A transfer of funds to Baron Rolfe.'

'Baron Rolfe?'

Parker knew nothing about his betrothal. 'I'll explain later. Go on with you.'

Parker rose and hurriedly put some bread and ham on his plate. 'Begging your pardon, sir, but I am astonished that you allow the children in the dining room.'

Parker was a confirmed bachelor who had even less need for children than he had for women. It was obvious to Brent now that Parker knew nothing of the children's needs.

He gave the man of business his coolest stare. 'I am astonished you would question my personal family affairs.'

Parker stiffened, then bowed, plate in hand. 'It will not happen again, my lord.'

'Thank you.' Brent took another sip of tea. 'You may ask Davies to bring you some tea.'

Almost immediately after Parker left, Anna and the children came in, Cal carrying his sword, Dory, her doll.

Brent caught Anna's eye briefly and smiled. She smiled back. It was a tentative smile at best, but then so had his been. But it was enough to encourage him that they could do this, help the children in spite of what hummed between them.

'Papa!' Dory ran over to give him a kiss.

He kissed her back, disarmed in spite of the memories of her mother that she evoked.

He left his chair to give Cal a hug. 'How are you this morning? Did you sleep well?'

Cal nodded.

Anna spoke up. 'As well as a boy could who slept with his sword.'

Brent ran his finger down the wooden blade of the toy sword. 'A knight must be ready at all times to defend the castle. Is that not so, Cal?'

Cal made a face. 'Not a knight. An officer.'

'An officer?' Brent felt a pang of tenderness every time Cal spoke. 'In the war, I suppose.'

Cal nodded and then caught himself. 'Yes.'

Dory thrust her doll at Brent. 'I slept with my doll, Papa.'

'So you did, Dory.' He obligingly admired the doll. 'Did she sleep well?'

Dory's expression turned serious. 'She did not make any noise all night long.'

As they'd been afraid to do while Eunice has been alive.

Anna clapped her hands. 'Put the toys aside now, as you promised, and come tell me what you wish to eat this morning.'

The breakfast was as calm and pleasant as Brent could expect. So why did he feel a tug of regret, as if he'd lost something he would never get back?

* * *

After breakfast, Brent met with Parker, then took the children to the Tower to see the animals. Kings had kept their menageries of exotic animals there for centuries, and now visitors could pay to see them.

The trip was an unqualified failure. Although seeing the porcupine and zebra were met with cries of delight, the stench was so oppressive that Dory spent the entire time holding her nose. When they came upon the lions and tigers and other wild cats, the children stood silent. The big cats paced back and forth in their cages, always looking through the bars as if yearning to be free.

Brent understood why the sight of the caged animals disturbed the children. They'd been caged, too, until recently.

He less understood why Anna's gaze was riveted to the panther cage.

'Shall we go?' he asked.

'Yes,' Cal said.

Dory, her fingers still pinching her nose, nodded.

Anna took one last glance at the panther. 'As you wish.'

She engaged the children as before, but spoke to him only when necessary. He mourned the loss of their easy camaraderie.

When they waited for the carriage outside the Tower walls, Brent looked back at the imposing stone structure and leaned towards Anna. 'I should not have brought them here, to see a prison and caged animals.'

'Perhaps not,' she responded noncommittally.

'The panther seemed to captivate you,' he tried again.

'The panther,' she repeated absently, but she did not explain.

The children were delighted to return to the town house and to the abundance of toys waiting for them upstairs. They barely noticed when Mr Parker immediately begged for their father's attention on an urgent matter.

Anna was left with nothing to occupy her, though. She had no wish to impose lessons on the children after the depressing outing to the Tower, but she could not bear to be confined like the cats in their cages.

No matter her good intentions or her promises, it had been agony to be in Lord Brentmore's presence.

'My lord. If you please, I do need to speak with you,' Mr Parker said in a clipped voice.

The marquess crouched down to the children. 'I will try to come upstairs later.' He gave them hugs.

'Please, my lord. Come to the library.' Mr Parker was full of anxious impatience.

Lord Brentmore glanced at Anna before turning to follow Mr Parker.

She spoke up. 'My lord, may I have some time off? Eppy can keep an eye on the children.'

He turned back to her and she saw in his eyes the heat of passion they were trying so hard to ignore. 'Of course you may, Anna,' he said in a low voice.

The children ran up the stairs and Anna started to follow them, to make certain they were settled in before she left.

'One moment, Anna,' Lord Brentmore called to her.

He left Mr Parker and walked back to her. She waited for him on the first step, her heart racing at his approach. When he reached her, her face was even with his and their eyes connected.

Without looking away, he took her hand and placed several coins in her palm. 'Buy something for yourself, Anna. A book. A hat. Anything that pleases you.'

Another dagger of kindness. 'Thank you, my lord,' she murmured.

He held her gaze. 'Do not linger past two o'clock.'

'I will not.'

Men loitered on Bond Street and around the shops after two. Respectable women did not visit the shops at that hour.

He closed her fingers over the coins and

squeezed her hand before releasing it and walking swiftly away.

Clutching the coins, warm from his hand, Anna climbed the stairway to tell Eppy and the children that she was going out. The children were already busy playing, Cal with his soldiers, Dory with the doll house.

'I'll keep a good eye on them, never you fear,' Eppy said.

As she walked away from Eppy, Anna finally looked in her hand.

He had given her five pounds! Never in her whole life had she possessed five pounds of her own. Goodness! Her salary for the whole year was only thirty pounds. She could buy a whole wall full of books for five pounds.

She put two pounds away with her other savings and carried the other three coins in her reticule. A few moments later she was walking towards New Bond Street. The weather was still cool for August, even as noon approached. She was glad she'd worn her spencer.

She walked past linen drapers and haberdashers, confectioners and watchmakers, shops she and Charlotte had visited when they'd first arrived in London. It seemed such a long time ago, not merely months.

She stopped in Griffin and Son to purchase a new pair of gloves and some hosiery. She peeked in the jewellery shops and admired glittering necklaces and bracelets, the sorts of items a gentleman might give a lady. As a betrothal gift, perhaps.

She quickly turned away.

At the stationers, she purchased new sketchbooks for the children and, on a whim, a journal, pen and ink for herself. She opened her heart to the simple pleasure of having money to spend and lovely things to purchase with it.

Her main intent was to visit Hatchard's Bookshop on Piccadilly to pick out a book for her very own. Once inside the shop, however, she could find nothing she wanted. A few short months ago, any book would have been a delight and all of them would have interested her. Now her mind seemed too restless to read.

She walked along the street to Jermyn Street and entered the Floris perfumery.

A clerk dressed almost as finely as a gentleman looked up from behind the counter. 'May I be of assistance, miss?'

'I would like a scent. Something new.'

This was frivolous indeed. She'd never purchased perfumery before, although she'd helped Charlotte make selections. Anna considered herself fortunate to have the lavender water she and Charlotte made themselves.

He sniffed. 'You wear lavender. An excellent scent, I agree, but for a young lady such as yourself, we have mixed something special.'

He placed a drop of scent on a piece of paper and lifted it to her nose.

It smelled light and floral, like being in a garden surrounded by flowers. 'Rose, obviously. And iris?' she guessed.

'Very good, miss, with a hint of jasmine.'

It was a lovely scent. 'Yes, that is perfect. I will have it. And some French-milled soap, please.' She might as well indulge herself completely.

'Would you like the scent in a throwaway? An *étui*? Or a larger bottle?'

Who knew when she might have another chance to spend without worry? A throwaway was a mere sample. An *etui* would be gone in a matter of weeks, even if she conserved it.

'A larger bottle,' she responded.

He showed her a range of pretty bottles. She selected one and paid him a pound. He returned her change on a velvet tray.

She'd never truly realised the power money gave a person. It was freeing to purchase whatever one desired. No wonder wealthy aristocrats spent great amounts on unnecessary things. It almost restored her to her old self. Happy and content.

She left the shop smiling as a lady and gentleman were preparing to enter.

'You!' the lady exclaimed.

Lord and Lady Lawton. She'd never dreamed they would be in London. Not in August. The plan had been for them to be in Brighton for the summer.

Anna curtsied. 'My lord. My lady.' She could not look at them. Could not look at Lord Lawton. Her father.

'What are you doing in London?' Lady Lawton demanded.

Anna reverted to old habits, saying or doing nothing to provoke Lady Lawton. 'My duties as governess.'

Her ladyship sniffed. 'As governess? What governess comes to London?'

Anna, eyes downcast, replied as if this were not a rhetorical question, 'I do not know, ma'am.'

But she glanced up at Lord Lawton, who did not look upon her any differently than he'd always done. With little interest. It suddenly infuriated her.

She straightened and looked him in the eye. 'I presume you were informed of my mother's death?'

His face turned red.

Lady Lawton said, 'Yes. Our condolences.' She made an annoyed gesture.

The poor woman. Made to endure seeing her husband's bastard child every day, the constant companion of her cherished daughter. Anna pitied her.

Her ire was confined to Lord Lawton. 'Did

you attend the funeral, my lord?' She knew he had not.

He could not look at her. 'Impossible. Too busy.'

'A pity,' said Anna, 'after all her service to you.'

Lady Lawton made a shocked sound and Lord Lawton actually looked at Anna, as if seeing her for the first time. He now realised she knew who he really was, she was convinced.

Anna curtsied again. 'I am delaying your visit to the shop. Good day. Please give my regards to Charlotte.'

She walked away without waiting for permission to take her leave.

Perhaps she would tell of this meeting when she and Lord Brentmore dined this evening. He was the only one who could appreciate her small triumph.

Or maybe she would say nothing of it. It felt too much like a return to their previous intimacy.

It turned out she did not have to make the choice. Lord Brentmore had been summoned to his club to discuss some Parliamentary matter. Davies conveyed his apologies to her. He would dine at the club and be home late.

'I believe I will have dinner with the children, then,' Anna told the butler.

She did not want to be alone with her thoughts, with her loneliness.

This was merely a sample of what life would be like. His life would be among the *ton* and with his wife. At best she would see him with the children. She might not even be able to consult with him about the children. Likely she would report to his new marchioness. She would never be able to share her small triumphs and trials with him, and she had no one else to tell.

Chapter Thirteen

The next day Brent saw the children and Anna briefly at breakfast and heard all about how they played with the new toys. Brent promised Cal he would help him set up the soldiers and show him how the real battle unfolded, but he did not know when he could manage it.

Parker commanded much of his time out of necessity. One of his estates had been badly managed and there was much to be done to rectify the problems. Brent could not postpone addressing these issues because his tenants' lives depended upon his actions.

No sooner had Parker left the library than Davies entered. 'You have a caller, m'lord.'

It was early for callers. 'Who is it?'

Davies handed him the calling card. 'Mr Kenneth Yates, m'lord.'

Brent's gaze flew up. 'What the devil does he want?'

Davies—and everyone else—knew precisely who Kenneth Yates was—the man Eunice was chasing when she suffered the fatal fall from her horse.

'He did not tell me the purpose of his visit, m'lord,' Davies replied.

Brent rubbed his face. He might as well get this over with. If Yates was back in the country, it would be only a matter of time before he would have to confront him. Better the first time be in private.

Brent rose. 'Send him in, Davies. I will see him here.'

A moment later Davies announced him. 'Mr Kenneth Yates, m'lord.'

Yates entered the room and the door closed behind him. He and Brent stared at each other before either of them spoke.

Yates finally said, 'Thank you for seeing me, Brent.'

The two men had known each other in school. Yates had been younger than Brent, but a decent sort of boy, not one to bully or ridicule. It made his betrayal with Eunice more surprising and doubly painful.

'I had not heard you were back,' Brent remarked. 'Where had you been? The Colonies?'

Yates tried a tentative smile. 'They prefer to call it America.'

Not that it mattered to Brent what the Americans called their country. 'Why did you come here, Yates?'

'To offer you my apology.'

It was a simple answer, but the reason to apologise was more complex. 'Why should I accept it?'

Yates drew a nervous breath. 'I cannot say whether you should or should not accept anything I say. I came to explain.'

'What good will that do?' He walked over to the window. 'What is done is done.'

If he hoped Yates would take the hint and leave, he was mistaken. Why had the man not remained in the Colonies?

Yates continued, 'It took me this year to understand what role I played in what happened. If I told you that I'd loved her, I am not certain now that would be the truth. I do know that my character was such that I could not resist her. She was captivating and I was weak. That might be the whole of it.'

How well Brent knew that Eunice could be captivating. She'd also possessed such exacting standards that she could never accept the truth about the maternal side of her husband's family.

'Are you asking for my forgiveness?' Brent countered, his tone sharp.

Yates's eyes widened. 'No. Not at all. But I

could not return to London without attempting this conversation with you.'

Brent wished the man had never returned. His presence would only cause more talk and remind Brent of painful memories.

'There is only one thing I wish to know.' He glared at Yates. 'Do you intend to cause me more trouble? Or more trouble for my family?'

Yates took a step forwards. 'Believe me, Brent. I give you my word as a gentleman. I came here to assure you that I will not cause you or your family any trouble. Society will never know what you and I both know.'

Brent felt his anger flash. 'If you break your word I will destroy you. Do I make myself clear? There are innocents I will not have hurt.'

Yates held his gaze with a steady determination. 'I would rather die than have anyone hurt further by my follies.'

Brent believed him. He turned his head away in thought. 'If we are seen as feuding, it will cause gossip. If we are cordial, people will soon pay us no heed.'

Yates nodded. 'I could not agree more. I will not assume such behaviour changes your personal feelings about me, but I wish you to know my esteem of you is genuine. Eunice and I have got what we deserved. My punishment is to live with my mistakes and regrets, but you have done nothing wrong.'

Brent knew that statement to be false. He had wronged his children. Abandoned them to suffer Eunice's unhappiness. He had vowed to amend his ways. Perhaps he could believe Yates capable of the same thing.

'Well!' Yates expelled a tense breath. 'I will not trouble you more. I have said all I needed to say. I bid you good day, Brent. Thank you for seeing me.'

He turned and walked to the door.

When he opened it, Brent said, 'It took courage to face me, Yates. I wish you a good day, as well.'

The tension in Yates's face eased. He bowed and walked out of the library.

Anna and the children burst into the hall just as a gentleman was leaving. The children ran into him.

'Children! Take care!' Anna cried, pulling them out of the man's way. 'Go upstairs and wash your hands and faces.'

They ran for the stairway.

'And do not run!' she cried, tossing the man a look of dismay.

He watched the children scamper up the stairs.

'Forgive me, sir,' she said to him. 'I thought a walk would deplete them of energy. Obviously it had the opposite effect.'

He blinked and dragged his gaze away from

where the children had been. 'They have grown since I saw them last.'

'Oh?' she smiled. 'You know Lord Brentmore's children?'

He looked rueful. 'I have seen them before…' His voice faded, then he seemed to collect himself. 'I am remiss. Allow me to present myself. I am Mr Yates.'

'A friend of the family?' she asked. There was something in his manner. Something unspoken.

'No.' He looked sad. 'Someone known to Lord Brentmore. I have newly returned to town and have paid my respects.'

She extended her hand. 'I am Miss Hill, the children's governess.'

He shook it. 'I remembered the governess as a lady with grey hair.'

He had seen Mrs Sykes? 'I am the new governess.' She suddenly felt uneasy about saying too much, not knowing who this man was, after all. 'Where were you that you have returned to town?'

'I—I spent a year in America,' he responded.

'America?' She forgot her reticence. 'I have read a great deal about America. The savages. The bison and bears. In fact, yesterday we saw a grizzly bear at the Tower.'

'You took the children to the Tower?' he asked.

She wished she had not mentioned it. She stepped back. 'I am keeping you from wherever you need to be. I bid you good day, sir.'

'Good day, Miss Hill.' He bowed.

Davies appeared in the hall. 'Did I hear Mr Yates leave?'

She nodded. 'Who is he? He seemed to know the family.'

Davies came close to her ear. 'Do not tell Lord Brentmore I said so, but he is the man with whom the marchioness had a long affair. It is said he broke it off and that is why she rode after him and fell from her horse.'

Her eyes widened. 'Why did he come here?'

Davies was clearly eager to discuss this. 'That is a puzzle. He wished to speak to his lordship, is all I know.'

'He said he came to pay his respects,' Anna shared.

'That is odd, indeed.' Davies seemed to catch himself. 'But I have said too much already. One must not gossip.'

'I will say nothing, Davies,' she assured him.

Lord Brentmore walked into the hall. 'Did he leave, Davies?'

'He did, m'lord.' Davies slid a glance to Anna, who started to climb the stairs.

Lord Brentmore spoke to her. 'How are you, Anna?'

'Very well, my lord.' She lowered her gaze and tried to dampen her response to him.

'Where are the children?' he asked.

'Washing up. We just came in from a walk.'

He frowned. 'I've seen so little of them.'

'They will be playing with the toys.'

He looked regretful. 'I wish I could spend some time with them. I have an appointment at Coutts and then I'm engaged to meet my cousin.'

It seemed each day took him further away.

He added, 'I plan to return for dinner, though.'

She glanced towards the butler. 'Discuss it with Davies. It is better for me and for the servants if I dine with the children.'

He looked disappointed. 'I suppose I deserve that. I have cancelled out on you each night since we've been here.'

She raised her eyes to his. 'London has changed things.'

As the days passed by Anna and the children adapted to this new routine. Lord Brentmore continued to share breakfast with his children, but any other time spent with them was snatched from his busy schedule. An hour here or there to show Cal with the tin soldiers some part of the Waterloo battle. A few minutes to see how Dory had rearranged her doll house. Quick instruction in fencing for them both, because Dory would not be left out of something so exciting and fun. Anna was never alone with him.

She resumed giving the children their lessons and did her best to devise outings for them, some enjoyable, some not. They were measured and fitted for new clothes, something that delighted Dory, but not her brother. They took walks around Mayfair and played with the ball and skittles in the Square or in the small garden behind the town house. She took them to the Egyptian Hall to see Napoleon's carriage and other artifacts from Waterloo. They visited the shops and had ices from Gunter's again, but it was not Anna's favourite place, reminding her of Miss Rolfe.

Lord Brentmore never spoke of Miss Rolfe to Anna. Never mentioned if the social events he attended at night were in her company. Never told Anna when the marriage date was planned so she would know when her life was about to change again.

Her outing with the children for this day was Hyde Park. They would spend a couple of hours there exploring its paths until the fashionable hour was upon them and the society carriages began circling the park. She and Charlotte had once sneaked into the park to witness this event. Anna remembered reassuring Charlotte that some day Charlotte would be riding in a gentleman's carriage, dressed in finery as lovely as any of the ladies they'd seen.

The children, dressed and ready for the park, were fidgeting in the hall, impatiently waiting for Anna to finish pulling on her gloves and tying her bonnet.

The door opened and Lord Brentmore walked in. The children ran to him for hugs.

'Where are you off to?' he asked Cal.

Cal hesitated, but said, 'Hyde Park.'

'Indeed? What will you do there?' he asked.

'Play,' replied Cal, lifting up his sword.

'I have never been to Hyde Park,' piped up Dory. 'I do believe Hortense will like it.'

'Hortense?' Her father's brows rose.

'My doll.' Dory was still trying out different names for her doll.

Lord Brentmore glanced over at Anna. 'Do you mind if I accompany you?'

Her stomach clenched. 'If you desire it.'

A few minutes later they were on their way. The children skipped ahead and Lord Brentmore fell in step with Anna.

'How are they faring?' he asked her.

'They seem happy enough,' she responded.

'And you?' His gaze was too penetrating.

She paused before answering, 'Well enough, my lord.'

He glanced around. 'This reminds me of our walks at Brentmore.'

She darted a look at him. 'Except for the town houses and the carriages and other pedestrians.' And the tension between them.

'There is that,' he agreed. His voice lowered. 'I miss our time at Brentmore.'

She took several steps before responding. 'I

suppose you will never have much time to spend there.'

They entered the park at Grosvenor Gate. The afternoon was so fine that there were several other people strolling through the park.

When they came upon an expanse of grass, Dory asked, 'May we run, Papa?'

Lord Brentmore answered, 'You may, but stay in our sight.'

Dory squealed in delight and she and Cal took off.

'Mind that sword!' Anna cried to Cal. He could fall on it and injure himself.

Cal didn't fall. Anna was forced to walk at Lord Brentmore's side, so reminiscent of more carefree days. At least the children were happy.

May it last for them, she silently prayed.

Lord Brentmore's arm brushed against hers, setting off memories of more tender touches. Was he happy? she wondered. She could not tell and would not ask.

'Anna,' he spoke. 'I have been meaning to tell you that I've seen Lord Lawton in town. The family are spending the summer here.'

'I know,' she said.

'You know?' He sounded surprised.

'I saw him at the shops.' She offered no more detail and he asked for none.

They walked on in silence.

Finally, Lord Brentmore murmured, 'Anna.'

She glanced at him and their gazes caught for a moment. His eyes darkened and filled with yearning. As did hers, she suspected.

They had almost reached the other side of the grassy area and the children ran back to them.

Cal tapped his father on the arm. 'May we walk to the Serpentine, sir? Anna said we might feed the ducks.'

Lord Brentmore touched the boy's cheek. 'Of course, but you must walk.'

Both Cal and Dory nodded and skipped ahead.

'You thought of feeding the ducks?' Brentmore asked Anna.

'Davies suggested it,' she answered. 'Cook gave us some bread.'

When they reached the water, Anna pulled from her pocket the pieces of bread wrapped in a napkin. She handed a piece to each child and instructed them on how to tear off bits and throw them to the ducks. Soon a flock of ducks surrounded them, quacking for more.

When they finished the bread they continued their walk, turning on a footpath heading toward The Ring, a circle of trees planted during the reign of Charles I.

From the carriage road a voice called, 'Lord Brentmore! Yoo hoo! Brentmore!'

He glanced behind them. There was a curricle stopped on the road and an older woman waved her handkerchief at them.

'I must greet them,' he said, turning back.

Anna watched him approach the curricle. A younger woman leaned forwards.

Miss Rolfe.

Anna swung away and walked quickly to catch up to the children. She let them go a far enough distance that she could not see the curricle. 'Dory! Cal! We must wait for your father.'

She saw a group of people approaching from the other direction and guided the children to a patch of grass nearby, so they would not be in the way.

The grass was dotted with patches of clover. 'See if you can find a four-leaf clover,' she suggested. 'It will bring good luck.' And keep them occupied.

Good luck was lost to her, she imagined. The children, however, took to the task with much enthusiasm.

The people, a woman and two gentlemen, came closer. Anna turned her back to them, making herself as inconspicuous as a governess ought to be. She heard their footsteps coming near.

'Anna?' The woman hurried up to her. 'Anna!'

It was Charlotte.

Her dear friend—her half-sister—gave her a hug. 'I did not know you were in London!' She glanced towards the children. 'Are those your charges? They are darling! But tell me why you are here. Why did you not tell me you were in London? Why have you not written to me?'

Charlotte did not receive her letters? Obviously her mother and their father had not shown Charlotte Anna's letters or told her of seeing Anna at the scent shop. But what good would it do Charlotte to know those things? 'Perhaps my letters were lost. I—I have been kept very busy.'

'With those two?' Charlotte gave them a fond look. 'They appear to be no trouble at all.' She turned to the two men who were accompanying her. 'But let me present you.' She gestured for them to come closer. 'Anna, this is Lord Ventry and Mr Norton. Gentlemen, this is my very dearest friend, Miss Hill.'

Their brows rose and their gazes darted to the children.

Charlotte went on, 'Miss Hill is the governess to Lord Brentmore's children.'

'Lord Brentmore?' Mr Norton's brows rose. 'Pleased to meet you.'

Lord Vestry inclined his head. 'I tell you, my governess looked nothing like you. I might have spent more time with my lessons if she had.'

Charlotte threaded her arm through Anna's. 'Isn't she beautiful? She quite puts me in the shade.'

Mr Norton smiled diplomatically. 'Together you make a very pretty picture indeed.'

Charlotte turned back to Anna. 'Lord Vestry and Mr Norton both called upon me at the same time to take a ride in the park, but it is such a beautiful day I suggested we walk instead.' She leaned into Anna's ear and whispered, 'I believe they are both suitors.'

Another gentleman walking on the path approached. He caught Anna's eye and tipped his hat. 'Good day, Miss Hill.'

'Mr Yates,' she responded.

He slowed when he caught sight of the children. 'I see you have gone for another walk.'

'Yes, indeed,' she replied.

He seemed to notice Charlotte and his expression changed. 'Good day, miss. Forgive my intrusion,' he said in a low voice.

The other two men jostled each other and whispered something.

Charlotte stepped forwards. Her manner towards her escorts had been cordial, but for Mr Yates her colour heightened and her voice became breathy. 'You did not intrude, sir.'

Anna had no choice but to introduce them. 'May I present Mr Yates to you, Charlotte.' She turned to Mr Yates. 'This is Lady Charlotte, Lord Lawton's daughter.'

Yates extended his hand and Charlotte grasped it. Neither seemed inclined to let go, but Charlotte finally collected herself. 'Anna is my dearest friend, Mr Yates,' she explained. 'I have not seen her for weeks and did not even know she was in London.'

'So this is a reunion,' he said.

Charlotte pressed her cheek against Anna's. 'A very welcome one.' She released Anna and looked into her face. 'But now we may see each other! Surely Lord Brentmore gives you time off. You can come call on me.'

She could not tell Charlotte how unwelcome she would be. 'I cannot, Charlotte. I have to care for the children.'

'But not in the evenings, surely! I know! You must come to our ball. Mama and Papa are giving a ball next week. It will not be a huge ball because there are not that many people in London, not as many as during the Season.' She turned to her companions. 'Gentlemen, Miss Hill should come to my ball, should she not?'

Mr Norton nodded. 'I should like that very much, indeed.'

'A lovely lady such as you would be welcome,' Lord Vestry added.

But a governess who was the natural daughter of the lord of the house would not be at all welcome. 'It is not my place to attend—' she began.

Charlotte cut her off. 'Nonsense! You are my dearest friend. You have always been with me.' She turned to Mr Yates and her tone grew softer.

'And will you come, too, Mr Yates? We need more gentlemen.'

He bowed. 'I would be honoured.'

Brent walked quickly to catch up with Anna and the children. He'd have to leave them again and the idea depressed him. He did not wish to see Anna's face—or the faces of the children—when he told them.

He found her surrounded by three gentlemen and another lady. At least two of the men whose faces he could see were smiling at Anna.

He quickened his step.

'Anna!' he called out, when he was in hearing distance. 'What is this?'

She turned to him and stepped away from her companions. 'Lady Charlotte, my lord.' She sounded upset. 'We met by chance.'

That did not explain the cadre of men around her. One of the men turned and nodded to him.

Yates.

What was he doing here?

'Where are the children?' Brent demanded. Had she forgotten them? Let them run off?

She pointed to where the children sat in the grass, absorbed in something or another.

'They are looking for four-leaf clovers,' she explained in a cautious voice. 'I have been watching them.'

Lady Charlotte left the group and came to

Anna's side. 'Lord Brentmore?' She smiled. 'Forgive me for stealing a moment of Anna's time. I have not seen her in so long.' This woman had been a child plagued with shyness? 'Oh, dear. We have not been introduced.'

Anna made the introductions.

'And do you know these gentlemen?' Lady Charlotte asked, gesturing to her entourage.

'Mr Yates and I are acquainted,' Brent said.

One of the other gentlemen elbowed the other. Obviously they knew the gossip, even though they looked as if they'd just been breeched.

'Good to see you, Brent,' Yates said.

Lady Charlotte presented the young gentlemen to Brent, who merely nodded to them.

He turned to Anna. 'I would speak with you for a moment.' He took her aside. 'Lord and Lady Rolfe desire me to take a turn around the park with them.' He refrained from mentioning Miss Rolfe to her.

She stiffened almost imperceptibly. 'Will you tell the children or shall I?'

'I will tell them.' He felt consumed with guilt, although it should be the most natural thing in the world to spend time with one's fiancée and her parents. 'Do you feel comfortable walking home alone with the children?'

Her chin rose. 'If you wish it, how can I object?'

If this had been a fencing match, her hit would

have earned a point. He nodded and walked off to tell the children.

'Papa!' Dory cried when she saw him. 'We are looking for lucky four-leaf clovers.'

He smiled at them. 'And have you found any?'

Cal looked at him. 'No.'

'Well, you will have to make your own good luck.' He tried to sound cheerful. 'I came over to tell you I am going to say goodbye to you here.'

'Why?' Dory asked.

'Did you see the people in the carriage? I walked back to talk with them?'

The children both nodded.

'Well, they want me to ride in their carriage, and because I have not seen them in a long time—' almost a week at least '—I need to go with them now.'

Dory's eyes widened. 'Will you come back?'

Another wounding question. Did she think he would leave them? 'Of course I will come back. I will see you later, before you go to bed.'

'Oh.' She relaxed. 'Then goodbye, Papa.'

'Goodbye,' Cal added.

When he walked back to Anna, Yates stood with her. 'Brent, I was on my way to my town house, but, if you like, I am at liberty to escort your governess and the children home.'

The young gentlemen were watching this exchange intently.

Brent raised his voice a little. 'Thank you,

Yates. That is good of you.' He glanced at Anna. 'I will see the children later at home.'

She did not respond.

Anna watched Lord Brentmore walk away. It seemed as if she'd been ripped to shreds and casually discarded, even though she had no right to feel that way, merely because he'd chosen to spend time with his fiancée.

'Will you walk with us, Miss Hill?' Mr Norton asked.

She'd forgotten about Mr Norton and Lord Ventry and anyone else. 'I must get the children home.'

'Oh, Anna!' Charlotte came over and hugged her again. 'I will see you soon, when you come to our ball. Promise me you will come?'

What reason would Charlotte accept? 'I did not bring a gown with me.'

Charlotte waved that excuse away. 'We can fix that.'

'No, Charlotte. I simply must say no.' She turned away. 'And now I need to get back to my duties.'

'Very well.' Charlotte sounded disappointed. 'But we must see each other. I have so much to tell you. And I want to hear all about being Lord Brentmore's governess.'

Lord Ventry and Mr Norton exchanged

glances, but she could not worry about what they thought of Lord Brentmore.

And there was too much Anna could not tell Charlotte. That they were sisters. That their father cared nothing for Anna or Anna's mother. That Anna was more like her mother than she could ever have guessed. That she wanted to be Lord Brentmore's lover as well as his children's governess. That another woman—and his scruples—prevented it.

'Perhaps if I have a day off,' she prevaricated.

'Lady Charlotte,' Lord Ventry called, 'shall we be on our way?'

'I have to go.' Charlotte gave her another swift hug, then hurried over to her companions.

Anna joined the children. 'Shall we walk some more?' she asked. 'Mr Yates is going to walk with us, is that not nice of him?'

'We didn't find any clovers.' Dory picked up her doll and popped her thumb into her mouth.

Anna gently pulled her thumb out again. 'Come on.' She took Dory's hand. Cal rose and walked with them.

Mr Yates stood waiting for them. 'If we continue past The Ring there will be a foot path leading directly to the Cumberland Gate. That will be the fastest way out.'

They passed The Ring, Mr Yates walking a little behind Anna, Anna holding each child's hand.

Dory dawdled, forcing Anna to pull her along. She was losing patience. 'Dory, faster, please.'

The little girl walked slower.

'She is tired,' Mr Yates said in a low tone.

'She's had a busy day.' Anna released Cal's hand and picked up Dory. 'Oh, she is heavy.'

Cal walked slowly, as well, hitting his sword on the path as he went.

Anna's arms and back quickly began to ache.

Mr Yates stopped her. 'Allow me to carry the child.'

'Thank you, Mr Yates.' Anna handed Dory to Mr Yates.

He turned his head to ask the little girl, 'Do you mind if I carry you, Lady Dory?' His voice was low and tremulous.

Why this emotion from him? she wondered.

'I do not mind,' Dory whimpered.

Both Mr Yates and Dory turned their faces to Anna.

She stifled a gasp.

Looking back at her were two identical pairs of eyes. There was also a very similar shape of the chin.

'Oh, Mr Yates!' she exclaimed breathlessly.

This man was Dory's father. Not Lord Brentmore. She was certain of it.

He shook his head as if to silence her.

Dory twisted around and laid her head on his

shoulder. He closed his eyes as if savouring the moment.

There was nothing to do but be on their way. Anna bent down to Cal, who'd sat down on the path to rest. 'Come on, Lord Cal. Time to start moving again.'

The boy took her hand.

Anna's own turmoil was momentarily forgotten. She could not think of anything but the secret she'd discovered. Did Lord Brentmore know? She could say nothing while with the children, but she must know more.

They walked in virtual silence back to the town house. Once when she exchanged a glance with Mr Yates, his eyes appeared moist.

Finally they arrived at the town house and were admitted into the hall by Davies, whose brows almost disappeared into his forehead.

'She is sleeping,' Mr Yates whispered.

Cal already was plodding up the stairs.

'Davies, would you be so good as to carry Lady Dory up to Eppy? I want to thank Mr Yates before he must leave.'

Davies reached for the little girl. 'Where is his lordship?'

Of course, he would not know. 'He—he encountered some friends and went with them.'

Davies frowned as Yates transferred Dory to him.

Anna gestured for Mr Yates to follow her to the drawing room right off the hall.

'You have guessed?' Yates said as soon as she closed the door. He sounded anxious and re-signed.

She met his eye. 'That you are her father? Yes, indeed.'

He leaned towards her. 'You must say nothing of this. Nothing. Ever! Do you understand me?'

She did not flinch. Instead she looked askance. 'Does Lord Brentmore know?'

'He knows.' Yates's eyes flashed. 'With Eunice dead, he and I are the only ones who know.' He glanced down. 'And now you.'

She peered at him suspiciously. 'Is this why you are back? Because of Dory?'

Had not this child's life been shaken enough?

'No!' He turned away. 'I came back to make amends. And because I cannot neglect my es-tate and business matters any longer. I did not know the child would be here in London. I never guessed…' His voice trailed off wistfully.

He swung back to Anna. 'But I will not allow her to be hurt. Do you hear? She must never know. Never! If you do anything to shatter her secure life, I will take my revenge on you and you will regret it.'

He loved the girl, she realised.

'You have nothing to fear from me, sir!' She, too, loved Dory. 'I want what is best for her.'

'Then she must grow up as Brentmore's daughter. She is his daughter in the eyes of the law. Do not ever tell her otherwise.'

Keep the truth from her, like the truth of Anna's paternity had been kept from her? One should always know the truth, should they not?

Would she have been happier not knowing the truth about her mother's character, her father's true identity? Would she have preferred to believe she had only one father who didn't love her?

Dory, apparently, had two fathers who loved her very much.

'I give you my word, Mr Yates.' She stared directly in his eyes. 'You must give me your word that you will never cause trouble for Dory. Ever.'

He looked solemn. 'That has been my vow since I learned of her existence. It will never change.'

'Then we are settled.' She blew out a breath. 'And I must thank you very sincerely for escorting the children and me, and for assisting me with Dory.'

'It was my privilege.' His eyes filled with pain. 'It may well be my only opportunity to hold her.'

She touched his hand in a sympathetic gesture. 'Oh, Mr Yates.'

She walked with him to the hall. 'Thank you again, sir. And good day to you.'

He nodded. 'Good day to you, too, Miss Hill.' He placed his hat on his head and opened the door, but turned back to Anna. 'Miss Hill, if—if she should ever need anything, if she is ever in trouble, will you tell me, so I may help?'

His words touched her heart. 'Yes, I will,' she promised.

Chapter Fourteen

Brent did not see Anna when he managed to return to the town house. He stopped by the room set up as the nursery, but she was not there.

Eppy was with the children.

'Where is Miss Hill?' Brent asked her.

The woman smiled. 'Taking a much-needed break, m'lord. Had a bit too much walking in the park, if you ask me.'

'Is she ill?' He would feel a complete cad if he'd left her when she'd been ill.

'No.' The nurse laughed. 'A fair bit weary, though.' She gestured to the children. 'These two scamps had a good nap and are full of beans.'

'We are not, Eppy!' Dory giggled. 'We have not eaten any beans!'

She and Cal had built an arrangement with blocks, putting the blocks side by side in a huge circle on the table and criss-crossing the circle with other lines of blocks. In one corner was a small looking glass. Two ducks from the Noah's Ark were placed on the glass.

'What is this, Cal?' he asked.

Dory put her hand over her mouth.

Cal finally answered, 'Hyde Park.'

'I can see it!' Brent exclaimed. 'The perimeter.' He pointed to the circle of blocks. 'The paths.' These were the criss-crossing blocks. 'And the Serpentine.' The looking glass. 'What else will you put in?'

Cal took a long thin block and set it on its end. 'Trees.'

Brent picked up a similar block. 'May I plant a tree?'

Cal nodded.

'I want to plant trees!' Dory cried.

Cal handed her some blocks.

Brent spent a pleasant half-hour with his children, building their replica of Hyde Park.

Dory ran to her doll house and brought back the doll family. 'This is Papa and Miss Hill and you and me,' she said to Cal.

She did not add any other dolls to the park.

A clock struck the hour and Brent realised he was late. He still had to change his clothes and meet Peter at White's. From there they would go to Lord Rolfe's to dine and attend a musicale together. He would come home too late to see Anna.

It unsettled him.

He wanted to see her, although he could not explain to her why he'd chosen to go with the Rolfes rather than stay with her and the children. He could not explain to himself why he did not tell her Miss Rolfe was in the carriage with her parents. He'd hoped to hear something from her about Yates. Had he behaved well with her and the children? Had Brent's trust been misplaced?

Mostly, Brent just wanted to see her.

Much more than he wanted to spend the evening with Miss Rolfe, her parents and his cousin.

The evening turned out to be pleasant, with nothing for Brent to complain of, except perhaps that he'd wished he were elsewhere.

The musicale had fine music—a skilled string quartet and a clear-voiced soprano—but it was torture to sit through it all, when his mind wandered back to his town house, his children. Anna.

At a pause in the music, Miss Rolfe leaned over and asked him, 'Are you feeling unwell, sir?' Her concern was genuine.

He shook his head. 'I am perfectly well. The music merely gives me too much time to think.'

Her brow wrinkled. 'Are you troubled?'

She was the sort of woman one could talk to and be guaranteed an understanding ear, but how could he confide in her?

He made a dismissive gesture. 'A business matter intrudes. It is nothing.'

'Perhaps Peter can help you,' she suggested. 'He is very clever at business.'

'That he is,' Brent agreed, although his cousin was not clever enough to accept the financial help Brent offered him. 'An excellent idea, Miss Rolfe.'

The music began again and he had no need to continue the conversation.

At the next break, refreshments were served in another room. Brent acted the suitor and fixed Miss Rolfe's plate for her. When he walked back to the buffet to fix his own plate, Lady Charlotte stopped him.

'Lord Brentmore! How delightful to see you here.' She seemed to have deliberately sought him out. 'Do you remember me? I met you in the park today.'

'Yes, Lady Charlotte, I remember you.' It was not likely he would forget in a matter of hours.

She boldly put her arm through his. 'Do you mind if I speak with you on a matter of importance?'

He glanced back at the table where Miss Rolfe and her parents sat. Peter seemed to be entertaining them very well. 'Of course.'

They stepped away from the refreshment table.

'As you must know, I am a very dear friend of Anna's—Miss Hill,' she began.

'I have heard her say so.'

That made her smile. 'Well, I want her to come to our ball next week and she refuses, because she must stay with the children, she says.'

He doubted that was the reason. 'She is very conscientious.'

'She is. I agree.' She took a breath. 'But I have a very special reason for her to come to the ball.'

'What is that?' he asked politely.

'Forgive me for saying so, but I do not think Anna should be a governess. I believe she can make a very respectable match if she is able to mix in society a little.' Her eyes twinkled. 'Why, the one entertainment she did attend with me, she was a great success! She had all sorts of gentlemen seeking to be introduced.'

A picture of Anna surrounded by Yates and those other two puppies flashed into his mind, as well as the rush of jealousy he felt upon seeing them gaze upon her.

Charlotte went on. 'I know she cannot reach so high as to a man with a title, but perhaps a younger son or some such.'

'You think she can marry?'

'I think she *should* marry! Do not you?' Charlotte seized his arm. 'Will you help me? I know it means losing a governess, but Anna is so lovely and so ladylike, she deserves to have a house of her own and children of her own.'

He had never thought that Anna might aspire to a respectable marriage, home and children.

The idea depressed him. 'What would you have me do?'

'Bring her to my ball!' she exclaimed. 'If you tell her she must attend, she will have to do it, because you are her employer.'

He frowned. 'What of your parents? Will they wish her to be included?'

She grew thoughtful. 'I dare say not, but they could not complain if a marquess escorted her. They will invite you, certainly. They do not expect you will come, but if you do attend, it will be a coup for them.'

Brent was not so certain of that. Perhaps Lord Lawton had considered him good enough to hire his bastard daughter as a governess, but would he truly want the scandalous Marquess of Brentmore to attend his ball?

Charlotte looked towards the table where Miss Rolfe sat. 'Your friends are invited. I know the Rolfes plan to attend, actually. Your cousin was invited, as well. Town is so thin of company, they have expanded the invitation list to include gentlemen who will certainly be suitable for Anna.'

Was Lady Charlotte including his cousin in that list? That idea disturbed him. 'You said she has already refused.'

Her eyes implored. 'You can command her to

come. Please say you will do it. If you have any regard for Anna, please say you will do it.'

Was he so selfish he would prevent her any chance to attract a suitor? He could offer her nothing but the lonely and thankless job of governess. No, her happiness must be considered.

'I will try, Lady Charlotte. That is all I can promise.'

She almost jumped up and down. 'I knew you would see it my way!'

'I must get back to my party,' he said, although the night had just become even more depressing.

'Me, too.' She smiled.

As he walked her back to the buffet table, he could not help but say, 'Lady Charlotte, I was under the impression from Miss Hill that you suffered from bashfulness.'

Her eyes widened. 'Oh, I do. I am horribly bashful!'

'Then how was it you could speak with me, with such little introduction?'

She grinned. 'When I am afraid, I merely pretend I am Anna and then I can be brave. I am pretending now and, I assure you, my stomach is full of butterflies.'

He nodded, admiring her courage for her friend's sake—no, her half-sister's sake, but Charlotte did not know that. 'You must never feel afraid to speak with me, Lady Charlotte. Your courage on behalf of Anna has won my admiration.'

Brent dropped a few pieces of cheese on to his plate and walked back to the table where Peter and the Rolfes sat.

Miss Rolfe smiled at him. 'That took you a long time.'

'My apologies.' He lowered himself into the chair. 'I saw someone with whom I needed to speak.'

'How nice for you,' she said.

At least he did not have to explain himself to Miss Rolfe. It was another of her virtues, to not care enough to question whatever he said.

Later when Brent and Peter were in the carriage on the way home, Peter chastised him. 'That was not well done of you, Brent, to leave Susan for Lady Charlotte. Not well done of you at all. I thought you wished to avoid gossip.'

'Heed who you are talking to, Peter.' Brent's head already pained him. 'I will conduct my own affairs.'

'*Affairs* is a good term for it, Brent,' Peter shot back. 'You make the appearance of courting other women while saying you are betrothed to Susan—Miss Rolfe. You are using her ill.'

He glared at his cousin. 'My conversation with Lady Charlotte was about a matter that does not concern you. If Miss Rolfe objects to my speaking to her, let her tell me. I will discuss it with her. Not you.'

'I cannot leave this alone,' Peter went on. 'You are not behaving like a betrothed man. It is an insult to Miss Rolfe and her family.'

Brent was not about to let his cousin continue. 'Enough!' he shouted. 'This was your idea, Peter. I went along because it suited my needs, but I'll not have you scolding me as if I were the veriest schoolboy. I can walk away from the whole matter, if I choose, and I might if I have to listen to you talk like this.'

Peter looked alarmed. 'You would not cry off! That would be the ruin of her reputation and the ruin of her family.'

A woman might cry off without censure, but if a man broke a betrothal, the woman was looked upon as damaged goods. Brent's threat was empty. He could not do that to a decent woman like Miss Rolfe. He also did not want her family's ruin to be on his conscience.

He'd had his fill of his cousin's lectures, however. 'If you do not stop plaguing me about this, I may indeed cry off.'

Peter backed off. 'Very well. Very well.' He was blessedly silent for a while, but started in again. 'There was something else I wanted to say.'

'Good God, Peter! You do not know when to stop.' Brent crossed his arms over his chest.

'It is a small matter, but I need to say it.' He looked as if he might burst if he did not speak.

Brent gestured for him to continue.

'Well, it is a matter of reciprocity,' he began.

'Reciprocity?' What the devil?

'You have dined at the Rolfes' several times, but you have never invited them to dine with you. It does not seem polite.'

Brent could not believe his ears. 'You want me to plan a dinner party now?'

'You would not have to do the planning. Turn it over to your servants. Or, better yet, have your governess plan the dinner party. She's been trained as a lady, you said. She should know how to hold a dinner party.'

Ask Anna to plan a party for his fiancée? That would be cruel indeed.

'It need not be an elaborate dinner party,' Peter said. 'Merely a family one, with Miss Rolfe and her parents.'

'And you, of course,' Brent added sarcastically.

'I would be delighted to come.' He seemed to miss the sarcasm. 'It would be a good time for Miss Rolfe to become acquainted with your governess.'

Have Anna dine with them?

He did see the logic in Peter's idea, though. Anna and Miss Rolfe needed to be known to each other if they were eventually going to work together on the children's behalf.

Unless he found a way to marry Anna off, like Lady Charlotte suggested.

Another dismal thought.

Two days later Lord Brentmore requested a moment to speak to Anna. She left the children in the nursery and attended him in the library, where he'd been ensconced with Mr Parker all morning.

Mr Parker, she was pleased to see, was gone. 'You wished to see me, my lord?'

He smiled, but it was not the easy, relaxed smile of their early days together. 'Ah, thank you for coming, Anna.' He rose and walked out from behind his desk. 'Shall we sit in the chairs by the window?'

She complied.

She'd seen little of him the past two days by her own design, at breakfast and in passing. She'd not been alone with him at all. They'd not talked about that day in Hyde Park or anything else, for that matter.

He looked tired and worn. And distant.

'What did you wish to see me about?' she asked, wanting to rid herself of the suspense. There could be little he would say to her that she would wish to hear.

A sad look came over his face, but only fleetingly. 'I need to beg a favour from you.'

'A favour?'

He took a breath. 'I am having a small dinner party tonight and I want you to attend.'

'Me?'

She'd known of the dinner party, even though he had not mentioned it. There were few things that happened in a house that were not known to everyone in it. She knew the guest list. His cousin. Lord and Lady Rolfe. His fiancée.

'Whatever for?'

It was going to be difficult enough to know the dinner was taking place. She'd planned to stay up in her room and hope the sounds of conversation and laughter did not reach her ears.

'Miss Rolfe is attending and I think it is an opportunity for you to become acquainted.' His voice turned low. 'You must some time, you realise.'

She averted her gaze. 'I do realise that, but I assumed it would not take place on a social occasion.'

'It is more a family dinner,' he explained. 'And I think it odd not to include you.'

She lifted her chin. 'Which explains why you waited until the day of the party to tell me.'

His eyes flashed. 'I did so because I knew you would have this reaction.'

'What reaction is that?' she shot back.

'This—' He searched for the word. 'Hesitancy.'

'I hesitate because it is not my place to dine

with you and your guests.' To watch him interact with Miss Rolfe would be so difficult. She was simply not ready for it.

'A governess certainly can be part of a family dinner,' he countered. 'I want you there, Anna.'

She straightened. 'Are you ordering me as my employer?'

Those words hurt him, she could see. 'If you wish to put it that way.' He stood and paced in the space in front of the chairs. 'Anna, I want you there. It is important to me.' He paused and looked down at her. 'But it is your choice.'

What did it matter? It was only one evening. She rose from her chair, but did not realise that doing so put her perilously close to him. Her senses hummed with the proximity.

'I will attend, if that is your wish,' she said in a quiet voice.

'Anna.' He reached for her, but withdrew his arm.

She could not bear it if he touched her, but she also could not resist looking into his eyes.

His eyes darkened in response. 'Anna,' he murmured again.

He stepped back. 'They will arrive at eight and we will dine at nine. I presume you have a suitable gown?'

'Yes.' She had brought one passable dress with her.

He smiled again. 'Excellent. It is kind of you to agree to this, when I know you do not wish it.'

She did not smile in return. 'I will manage, my lord.'

That afternoon as Brent walked back from St. James's Street, he encountered Yates, walking in the same direction. After exchanging greetings, they wound up walking together.

Yates looked burdened.

'Are you in some difficulty, Yates?' Brent asked.

Yates looked surprised. 'Does it show? Forgive me, Brent. It is nothing of consequence. A tangle with my investments right when I need some ready cash for the estate.' He smiled ruefully. 'And I just had to let my man of business go.'

'It sounds like something of consequence indeed,' Brent commented. 'Is there some way I can help?'

Yates gaped at him. 'Brent, you are the last person I would prevail upon for help.'

Brent agreed. 'Yes. It is unlikely for me to offer.'

In some ways he felt a kinship with Yates. They'd both hurt Eunice irreparably.

Brent went on. 'I have another unlikely idea to offer. Come to dinner tonight. I am having a very small party. Just my cousin and Lord and

Lady Rolfe. And their daughter. I am to marry her, you might as well know.'

'Marry?' he cried. 'Did I miss this announcement?'

Brent shook his head. 'We have not formally announced it.'

Yates responded, 'I should not intrude on your dinner party.'

Brent frowned. 'It would be a good thing for you to attend. Undoubtedly the Rolfes know of our—our previous relationship. It will reassure them that the scandal about us is gone.'

Yates looked sceptical.

'Besides, my cousin and Mr Rolfe might have some ideas about how to untangle your financial difficulties.' He added, 'You will not be the only person outside the family. Miss Hill will be attending as well.'

'Then perhaps I will attend.' Yates glanced at Brent. 'I mean, I would be honoured to attend.'

Chapter Fifteen

Anna's maid and Eppy both became quite excited that she would be attending this dinner. She had packed one good dress, but it was a rather plain white muslin. Eppy found some dusty pink ribbon and white lace, goodness knew from where, and worked all day at embellishing the gown. The maid made a special effort to arrange her hair, threading some of the ribbon through her tresses. Anna added the very lightest tint of pink to her lips and wore her new gloves and stockings. She dabbed her new scent on her neck and in the peek of *décolletage* the neckline of her dress revealed.

The three women surveyed the result in a full-length mirror.

The peek of lace softened the neckline and sleeves, and the ribbon encircled the empire waist and draped into a bow whose tails fell nearly to the gown's hem.

Eppy declared, 'You look the very image of a fashion print!'

Anna hoped that was true. She was usually not so vain, but this night she wanted her appearance to compare favourably with Miss Rolfe's. Anna knew that Miss Rolfe came close to the perfect image of feminine beauty and Anna did not, but she at least wanted to look her very best.

She surveyed herself. 'It wants jewellery of some sort, but I suppose a governess is not expected to own jewellery.'

'You look every bit like a lady,' insisted the maid.

The clock struck the quarter-hour. Anna was running late.

An attack of nerves hit her and she pressed her hand against her stomach. 'I should go now. Thank you both very much.'

'Lord Brentmore will be dazzled.' Eppy grinned.

Anna had to admit that was what she wanted most—to dazzle Lord Brentmore.

It was not at all admirable of her to wish to command his attention. She should, by rights, dress to blend into the woodwork, as Lady Lawton always insisted she do and as the daughter of a laundress ought. Half her blood, however, was aristocratic and, just this once, she wanted to show that part of her.

With butterflies still fluttering inside her, she walked down the stairs and entered the drawing room.

Two gentlemen turned.

'Mr Yates!' Anna exclaimed.

He stepped forwards. 'It is good to see you again, Miss Hill. I trust you are well.'

'Yes, I am,' she responded. 'I did not know you would be here.'

The other gentleman in the room was, of course, Lord Brentmore. 'I invited him this afternoon.'

She felt Lord Brentmore's eyes flick over her, but his expression gave away nothing of his opinion of her appearance.

Mr Yates was more forthright. 'May I say you are in excellent looks this evening, Miss Hill.'

'I hope I will do.' She slid a glance to Lord Brentmore.

The marquess turned his back. 'May I pour you a glass of port, Anna?' he asked.

She was tempted to use port to calm her nerves. 'I will wait for the other ladies, I believe.' She turned to a chair in the corner. 'Please continue your conversation. I do not wish to intrude.'

'You do not intrude, Anna,' Lord Brentmore said, an edge of annoyance in his voice. He took a sip of his port.

'How do the children fare?' Yates asked her.

She could tell he tried to keep his voice neutral. 'Very well, thank you.'

'Have you taken more walks in Hyde Park?'

She could tell he had chosen his words carefully and that he yearned to ask her more, but could not with Lord Brentmore present.

She wanted to give Yates something of the happenings of his daughter's life. 'We have been busy with dressmakers and tailors.' She inclined her head to Lord Brentmore. 'Their father has generously wished them to be fitted for entire new wardrobes.'

'How nice for them,' Yates said in a polite voice.

'I dare say they detested the task,' Lord Brentmore added.

She wondered why he had invited this man, but because she was not supposed to know who Yates was, she could never ask.

'Have you called upon Lady Charlotte?' Yates asked her.

He would have overheard her entire conversation with Charlotte.

She lowered her voice. 'I have not the opportunity.'

Brentmore walked over, taking Yates's empty glass from him. 'Did she wish you to call, Anna?'

She lifted her gaze to him. 'She asked, but I cannot call upon her.'

Brentmore returned to the side table and filled Yates's glass. He walked back to hand it to him.

'How are you acquainted with Lady Charlotte?' Yates asked her.

'I was her companion before becoming governess to Lord Brentmore's children.' She hoped he did not ask for more explanation than that.

He did not. 'Will you attend her ball?' he asked instead.

'No,' she murmured.

'You should attend, Anna.' Lord Brentmore still sounded annoyed with her.

She faced him. 'You know I cannot.'

She caught Yates looking from her to Brentmore.

Davies came to the door. 'Lord and Lady Rolfe, Miss Rolfe, Mr Caine.'

Lord Brentmore crossed the room to greet them. 'Welcome,' he said.

Anna remained where she was, as did Yates. She braced herself to witness Brentmore's manner towards Miss Rolfe.

He bowed to her and to her mother and shook hands with her father and his cousin. Miss Rolfe curtsied.

As the group exchanged more pleasantries, Yates remarked to Anna, 'One wonders about this betrothal. It came as a surprise to me.'

And to Anna, of course.

When the greetings were done, Lord Brentmore glanced over at Anna.

She and Yates joined them.

Anna was presented to Lord and Lady Rolfe.

'You are known to Miss Rolfe and my cousin,' Lord Brentmore added.

Anna curtsied. 'How do you do, Miss Rolfe?'

'I am so pleased to see you again,' Miss Rolfe said, sounding very genuine.

When Brentmore introduced Mr Yates to Lord and Lady Rolfe, Anna saw the shock of recognition on their faces. They knew who Mr Yates was to the marquess.

Poor Mr Yates. He saw their expressions as well.

Lady Rolfe led her daughter around the room, remarking at the décor, and probably thinking that it would all be her daughter's one day. The gentlemen busied themselves with more port.

Anna stepped back, out of the way, convinced more than ever that she did not belong in this party.

Lady Rolfe finished her survey of the room. She addressed Lord Brentmore, 'Brentmore, my dear, I would love a tour of the house.'

'Mama!' Miss Rolfe turned a bright shade of pink. 'You mustn't ask.'

Brentmore said, 'I ought to have offered. Of course, you will be curious about the house. I don't like to leave the gentlemen....' His voice trailed off. He directed his gaze at Anna. 'Would you take the ladies on a tour of the house while there is still some daylight, Anna?'

She stiffened, but replied, 'As you wish, my lord.'

She led them out the door and started the tour with Lord Brentmore's library on this level, trying hard not to recall her encounters with him in the room.

After the library she said, 'Let us go to the first floor. You will see the dining room later.'

They climbed the stairs and she showed them the two large drawing rooms there. 'There is a folding door that, when opened, doubles the size.'

'Perfect for a ball, Susan,' Lady Rolfe remarked to her daughter.

Anna waited near the door while Lady Rolfe completed her inspection. She next showed them a cosier sitting room behind the other two rooms.

She took them next to the second floor. 'There are two bedrooms on this level.' She gestured to one closed door. 'That is Lord Brentmore's bedchamber.' She opened a second door. 'This room was once the marchioness's.'

Lady Rolfe entered the room eagerly. Her daughter merely stepped inside.

'Is there a connecting door between the two bedchambers?' Lady Rolfe asked.

Anna felt sharp pain inside her. 'I do not know, ma'am.'

She showed them the dressing rooms and the lady's maid's room, as well.

She merely pointed to the third floor. 'There are five bedrooms on that level, currently being used as the nursery, for the children, their nurse and me.'

'The children must be sleeping,' Miss Rolfe said in a kind voice.

'Yes. If you will forgive me, I'd prefer not to take you up there and risk waking them.' She also did not want them looking into her room.

'I agree,' Miss Rolfe said.

They walked down the stairs again to the ground level. 'The kitchen and the servants' rooms are below, of course.'

They returned to the gentlemen.

'Did you make a full inventory, my dear?' Lord Rolfe asked his wife.

She smiled. 'It was very helpful to see where our daughter will some day be in residence.'

Miss Rolfe turned to Anna. 'Will you sit with me, Miss Hill?'

'Of course.' How could she refuse?

'Tell me about the children,' Miss Rolfe requested. 'I know so little of them.'

Lord Brentmore apparently did not discuss the children's troubles with his fiancée. Anna was certainly not going to be the one to talk of Cal and Dory's difficulties.

'They are very clever.' Anna talked about their

lessons, matters that would likely be expected of a governess.

Finally Davies announced the dinner. Anna was surprised to see that Lord and Lady Rolfe were seated at each side of Lord Brentmore, who headed the table. Miss Rolfe sat next to her father and Mr Caine sat next to her. Mr Yates was placed next to Lady Rolfe and Anna next to him.

Lady Rolfe did not seem to have much to say to Mr Yates, and, across the table, Miss Rolfe and Brentmore's cousin seemed to have a great deal to talk about together and with Lord Rolfe. Yates and Anna were left with each other.

It was an excruciatingly long dinner.

Anna's attention could not help but be drawn to Miss Rolfe. It was a puzzle. She and Lord Brentmore were little more than cordial to each other, but, seated next to his cousin, Miss Rolfe seemed to blossom.

At one point, Yates bent to her ear. 'Do you make the same observation as I do?'

She watched more intently before responding, 'They are clearly attached.'

'Very attached, would you not say?' he added.

'But, then, why—?' She did not need to complete her thought.

Mr Yates explained, 'Word is that Rolfe is in financial distress. His daughter needs to make a good match to a generous and wealthy man. Mr

Caine owns property, but his finances are only marginally better than Rolfe's.'

She peered at him. 'How do you know this?'

He gave a sad smile. 'Word gets around. The end of the war has left many of us struggling, and this summer's crops are not doing well with all this cold weather.'

The weather was part of the reason so many of the *ton* were still in London in August.

Anna glanced from Miss Rolfe to Lord Brentmore. His gaze caught hers. He continued to appear displeased with her. It baffled her. She'd come to his party and made the best of it. What had she done to displease him?

'The web becomes more tangled as we speak,' said Mr Yates.

Brent held Anna's gaze for a moment. Was she deliberately seeking Yates's attention, or was it merely because they were seated together? He wished he had paid more attention to Davies's question of where to seat everyone.

He wished he had not invited Yates.

It had seemed like a good idea at the time, but now it felt like a repeat of history. Except Anna was not Eunice and not obligated to keep any wedding vows.

If she had been Eunice, then undoubtedly the flirtation would have been a deliberate ploy to shame and embarrass her husband. How many times had he watched Eunice initiate a seduction right in front of his eyes, all the while appearing as if she merely was engaging in conversation?

Anna's face, however, showed nothing of Eunice's contempt. She looked confused and hurt.

Perhaps he should be wary of Yates. Was the man deliberately seeking out Anna, and, if so, was Yates trying to wound him further?

Brent forced his eyes away and asked Lord Rolfe a question.

When the man launched into a loquacious response, Brent's gaze wandered back to Anna.

He had to admit she looked beautiful this evening with her upswept curls and unadorned dress, like a statue of Aphrodite he'd once seen in his travels. She'd so taken his breath away when she'd entered the drawing room that he'd had to look away.

The last course was finished and it was time for the ladies to retire and the gentlemen to remain for brandy.

Anna, her head held high, left the room with Miss Rolfe and her mother. Brent had not thought the evening through in enough detail to realise Anna would be left with the two ladies. He felt guilty for making her do what she so clearly did not wish to do, but he still believed he was right. She and Miss Rolfe needed to become accustomed to each other.

Miss Rolfe. More reason for him to feel guilty.

He'd hardly spoken to her all evening. He must make certain to rectify that.

Peter, Lord Rolfe and Yates were talking about the financial stresses of the times.

'I do not know what we would do without the Corn Laws,' Lord Rolfe said. 'If Great Britain were to import foreign grain, it would be the end of me, I'll tell you that.'

'It has caused a great deal of unrest,' Yates commented.

People were hungry, Brent thought, remembering long days in Ireland when he and his grandfather had not enough to eat.

He let the discussion wash over him, without debating either side of the issue. His fortune could weather these difficult times. He and his children would never want for anything and he could still afford to help those most unfortunate.

And men like Lord Rolfe, who had indeed accepted the money Brent transferred to him.

They finished their brandy and Peter suggested they return to the women.

When they walked out of the dining room, Yates fell into step with Brent. 'You were quite quiet during the discussion, Brent. Is there anything amiss?'

Brent was taken aback. 'I didn't realise. No, nothing is amiss.' He did not realise his preoccupation showed, he meant.

'I hope you do not regret inviting me,' Yates said.

'Why would you think so?' Brent asked.

'I noticed you looking my way from time to time.' Yates slid him a glance. 'Or perhaps it was Miss Hill who concerned you.'

'Concerned me?' Yates saw too much, Brent thought. 'I think it was more a case of my rethinking the seating arrangement.'

'Putting me near the Rolfes would have proved awkward,' Yates responded. 'They seem uncomfortable conversing with me.'

'I am sorry for it.' Brent slowed his pace as he and Yates crossed the hall. 'I still think it is a good idea to be seen together. If we can forget the conflict between us, the *ton* will soon forget, as well, but if we continue to feud, we keep the talk alive.'

'I hope you are right,' Yates said. 'But perhaps this private party of yours was not the best place to start.'

'It was for me,' Brent told him. 'I need to get used to seeing you without animosity.'

They entered the drawing room and Brent saw right away that Anna was seated in a chair adjacent to the sofa where Miss Rolfe and her mother sat. Her back was to him. Miss Rolfe was busy pouring tea for Peter and laughed at something he said.

He and Yates walked over to them.

Anna rose. 'You may have my seat, my lord,'

she said to him. 'I am certain you wish to sit next to Miss Rolfe.'

It was where he ought to sit.

'You do not have to move, Anna.'

But she moved anyway, her skirt catching in her legs, showing their shape beneath the thin muslin. Brent felt a flash of arousal. He quickly turned away, taking a moment to dampen his desires before his body betrayed him.

He sat in the chair Anna vacated for him. It was still warm from her. He watched Anna withdraw.

Miss Rolfe switched her attention from Peter to Brent. 'Let me say, Lord Brentmore, that the food this evening has been superb. As has the company.'

'Thank you,' he responded. 'I am glad to have pleased you.'

She smiled.

He glanced away. 'Did you and your mother find something to converse about with Miss Hill?'

'The children, of course,' she replied. 'And Mother had several questions about how many servants you keep, if the meals are always so well prepared, if the house runs smoothly.'

'That is fine,' he said.

He wished he had discussed with Anna what to say about the children. Miss Rolfe did not need to know about Cal's affliction, nor about the abuse the children had suffered. There was so much he had not considered.

He glanced over at Anna. Yates engaged her in conversation.

'Is Mr Yates her suitor?' Miss Rolfe inclined her head in their direction.

'I beg your pardon?'

She turned to him. 'I thought perhaps Mr Yates was Miss Hill's suitor. I thought perhaps that is why they were included.'

'Miss Hill attends so you can become acquainted with her as the children's governess.' His tone was clipped.

'Of course,' she said mildly. 'But I thought perhaps Mr Yates was here because of her.'

'Do you know who Mr Yates is?' he asked.

She lowered her gaze. 'Peter told me. That is why I am trying to make sense of why he is here.'

It seemed too much effort to explain to Miss Rolfe the strategy behind inviting Yates. 'I have known him since my school days and, no matter what has happened, I hold no ill will towards him.'

She gave him a placid look. 'That is very commendable.'

Lady Rolfe broke into the conversation. 'Are you attending Lord Lawton's ball next week, Brentmore? We are attending, are we not, my dear?'

Her husband replied, 'We are indeed.'

'And you are attending, too, Peter. Is that not right?' she went on.

'I would never pass up an opportunity to attend a ball,' his cousin said.

Lady Lawton twisted back to Brent. 'Will you come? It promises to be a fine ball, as fine as if it were during the Season.'

'Perhaps,' Brent replied, adding, 'I have been asked to escort Miss Hill to the ball.'

'What!' Lady Rolfe's voice rose in shock.

Anna looked alarmed.

'I spoke with Lady Charlotte at the musicale the other night,' he explained. 'She asked me to bring Anna. They—they grew up together.'

'Oh, they grew up together.' Lady Rolfe looked relieved. 'You would be doing a kindness, in other words.'

Miss Rolfe glanced at Yates. 'Are you attending, sir?'

'I was invited.' He did not explain more.

She looked over at Anna. 'You must come, Miss Hill. It will be a delightful party.'

Brent watched Anna's expression. He could see in her eyes the hurt and anger, an anger he deserved. What possessed him to inform her of Charlotte's request in this manner? Was he punishing her for talking to Yates? Or for looking so lovely he could not take his eyes off her?

Whatever it was, it did him no credit.

How could he profess to be her friend when he treated her so shabbily?

'What say you?' Miss Rolfe pressed.

Brent watched Anna lift her chin, a gesture he now knew well. 'It is kind of Lady Charlotte to wish to include me and kind of Lord Brentmore to be willing to escort me.' She kept her eyes directly on Brent. 'But I will not attend the ball.'

Miss Rolfe said, 'I do hope you change your mind.'

Brent walked his guests to the hall and bid them goodnight. Anna waited outside the drawing room. When the door closed behind them, she crossed the hall and started up the stairs.

He hurried after her. 'A moment, please, Anna.'

She whirled on him right on the staircase. 'Do not speak to me, my lord. I am much too angry.' She lifted her skirts and doubled her pace.

He caught up with her again on the first floor. 'We must talk.'

He seized her arm and pulled her into the nearest room, lit only by light from the streets. Below them carriage lamps blazed while the Rolfes settled into Brent's carriage, which would take them to their rooms on Somerset Street.

Anna struggled against his grip. 'Release me, sir!'

'No. Not until you promise to listen to me.' This was becoming more unreasonable by the second, but he could not stop himself. He backed her against the wall between the two windows.

She suddenly stilled. 'Very well. Say what you wish to say, so I may go!'

What words could he say? He hardly knew.

'I am sorry, Anna,' was all he could manage.

'Sorry?' she cried. 'This is how you show you are sorry? By bullying me and putting your hands on me?'

He let his hands slip down her arms. 'I could not let you go to bed before letting you know how wrong I was. I should not have told you about Lady Charlotte in front of them all. I do not know why I did it.'

He heard the carriage drive off. The room plunged into darkness.

She went on. 'I did not want to attend your dinner party in the first place and then suddenly I must take your lady guests on a tour, as if I was their hostess and this was my house. But that was not enough, was it, my lord? You obviously withheld from me your conspiracy with Charlotte. You, of all people, know why I do not wish to go to that ball. You should have supported my wishes with Charlotte, and told me that she had spoken to you. Instead, you blather about it with people who are strangers to me.' Her voice cracked. 'I do not need this treatment, my lord. I do not deserve it.'

'You are right. You are right.' He cared about her. Why had he deliberately hurt her? 'Anna, I do not know why I did any of it. I only know I could not have a dinner party and leave you sitting alone in your room. And, then, you looked so very beautiful and Yates paid you such particular attention—'

'That was another thing. You did not do that poor man a favour by inviting him. Who else was he to converse with? Your cousin and the Rolfes made no effort to include him. Or you. You left him to me.'

Had he done so? Had he handed her to Yates, as if she were another course for dinner?

No, she was wrong. He might have acted on impulse inviting her, inviting Yates, but she had played her part in this.

'What of you, Anna?' he countered. 'You knew you were included to become acquainted with Miss Rolfe, but you treated her more as a rival than the prospective marchioness—'

'A rival!' Her voice rose. 'How can you say such a thing?'

'How?' He placed his palms on the wall, caging her between his arms. 'Tell me you did not deliberately dress to be alluring.'

She gasped.

He was so close to her that he felt her breath. She was only a shadow in the dark room, but her allure was stronger than ever.

'Roses,' he murmured. 'You smell of roses.' An intoxicating scent, he decided. 'That is a new scent for you. Tell me you did not choose that scent tonight for a deliberate reason. Was that for me?'

She rose up in defiance. 'Does it work?'

By God, it worked very effectively.

He placed his hands at her waist and lowered his lips on to hers.

Her arms twined around his neck and he pressed her hard against him, as she hungrily kissed him back.

'No!' She pushed on his chest.

He regained his senses, if not his tongue. 'Is that what you hoped for, Anna?'

He backed away, wishing he could take those words back.

She shot back at him, 'Is that what *you* hoped for, my lord? Are you trying to prove to me how like my mother I am? I need no proof, my lord. It was I who told you so.' She took a breath and her voice dipped low and tremulous. 'Well, I will not *be* my mother. Do you understand? I choose not to be her.'

'Anna—' he began, but what could he say?

In the dim light he could see she rubbed her arms. 'If I had some place to go, some place with someone who knew me and would take me in, I would be gone from here!' She advanced on him, only to push at his chest again. 'I have no one and you know it. You, of all people, know it and still you take advantage!'

She shoved him one more time and rushed past him out the door. He heard her footsteps running up the stairs.

Chapter Sixteen

By the next morning Anna realised she must do something to determine her own fate. Always she'd accepted whatever others decided for her, provided for her.

And what they denied her.

She no longer had to do that. She could choose to leave Lord Brentmore's employ, if she wished it. She could investigate agencies in London and she had a little money, thanks to his generosity.

She'd counted her money—over five pounds. She could live on that amount for a time.

Although, what would she do if a position did not present itself?

When she entered the children's room, though, her resolve fizzled.

Dory greeted her with a hug and a kiss, as enthusiastically as if she'd thought she'd never see her governess again.

Cal grinned at her and said, 'Good morning, Miss Hill.'

She gave him a hug and a kiss as well.

Anna loved these children. She wanted to stay with them. She wanted to cosset them and protect them and never see them hurt again. Surely it would hurt them if she left.

'Do we have to go to the dressmaker today?' Dory asked in an exasperated tone.

'I thought you liked the dressmaker,' Anna said to her.

The child made a face. 'The first time, I did.'

Anna smiled at her. 'No, we do not have to go to the dressmaker today. Today we will have lessons and then, if you have worked very hard at them, perhaps an outing.'

'Will Papa come with us?' Dory asked hopefully.

'Papa will be busy, Dory,' Cal said. 'A marquess has much to do.'

'He didn't have much to do at Brentmore!' Dory whimpered. 'I want to go back there. I miss my pony. I want to go home.'

Home. To Brentmore Hall. There she would be free to love the children without distraction.

She gathered Cal and Dory together and hugged them both. 'Perhaps we will not be in London too much longer.'

'Will I have to leave my doll house and Hortense?' Dory asked.

'No, silly,' Cal said. 'Papa will allow us to take the toys home.'

Cal was assured of his father's devotion. That was a good sign. The children would adjust to not seeing him daily.

As she must do.

Anna resolved to talk to Lord Brentmore today. She would tell him to send them back to Brentmore.

As she and the children walked down to the dining room, Anna's improved spirits flagged. Facing him was the hard part.

His kiss of the night before haunted her. She'd pushed him away, but really yearned for more.

Lord Brentmore was not in the dining room. Would he not show? What would be worse—to see him this morning or have him avoid her?

She fixed the plates and she and the children were settled in their chairs when he finally entered.

'Papa!' Dory jumped from her chair to hug his legs.

'Good morning, Papa,' Cal said.

He smiled at his son and kissed Dory on the top of her head.

His gaze turned to Anna. 'Good morning, Anna.'

Her heartbeat accelerated. 'Good morning, my lord.'

He looked as if he'd not slept at all and, in spite of herself, her sympathy went out to him. He'd not been wrong to accuse her of dressing to attract him, to compete with Miss Rolfe. Miss Rolfe had been cordial to her, even friendly, you might say. It had been Anna who'd wrestled with her emotions.

Lord Brentmore selected his food from the sideboard and sat, chatting with the children who were delighted to respond. Anna alone perceived his sadness.

'Papa, will you take us on an outing today?' Dory asked. 'Miss Hill says we may go on an outing after lessons. No more fittings.'

He seemed to gaze at Dory intently. Did he struggle with the knowledge that she was not his child? Did he see Yates when he looked at her? Lord Brentmore had always been more reticent in his response to the girl. Now his behaviour made sense. Now his genuine devotion to the child made Anna ache in empathy with him.

He smiled at Dory. 'Perhaps I can break away for a little while.'

'Take us to Horse Guards to see the horses?' Cal asked.

'Perhaps not today.' He ruffled Cal's hair and his tone was almost mournful. 'But maybe soon

I can take you to see the Guards exercising the horses.'

Anna felt responsible for his misery. No doubt they must be parted.

The marquess finished his breakfast more quickly than usual. 'I must go, children. I will try to get back this afternoon.' He stood.

Anna also rose to her feet. 'May I speak with you a moment, my lord?'

He hesitated before finally nodding. 'In the library?'

'May we go up and play?' Cal asked.

'Of course you may,' Anna said.

The children scampered out of the room and up the stairs. Anna walked a little behind Lord Brentmore across the hall to the library.

'Cal is talking so well today,' she remarked, although she forced out the words.

'Remarkably well,' he agreed, but in a flat voice.

He opened the door to the library.

Anna heard a voice from within. 'Good morning, my lord. I have some papers for you to sign.'

Lord Brentmore turned to Anna. 'Mr Parker.' He gestured to the drawing room. 'We may talk in there.' To Mr Parker, he said, 'I'll return in a moment.'

'But, my lord—' Parker implored.

Anna entered the room where she and the

marquess had created such unhappiness for each other the night before.

As soon as he stepped inside and closed the door, he said, 'What is it, Anna?'

She feared any apology she attempted would come to the same end as his had done the night before. Best they pretend none of it happened.

'I want to take the children back to Brentmore,' she said simply.

Brent's muscles relaxed. He'd been prepared to hear her say she was leaving for good.

'I cannot leave London for a few more weeks at least,' he told her. 'We can go back for harvest.'

'No.' She gave him a steady look. 'I want to take the children back now.' She lowered her voice. 'I think it will be for the best.'

He turned away and walked to the window, looking out on to the square where he'd first set eyes on her. To be here without her and the children? It would be desolate.

As he'd lain sleepless in his bed last night, he'd formulated another plan. To help her find a happy life for herself with a husband and children of her own, a family with whom she truly could belong.

He swung back to her. 'I want the children with me.'

She looked about to protest.

He raised a hand. 'But I am willing to compromise.'

'How?' She peered at him with suspicion.

'Stay a few more days, at least,' he said. 'Attend the Lawton ball—'

'Attend the Lawton ball!' The colour rose in her face.

'After the ball you and the children may go back to Brentmore.'

Her eyes flashed. 'Why must I attend the ball? Why would you put me through such an ordeal?'

So she could see how easily she would attract suitors and perhaps attract a man who would be good to her.

No matter how depressing that thought was to him, it was the least he could do to repay her for all she'd done for him and the children.

'It does not have to be an ordeal, Anna. You might enjoy yourself.' He did not need to tell her why he was doing this. 'Your friend wishes you to come.'

'My sister, you mean.'

'Very well. Your sister.' He met her defiant gaze. 'If Lord Lawton had any decency in him, he would have raised you to be a lady who attends balls.'

She glanced away. 'It is ridiculous to require me to attend a ball in order to take your children back to Brentmore.'

He remained firm. 'That is my stipulation.'

She whirled around and left the room.

Brent pressed his fingers against his temples.

He'd done it. He'd set it up so Lady Charlotte could attempt her matchmaking. Unlike last night, he still must stand aside and not interfere, not sabotage. Perhaps if he and his children were very lucky, she'd choose them over a life of her own.

He walked slowly back to the library.

As soon as he walked into the room, Parker pounced. 'My lord, we really must go through these papers. You mustn't allow anything—or anyone—interfere.'

That set Brent's teeth on edge. He crossed the room and sat behind the desk. 'Who is it interferes with what I wish to do?'

Parker put down the inch-thick stack of paper he'd been gripping and faced him. 'If I may speak plain, sir, it is that governess. She is always luring you away from your business matters for one triviality or another—'

Brent glared at him. 'Take care, Parker.'

His man of business did not heed the warning. Instead, he picked up the papers again and swung them through the air as he spoke. 'I mean, it just is not done! She has you acting the nursemaid. You! A marquess!'

'Enough!' Brent rose from his chair. 'You forget your place, sir.' He stood face to face with the man. 'What I do, how I spend my time, who I spend it with, is not the sort of business to which you are paid to attend.' His anger was perilously close to exploding. 'Heed what I say. Discussion of my children or their governess is prohibited to you.'

Parker continued. 'She has changed you! She is pulling your strings as if you were a marionette. You cannot see it.'

Brent leaned forwards, his fists on the desk. 'That is it, Parker.' He lowered his voice to a growl. 'Leave now. Come back in a week's time and I will have a letter of recommendation for you and you will be paid for the year.'

'You are discharging me?' Parker eyes grew wide with shock. 'You cannot! We are in the midst of all this work.'

'I can and I did and I am not above tossing you out on your ear, as well.' He gave Parker his sternest look. 'Go now if you want any pay at all.'

'But—' Parker sputtered.

'Go!' Brent bellowed.

Parker dropped the papers and ran out.

Anna and Dory sat in a sunny spot in Anna's room, sewing. When Eppy had searched for the trim for Anna's dinner dress, she'd discovered a trunk with a sewing basket and scraps of fabric, lace and ribbon. Anna told Dory they might make new dresses for her doll with this treasure trove, and Dory was so excited about the prospect she willingly gave up an outing to the Horse Guards with her father and brother.

It suited Anna to miss that outing as well.

Dory had chosen a scrap of white muslin and pink ribbon for the first dress. 'Hortense will look as pretty as you,' Dory said.

First Anna showed Dory how to make simple stitches. She gave the child a scrap of linen on which to practise while she sewed the replica of her dinner dress. With every stab of the needle she saw Lord Brentmore's face in her mind.

She looked over at Dory. 'Keep your fingers away from the point of the needle.'

Dory was unusually quiet and intent on her stitches. 'I like sewing very much,' she said.

Anna could not help but smile. How could she ever have considered leaving these children?

There was a knock on her door.

Davies opened it and stuck his head in. 'Miss Hill, Miss Rolfe has called and requests a moment of your time.'

'Miss Rolfe? For me?' What could she possibly want?

'For you. She did not ask for his lordship.' He sounded as surprised as she. 'She is waiting in the drawing room.'

Anna set aside her sewing and stood. 'Would you find Eppy and have her come stay with Dory?'

'Very good.' Davies left.

'Dory, I'll be back soon. Eppy can help you sew while I see this caller.'

'Papa's fiancée,' Dory said without looking up from her sewing.

Anna took off her cap and the apron that covered her dress and quickly tidied her hair, all the while realising she wanted to appear at her best in front of this woman, just as Lord Brentmore had accused.

When Anna entered the drawing room, Miss Rolfe stood staring at the same Gainsborough portrait that had captured Anna's attention that first day.

She turned and smiled. 'Miss Hill, how kind of you to see me.'

'Miss Rolfe.' Anna curtsied. 'Please do sit down. Shall I have Davies bring some tea?'

'Oh, no, please do not go to such trouble for me.' Miss Rolfe lowered herself on to the same sofa on which she sat the previous night.

'It is no trouble to serve you.' Anna was still puzzled by her presence. 'You will, after all, become the marchioness.'

The young woman brushed a curl off her forehead. 'I suppose you are correct, but I still would prefer not to have tea.'

'As you wish.' Anna sat in the adjacent chair.

Miss Rolfe smiled nervously. 'You are probably wondering why I am here.'

'I am certain you will tell me.' Anna could not help but try to put her at ease; she was so obviously troubled.

'I—I came to ask you something…' She placed her hand over her chest as if to try to calm herself.

What would cause a future marchioness to be nervous about speaking to a governess?

Anna waited.

Miss Rolfe tried again. 'My mother made a comment upon which I have pondered all night.'

'A comment?' She tried to sound encouraging.

'She said it half in jest, but it troubled me.'

Simply come out with it, Anna wanted to say. 'What was it?'

The young woman took a breath. 'She—she said that you and the marquess did not talk to each other like any employer and governess she'd ever known. It made me wonder—wonder if there was more to your relationship with the marquess than that.'

Anna's own nerves flared. 'More to our relationship?' She must answer this very carefully. 'The marquess acted as a friend to me on the occasion of my mother's death, but—but there is nothing more.' Nothing spoken—nothing acted upon. At least not fully acted upon, not fully disclosed.

'You are not lovers?' Miss Rolfe blurted out.

Anna lowered her gaze. 'We are not lovers.' Merely a hair's breadth from being lovers.

Miss Rolfe's face screwed up in anxiety. 'Because I am very desirous of making my marriage a good one. I—I should need to know if—

if the marquess had other interests. I would hate to act the jealous wife.'

Anna gaped at her. 'You would tolerate such a thing?'

The young woman lifted a shoulder. 'What else can a wife do?'

Anna's brows knitted. 'May I ask, is this marriage a love match for you?'

Miss Rolfe's expression lost its tension. 'Oh, no, but Lord Brentmore understands that. Marrying me suits his need for a respectable wife and it suits me because his money saves my father from ruin and provides for the futures of my sisters and brothers.'

A marriage of convenience.

The young woman went on. 'It is all very civilised. Peter assures me his cousin is a fine man and I will be treated very well by him.'

'He is a fine man,' Anna murmured. She peered at Miss Rolfe. 'In this marriage would you also take lovers?'

She looked shocked. 'Oh, no. I cannot even imagine it.'

'Not even with your Peter?' Anna spoke in a low voice.

Miss Rolfe turned bright red. 'Peter? Why would you say such a thing?'

Anna spoke quietly. 'I noticed the way you looked at each other.'

Miss Rolfe, appearing alarmed, reached over

and gripped Anna's arm. 'Do not tell the marquess, please!'

'I will not,' Anna assured her.

Miss Rolfe released her and expelled a relieved breath.

Anna went on. 'How do you see this, marrying Lord Brentmore and being in love with his cousin?' If Miss Rolfe knew how to accomplish such a thing, perhaps she could teach Anna.

The young woman lowered her head into her hands. 'He—Peter—is going to move to the Continent. He says it will cost him less to live there, so it is a good thing for him.' She raised her head and her eyes filled with tears. 'You see, Peter has no money. Marrying him is out of the question. I—I do not care for myself whether we have money, but I'll not have the ruin of my whole family on my conscience.'

Anna felt sick. She might be able to bear it if Lord Brentmore made a marriage that brought him happiness and devotion, but this sounded dreadful.

Miss Rolfe took out a lace-edged handkerchief from her reticule. She dabbed at her eyes. 'It—it makes it all easier to know you and Brent are not lovers. I confess, I did not know how I would do, knowing such a thing and acting the good wife. I—I must be a good wife to him. He is the salvation of my family.'

And Miss Rolfe, apparently, was the sacrificial lamb.

A memory flew into Anna's mind. Her mother greeting Lord Lawton at the cottage door, telling Anna to hurry back to the house and to Charlotte.

Would this be Anna and Brentmore at Brentmore Hall some day? Snatching passionate encounters with each other, all the while knowing his wife suffered for it? Could they really resist it when their passion was as alive and as powerful as Miss Rolfe's for Peter?

Anna glanced towards the drawing-room door. What a deplorable muddle and who would be right in the middle of it?

The children.

Chapter Seventeen

Anna bided her time the few days before the ball and before she and the children could return to Brentmore Hall. She and Lord Brentmore existed in an uneasy peace that was every bit as painful as their volatile confrontations. She kept Miss Rolfe's visit from him, but it haunted her every hour.

Charlotte sent over a ball gown, complete with matching shoes, gloves and shawl. Anna recognised it as one of Charlotte's outfits of the last Season. Only a few short months ago, Anna had helped Charlotte select its design for the modiste. The gown, a pale blue silk with a sheer overskirt, was adorned with fabric flowers on the bodice and hem. Anna instructed Eppy to remove the flowers. A governess ought not to wear such a fancy dress.

When the night of the ball finally arrived, Eppy and Anna's maid helped Anna dress, just as they had for Lord Brentmore's dinner party. While they were putting the final polish on her appearance, Davies knocked on her bedroom door.

He bore a jewellery box. 'Lord Brentmore said you are to select whatever you wish from this box. The jewels belonged to the marchioness.'

When the women opened the box, they gasped. Diamonds, rubies, emeralds were all thrown in a jumble that glittered in the lamplight. Most of the necklaces, bracelets and earrings were much too opulent for Anna's station, but she found a blue sapphire pendant surrounded by seed pearls and hung on a delicate gold chain that would do. Digging further into the jewellery box, they pulled out teardrop pearl earrings to match.

Once Anna would have been delighted to dress for a ball. She and Charlotte had attended many near Lawton, where everyone knew precisely who she was. This night, though, brought Anna no joy. She did not aspire to dazzle anyone, merely to be presentable enough not to embarrass Lord Brentmore or Charlotte. All she really wished was to blend into the wallpaper.

But Eppy and the maid had other ideas. They'd visited Ackermann's and looked through the fashion prints in *La Belle Assemblée*. They aspired to make her as fashionable as possible.

'I'll defy any of those society ladies to hold a candle to you!' the maid said, pinning one of the fabric flowers into her hair.

'You are a picture!' Eppy agreed.

Anna thanked them, but hoped Lord Brentmore would not think she was attempting to look alluring.

Davies knocked at the door again. 'His lordship is waiting, Miss Hill. The carriage is here.'

'I am coming.' She hugged her maid and Eppy and hurried down the stairs.

He stood at the bottom, leaning against the banister.

Her breath caught.

He looked exceptionally handsome in his superbly fitting formal wear. His black coat, set against the pristinely white linen of his shirt and neckcloth, merely enhanced the impression.

His eyes followed her as she descended and her heart beat wildly.

'I am sorry to keep you waiting,' she said, walking past him to the door.

As she reached the door it was opened by a footman. She passed through to the outside and to the carriage, where another footman waited to assist her inside. She did not look back to see if Lord Brentmore followed, but she felt him behind her.

Inside the carriage, they faced each other as they had that first day when he'd given her a ride in the rain. It was no easier to converse with him this night than it had been that day.

When they pulled up to the Lawton town house, he said, 'If Charlotte wants you here, you will be welcome, Anna.'

Her gaze flew to his face. She knew her father did not welcome her.

The carriage door opened and a footman put down the steps.

When Anna reached out her hand for him to assist her, the footman grinned. 'Why, it is Anna! How'd you do, Anna!'

'Hello, Rogers,' she responded. 'I hope you are well.'

'Quite well.' His smile vanished when Lord Brentmore emerged. He resumed his formal role.

Lord Brentmore did not offer his arm, nor would Anna have taken it if he had. After what Miss Rolfe had suspected, she wished to be careful what impression she gave.

They entered the town house, where another footman greeted Anna and took their things. As they walked up the stairs to the ballroom, she felt an attack of nerves.

'Steady, Anna,' Lord Brentmore murmured.

The butler gave her a wink before stepping in the room and announcing, 'Lord Brentmore and Miss Hill.'

The chatter ceased for a moment and Anna suffered the gaze of many eyes upon her, followed by a hum of whispers. Lord and Lady Lawton stood to the side greeting guests, displeasure written all over their faces.

She felt Lord Brentmore's hand on her elbow. They approached the Lawtons together.

'Anna, this is not well done of you!' Lady Lawton glared.

'See here—' Lord Lawton huffed.

Lord Brentmore faced them both. 'Your daughter invited Miss Hill and begged me to bring her. It is the sole reason I attend.' His voice sounded dangerous. 'You will be civil to her or answer to me.'

'Anna, you should have known better,' Lady Lawton cried, as if the marquess had said nothing. 'No matter what Charlotte wanted you to do.'

Anna stood tall. 'I did know better, my lady. But Lord Brentmore insisted I attend and, since I am in his employ, what other choice did I have?' She turned to Lord Lawton. 'I would have nowhere to turn if I did not have the position he provides me.'

Lord Lawton flushed.

At that moment, Charlotte rushed over in a flurry of skirts. 'Anna! You came!' She gave Anna a quick hug and smiled at Lord Brentmore. 'I knew I could rely on you, sir!' She took Anna's hand. 'Come. There are so many gentlemen I should like to meet you.'

The names and faces of the gentlemen to whom

Anna was introduced blurred after a while. Lord Vestry and Mr Norton, the men she'd met at Hyde Park, were among many others. This was not at all how Anna had wished to pass the time at the ball. She'd planned to find a chair near a big plant and wait out the entire thing.

She caught Charlotte between gentlemen for a brief moment. 'Charlotte, you must stop pushing me off on these poor gentlemen.'

Charlotte squeezed her hand. 'Never! I intend to find one who will fall madly in love with you and then you shall no longer need to be a governess.'

Anna felt the blood drain from her face. Was that what this was about? Was Lord Brentmore in on the scheme?

She scanned the room and found him. He stood with Miss Rolfe, who was at that moment speaking to Peter Caine. Brentmore looked burdened. His gaze slid to her and held for a moment before he lowered his head and eventually turned away.

Anna felt a wave of sadness for him. She was not the only one who suffered.

'Oh, Anna!' Charlotte took a deep breath and pressed her hand against her stomach. 'I feel all tied in knots inside. How am I doing? Am I talking too much? I feel like I am, like people are watching me. All I wish to do is run up to my room and hide.'

Anna fell into her familiar role. 'You are doing

splendidly. You are the very picture of a lively and delightful hostess.'

'I am just pretending, Anna.' She released a long breath.

Anna knew Charlotte could very easily freeze up when she started talking like this. Anna did what she'd always done: distracted her. 'Are there any of these gentlemen who particularly interest you, Charlotte?'

Charlotte surveyed the room. 'There is one man… But I do not see him yet.' She shot a glance over to Lord Vestry and Mr Norton. 'Not those two, though. They are so childish.'

Lord Vestry and Mr Norton were whispering together like two dowagers with nothing to do but gossip. They caught Anna looking at them and quickly turned away.

The musicians began tuning their instruments.

'The dancing should begin soon,' Charlotte said. 'It is so much easier to dance and not talk.' She peered at Anna. 'Tell me you will dance.'

Anna shook her head. 'I should not—'

Charlotte pressed her arm. 'Oh, please say you will dance.'

Anna sighed. 'Very well. If anyone asks me.'

Charlotte gripped her arm harder. 'Oh, look. Here comes Mr Yates.'

Mr Yates walked up to them and bowed. 'Good evening, Lady Charlotte. Miss Hill.'

Charlotte smiled at him. 'I am so glad you

came. Did—did you have any difficulty? I gave strict instructions that you were to be admitted.'

'No difficulty at all.'

One of Charlotte's gentlemen guests came to claim her for the first dance and she excused herself.

Mr Yates turned to Anna. 'So you are here after all.'

She nodded. 'Very unhappily.' She stole a glance towards Lord Brentmore. 'Very unhappily, indeed.'

Brent's gaze continued to seek out Anna. He was almost resigned to it, although he hoped it was not obvious to anyone else. Certainly in his party—Peter, Miss Rolfe and her parents—no one seemed to take notice.

She could not have looked more beautiful. Her gown flowed around her like water. Its blue colour brought out the blue in her eyes, so vividly that in the carriage he'd had to look out the window to avoid staring at her.

He watched her dance, her grace and her flowing skirts making it seem as if she floated on the air rather than be attached to this earth.

He was also aware that other men noticed her, too. Perhaps Charlotte's plan for Anna would reach fruition. How could any man resist her?

That thought depressed him even more than watching Yates speak with her.

Lady Charlotte rarely left her side, except to dance, and after each set, quickly returned to her. Would the young woman want to know she and Anna were sisters?

After one set in which Yates danced with Anna, Charlotte dragged them all to where Brent stood with his cousin and the Rolfes.

'I do hope you are enjoying yourselves,' Charlotte said.

While the others were speaking—except for Anna, who looked distracted—Charlotte whispered to Brent. 'I do think she is a success, do you not, sir?'

'You are doing an excellent job of ensuring it, Lady Charlotte,' he responded.

In fact, as the night had gone on, Anna seemed to be gaining more approving glances from the men in the room.

The next set began. 'Let us all dance!' Charlotte insisted.

Brent glanced at Anna, who looked away. He asked Miss Rolfe to dance. Yates secured Lady Charlotte and Peter politely asked Anna.

The dance required groups of three couples to perform the figures. They began by facing each other in a line, ladies on one side, men on the other. They crossed and turned as the dance dictated, its music slow and sinuous. As Brent crossed the line and met Anna in the middle, their gazes caught. When they joined hands and danced in a circle, he clasped her hand. He could not say how any of the others moved or what expressions their faces held. It was, to him, as if he danced only with Anna.

God help him. He was to marry a woman who could occupy only fleeting thoughts in his brain, while Anna consumed all of him.

Finally the dance was over and he could try to break the spell that always seemed to weave itself around him when she was near.

He was only partially successful. He still could only make a pretence at conversation with others, when, all the while, he watched her.

She became more and more upset, he noticed. Something had happened, something that made her look like the caged animals at the Tower, as if she could do nothing but pace the cage and long for escape.

She broke away from Charlotte with some whispered excuse and made her way out of the ballroom. Brent followed her, determined to discover what had suddenly gone so wrong.

Other ladies walked in the direction of the retiring room, but Anna turned the opposite way, towards what Brent supposed would be the servants' staircase. He hurried after her, found the door and opened it.

She stood on the landing and whirled around when he entered the staircase.

He closed the door behind him. 'What is it, Anna? What is wrong?'

She hugged herself and rocked on her heels as if trying to soothe herself. 'May we leave now?' she asked. 'I really wish to leave now.'

He stepped towards her and seized her shoulders, trying to make her look at him. 'What is it? What happened?'

She kept her gaze averted.

He was puzzled. 'You have been dancing. You have received plenty of attention—'

'Attention,' she repeated sarcastically.

'Lady Charlotte meant for you to be such a success that you would have gentlemen proposing to you on the spot.'

'Proposing?' Her eyes looked wild. 'Not precisely.'

'Tell me, Anna.'

She met his eye. 'So you were in on Charlotte's scheme? Were you also in support of the idea that I needed to be married off?'

He frowned. 'You take this all wrong,' he snapped. 'Do you not see that marriage would be the best thing for you? You would have a home of your own, children of your own, something that is yours, not your employer's.'

Her eyes shot daggers at him. 'My whole life I have been manoeuvred and manipulated with others deciding what I should do. Now you, too, are deciding for me.' She leaned forwards. 'Do you wish to hear about the proposals I have had this night, Lord Brentmore? Because I have had many.'

'You have received proposals? Of marriage?' He felt sick inside. He would lose her after all.

'Oh, the proposals I've received are not of marriage.' She lifted her chin. 'It seems that Lord Vestry and Mr Norton have it on good authority that you and I are lovers and that when you marry Miss Rolfe, I will need a new protector.'

'No.' He felt as if punched in the stomach.

Gossip. Scandal. It followed him in spite of his efforts to avoid it. And now it wounded Anna.

She swung around and gripped the banister. 'I am sick to death of this! It becomes worse and worse. I find out I am not who I think I am, but I quite easily could become what they accuse me of. Even if I do nothing more to earn that reputation, I will somehow stand between you and your wife, because you and I—' She did not finish that thought. 'I will be honest,' she continued, her voice more composed. 'What is between us will not disappear.' She glanced away. 'What is between your cousin and Miss Rolfe will not disappear either, no matter how many miles he puts between them.'

'What the devil are you talking about?'

She clapped her hands against her head. 'Never mind! I'll not stay, do you understand? I'm leaving! I'll walk back to Cavendish Square if I must.'

She whirled around and ran down the stairs, her skirts flying, her shoes beating a frantic tattoo.

He ran after her, but by the time he reached the floor below, her footsteps were silenced and she was gone.

He rushed to the first door he saw, but was disoriented momentarily when he walked through. He emerged into the hall.

'Did she run through here?' he demanded of the footmen attending the hall.

'Who?' one asked.

He didn't pause to explain. He ran out of the town house and looked in both directions, but he could not see her. The streets were not safe for a woman alone.

He seized hold of one of the outside footmen. 'What direction did she go?'

The man pointed.

Brent shouted to him, 'Find my coachman and have him find us or go home.'

He ran off.

Anna ran as fast as her legs and ball slippers could carry her. She wished she could run all the way to the sea, like Lord Brentmore had done as a child, anything to escape the disorder that had become her life.

She was like her mother, in love with the lord and more than willing to bed him. There was no use denying it to herself. The rumours those young gentlemen had contrived were based on something, a glimmer of the truth the men had gleaned from the way she and Brentmore looked at each other, perhaps. The sparks of attraction between them were so strong she would not be surprised if they were visible.

She could no longer talk herself into believing that she and Lord Brentmore could learn to resist each other. It was only a matter of time before they would fall in bed together.

She must be like his cousin and put distance between them. She must leave, no matter that she would be leaving the children—the poor children! She must go and trust that he would help the children to recover from her loss.

She reached Grosvenor Square and leaned against the wrought-iron fence, to catch her breath.

She heard footsteps ringing against the cobbles of the street behind her and knew it was him. She turned and he emerged from the darkness. She watched him stop and scan the area, and knew the instant he saw her. He rushed directly for her.

When he reached her, he gripped her arms. 'Are you mad? You put yourself in danger, running off alone.'

'I am alone,' she countered. 'Why pretend otherwise?'

'Enough of that nonsense.' He shook her. 'You have me.'

The sound of carriage broke into the silence of the street. 'That will be our coachman.' He dragged her into the street and waved to the man, who stopped the horses.

Lord Brentmore picked her up and carried her to the carriage. He lifted her inside and climbed in after her. 'Home,' he called to the coachman.

He sat next to her, but she slid quickly over to the far side of the carriage.

'Do not say more,' she cried. 'I know it was foolish to run, but I had to get away. I still have to get away.'

He seized her wrist. 'No more running. We face this now.'

'I have faced it, my lord,' she said. 'Nothing will change as long as we are together.'

He touched her face. 'No more of this. Call me Brent or Egan. Call me who I am, not my title.'

She turned her head away.

He moved closer to her and drew her into his arms, settling her against him, as he had done in the inn's tavern. 'I am sorry for the talk about you and me. I wish I could stop it. Nothing stops gossip but time. Protesting it only makes it worse.'

'The gossip is correct,' she said. 'We have not made love, but we both know I am too much like my mother—willing to take what I can and ignore the consequences.'

'Was your mother beautiful?' he asked.

She was too tired to ponder why he was asking. 'Very beautiful.'

He went on. 'Was she passionate?'

'I suppose so.' She shrugged.

He planted a kiss on her temple. 'Then you must be like your mother.'

She tilted her head. His lips were close, very close.

She slowly raised her lips to his, touching them lightly, tasting them with the tip of her tongue. She felt his body tense.

'Anna,' he rasped.

And took possession of her with his mouth.

She dug her fingers in his hair and indulged in the kiss while her body erupted in flames.

His hand cupped her breast and she longed to remove her gown, all her clothing and to finally feel his skin against hers. She yearned to finally learn the pleasures of joining with him.

This time there was no stopping. She wanted him, urgently wanted him. Before she left him, she wanted to know the glory of making love with him.

The carriage stopped. They were home.

Chapter Eighteen

Brent lifted her from the carriage and held her hand tightly in his as they hurried to the door.

A sleepy footman gave them entry. If he was surprised that Brent did not have his hat and Anna did not have her wrap, he did not say.

Brent and Anna walked past him, up the stairs. When they reached the second floor, Brent lifted her into his arms and carried her into his room, glad he'd told his valet not to wait up for him. The light from the fireplace cast the room in a soft glow, enough to see by. He carried her to the bed and set her down, kissing her again, a kiss of promise.

He pulled off her shoes and, kicking off his own, shrugged out of his coat and waistcoat.

She presented her back to him and he quickly undid the line of buttons there. She immediately lifted the dress over her head and waited for him to untie the laces of her corset. Then she spun around and watched as he rid himself of his shirt, breeches and stockings.

He had not considered that this was most likely her first view of a real naked man, but she was game. Her gaze flicked over him with approval and pleasure as she removed her stockings. He climbed on the bed next to her.

'I'll be gentle with you,' he assured her as he slid his hand over the soft thin fabric of her chemise.

She pulled the flowers out of her hair and used her fingers to comb out the tangles. 'I do not know if that is what I wish or not.'

She rubbed her fingers over the muscles on his back and he thought his senses would soar to the heavens. He edged her chemise up and she raised her arms so he could pull it off.

He gazed at her, becoming even more aroused to finally drink in the sight of her full breasts, dark-rose nipples, narrow waist and the dark hair at the apex of her legs. His eyes wandered back up the length of her.

He touched the necklace she wore.

'Should I take it off?' she asked.

'No need.' Odd that she should have selected that piece. His wife had looked at it and thrown it on the floor, uttering, 'Cheap trinket.'

Her brow creased. 'What is wrong? Do I disappoint?'

He knew now that the pendant, so perfectly matching her eyes, had always been meant for her. 'You could never disappoint,' he told her. He peered into her eyes. 'Are you certain of this, Anna?'

'Very certain,' she murmured. 'Show me. Show me, Egan, how loving you feels.'

His name on her lips, a name no one else spoke, made his heart swell. He loved her, he realised. There would be no going back if he consummated that love.

He'd find some way to make it all right, to face the scandal, to show the children how to surmount it.

He wanted to rush to that moment of no return. It was the place he wanted to be, a place they both belonged, the inevitable result of that first glimpse of her. He wanted all of her, wanted to feel himself inside her, wanted to feel her pleasure vibrate around him.

He whispered to her, 'Do not be alarmed. I am going to touch you. To prepare you.'

He slid his hand between her legs and gently stroked the part of her that was the key to her pleasure.

She gasped and arched her back, moving against his hand as she would soon move against his body.

'Never dreamed of this,' she managed.

'Neither did I,' he rasped. He'd never dreamed making love could feel like this. So important. So momentous. So right.

He withdrew his hand and rose over her. She smiled at him, a sensuous smile that stoked his masculine pride.

His body wanted to plunge into her and take his pleasure in a wild frenzy, but his heart wanted to make this first time as easy and pleasant for her as possible.

He forced himself to enter her slowly, a little at a time, giving her body a chance to adapt to him. She moved against him so that he slipped in easily.

He thought of the dance they'd briefly shared earlier, of the music and the rhythm, of moving closer and away. He moved now as if to the music, a dance that belonged to the two of them alone.

The music's tempo increased and he moved faster. She kept perfect pace, building his need little by little, extending the glory of her warmth enveloping him. A slow sensuous pleasure unlike he'd ever had before.

Anna was the first woman he'd cared enough to draw out the experience. No rushing to give the woman pleasure and take his own.

Anna made a compelling sound and he crossed the boundary between thought and sensation. His body took over and quickened the pace, building the need higher and higher.

She cried out and writhed beneath him, her climax coming in waves that pushed him over the edge. His seed exploded within her in an ecstasy of release. Together they reached the peak of sensation, the ultimate of pleasure.

And just as quickly the languor wended though him. Brent's bones seemed to melt like candle wax. He collapsed atop her and slid to the side, lying on his back, trying to make his arms and legs work again.

'No wonder,' she murmured.

'No wonder what?' he asked.

She turned her head and looked into his eyes. 'No wonder my mother wanted this.'

He caressed her cheek. 'Anna, believe me. This is more than what your mother ever had.'

To prove his point, as soon as his body recovered, he made love to her again.

And a third time, before he fell into a deep, contented sleep.

Anna rose from Brent's bed when the first peek of dawn appeared in the windows. She slipped on her chemise and gathered the rest of her clothing. With it bundled in her arms she gazed back at him.

He looked like Cal in his repose, so boyish and untroubled.

Making love with him had altered her. She felt now that a part of him would live in her for ever. For this brief time—these three brief times— they'd truly become one.

She resisted the urge to kiss him now. He might wake and that would make everything more difficult.

She rushed out of the room and ran up to her bedchamber. She dressed quickly and sat at the window to write two letters: one to Brent and one to the children.

There was no going back after this night that they had shared. No longer could she pretend she could see him briefly and act as the mere governess of his children. Brent—Egan—she was certain would understand. He, after all, faced the same situation. How could he build a marriage if he wished to bed the governess and she, him?

It was the children she grieved for the most. They would not understand. Perhaps they would never understand, even when they grew older. They would merely feel abandoned once more.

She knew, though, that the unhappiness her presence would cause would also spill over to them. Leaving was the best thing she could do.

And was the hardest.

Truth was hard, but not as difficult as living a lie. Truth opened the heavens and brought clarity. She knew now that she would some day tell Charlotte the truth about their connection. She wished she could ensure that Dory, too, would know who she was some day.

But she would never have that chance.

She'd packed a portmanteau in anticipation of travelling back to Brentmore Hall, a place she would never see again. It made leaving easier, before anyone saw her.

She tiptoed down the stairs and slipped out the front door. She was headed to the one person last night whose proposal she could accept.

She headed to Mr Yates.

Brent woke to the door opening. The room was bright with sunlight and the bed was empty next to him.

His valet stuck his head in. 'Do you wish to rise yet, m'lord?'

He felt the bed linens next to him, remembering she had slept there. Clever of her to rise early. Had she gone to her own room before anyone could take notice?

'I'll get up,' he mumbled. 'What time is it?'

'A little after ten, sir,' the man said.

Brent groaned. He had probably missed breakfast with the children.

He dressed hurriedly and went straight upstairs to the nursery. Anna and the children would have started their lessons already.

As soon as he walked in the nursery, Dory ran

up to him. 'Papa! Miss Hill is gone! She is gone! Will she come back?'

He glanced around the room. Cal sat with his head bowed and his arms wrapped around himself.

Eppy rose from a chair. 'She left some letters in her room.' She pushed past him and gestured for him to follow her. 'I left them right where they were,' she whispered. 'Her portmanteau is gone.'

He entered Anna's room and broke the seal of the one addressed to him.

He read:

Dearest Egan,
Last night with you was the loveliest time I have ever spent. It also shows me how wrong it would be for me to stay. I've struggled with this for a long time, but now I know I must make a decision. I must leave or the happiness of too many people will be impossible.

Remember, please, that I love you and the children and it breaks my heart to leave you, but it is the best thing.
Yours always, Anna

He crumpled the paper and cried aloud, 'No!'

He would not let her go. He opened the children's letter, which said only that she had to leave and that she loved them above all things.

'What do they say?' Eppy stood in the door.

'That she has left us.' He felt empty.

Eppy nodded and dabbed at her eyes with the corner of her apron. 'I was afraid she would do something like that. What will you do, m'lord?'

'Find her,' he said. 'Stay with the children, Eppy. Tell them I've gone to bring her back.'

There was only one place she could be.

He could walk the distance faster than he could have a horse or carriage ready. As it was he practically ran to the Lawtons' house.

Lord and Lady Lawton were still abed, but Charlotte agreed to see him.

He paced the drawing room until she walked in. 'Where is Anna?' he asked.

Her eyes widened. 'Is she missing? I—I know she left the ball early. Disappeared, really, but you did, too, so I thought—'

'Lady Charlotte.' He spoke in his severest voice. 'Is she here? I beg you to tell me if she is.'

'She is not here,' she cried earnestly. Her fist covered her mouth. 'Do you think she has met with an—an accident?'

'No.' Where was he to look from here? 'I think she left deliberately, but how and to where, I cannot guess.' He strode to the door. 'But I will find her.'

He walked to the hack stand nearest Cavendish Square to see if any of them had taken her somewhere. None had. He checked at various coaching inns, also to no avail. Walking back, he thought over everything she had said to him the previous night.

Grasping at straws, he decided to call upon Yates. Perhaps she had said something to Yates the previous night that would provide some clue. Yates's London town house was on George Street, not far from Hanover Square.

'Mr Yates is not here,' his manservant said. 'He went out earlier. You are welcome to wait, but he did not say when he would return.'

'Tell him Lord Brentmore wishes to see him on an urgent matter.' What more could Brent do?

He started to leave, but turned back. 'Tell me. Did a lady call upon Mr Yates this morning? A pretty young lady with auburn hair and blue eyes?'

'Why, yes, my lord,' the man said. 'She carried a portmanteau and Mr Yates left with her. He has not come back since.'

Brent felt as if a shaft had run through him.

He'd believed in Yates. Trusted him that his former betrayal had been Eunice's doing. He'd more than extended the olive branch to the man and Yates had turned around and acted the libertine at the first opportunity.

Brent's anger escalated as he walked back to his town house. How big a fool could he be?

* * *

When he opened the town-house door and stepped into the hall, Davies hurried up to him. 'Mr Yates has been waiting for you, m'lord, for almost as long as you've been gone.'

Brent strode into the drawing room. 'Why are you here, Yates?' he growled. 'What tale did you tell Anna to get her to go to you?'

Yates held up a hand. 'Wait, Brent! I can imagine what you think, but let me explain.'

Brent folded his arms across his chest. 'Explain why you took her from here? From my children?'

Yates gave him a sympathetic look. 'From you, you mean.'

Brent started to protest.

Yates shook his head. 'I could see the two of you were besotted with each other, even though you are intent on marrying another woman who does not love you. I do not know what happened last night between you and Miss Hill, but I expect you could tell me.'

Brent glared at him. 'You said *you* would explain.'

Yates nodded. 'She came to me this morning needing a place to stay. I could not have her stay with me in London, so I sent her to my estate.'

The estate near Brentmore where he had carried on his affair with Eunice.

Brent peered at him. 'To what purpose?'

Yates stepped back and lowered his voice.

'Brent, I promised you that I had reformed and that I want to atone for what I did to you. I have not changed. Last night when I saw Miss Hill so distressed, I told her I would act as her friend, if she needed one.'

Exactly what Brent had done. Offered friendship, but Brent had known there was more between them than friendship.

Yates went on. 'This morning she arrived with a portmanteau, asking for help. I suspected something had occurred between the two of you, but I did not ask and she said nothing. Only that she needed a place to stay until she could rally.' He looked Brent in the eye. 'You could reach there before dark if you left now.'

Brent looked away. 'I cannot. I have matters to attend to here.'

Chapter Nineteen

It had been a mistake for Anna to go on the long walk she'd taken, but after two days, she'd been so restless, so disconsolate, that she'd needed exercise and country air.

What she had not needed was to climb a hill only to discover it looked down upon Brentmore Hall.

She could see the archway she had passed through when first arriving at Brentmore and where Brent had kissed her. A corner of the kitchen garden was visible. Were there still peas to be picked? she wondered. Would the children plant other vegetables without her? Beyond the house were the stables and paddocks where the children had ridden their ponies and where Cal had begun to speak.

The pain of their loss brought her to her knees

and it was a long time before she could make herself rise and embark on the long walk back to Mr Yates's house, not as grand as Brentmore, but a comfortable, prosperous property.

His servants had been gracious to her. She did not know if they really believed she was the down-on-her-luck sister of an old school friend who had died in the war, but they certainly could tell merely by the shadows under her eyes that she was down on her luck.

She had not yet written letters to seek a new governess position. The idea of taking care of children other than Cal and Dory was, at present, too difficult to contemplate. Perhaps she would seek a companion position instead. Or teach in a school.

She pressed a hand to her abdomen. If she was not with child, that was. It seemed impossible to her that such a night of loving could fail to produce a child. His child. Her heart fluttered merely to think of the joy of holding his baby in her arms.

Even though she would have no way to care for the child herself.

Most of the walk back, though, she thought of Brent. Would he find happiness with Miss Rolfe? Would she indeed transfer her affections from his cousin to him?

She knew Mr Yates would tell Brent where she was. A part of her had hoped he would come for her, but that was mere reverie. He would see the logic in her leaving. He would accept it.

But no on could take away that one glorious night with him.

She crossed the field and soon would be in sight of Mr Yates's house. She walked along the road that led to the village. It was fortunate there was no chance she would encounter Brent and the children at the village. Brent would remain in London for weeks, he'd said.

From behind her she heard a horse approach, moving fast. She stepped off the road so the horse and rider could pass.

Instead, she heard her name. 'Anna!'

She turned—and saw Brent, riding his horse Luchar towards her.

Breathing, thinking, feeling became impossible. All she could do was watch him, his coattails flying behind him, his strong thighs hugging the horse's sides.

He dismounted before the horse came fully to a halt.

'Anna!' he cried again, advancing on her.

'My lord,' she managed.

He held her arms. 'What did I tell you? No more *my lord.*'

'Are—are you and the children at Brentmore?' She must be meeting him on the road by chance, exactly what she feared, being so close to Brentmore Hall.

'We are.' His expression sobered. 'I came for you, Anna.'

She glanced away. 'I cannot, my lord—Brent—*Egan*.' Her voice lowered to a whisper when she spoke his given name. 'I cannot be your governess. Not after—after making love with you. You once said it would change things. It has.'

'It has changed things for me, too, Anna.' He released her. 'May I walk with you and tell you?'

'It is no use,' she said, feeling anew the agony over their situation.

'I will tell you anyway.' He held Luchar's reins in his hand and walked beside her. 'After you left and I was searching for you, I came up with the solution to everything.'

She pressed her hand against her abdomen again. 'I cannot be your mistress.'

'I do not want you to be my mistress, Anna.' He stopped and held her face in his hand. 'I love you. I love you like my Irish grandfather used to tell me my father loved my mother. My father gave up everything for her. I am giving up worrying what other people think, worrying that my children will suffer the taunts I received, worrying that they will not be able to handle themselves in the face of it. They have been through much worse than taunts and slurs.' He made her look into her eyes. 'Do you comprehend what am I trying to say? I want to marry you.'

'Marry me!' Her heart pounded. 'A marquess cannot marry the daughter of a laundress!'

'He can. Had my parents lived, my father would have been a marquess married to the daughter of a tenant farmer.' He paused. 'Besides, you are also the daughter of an earl.'

She looked away. 'What of Miss Rolfe? And her family? You will ruin her. Her whole family will suffer.'

'I fixed that.' He grinned. 'I paid all of Rolfe's debts and I settled an amount of money and property on my cousin so generous he can marry Miss Rolfe and take on helping her brothers and sisters should they need it.'

Her eyes widened. 'That must have cost a fortune. You would give away such a fortune for me?'

He grew serious again. 'You are worth twice that.'

She felt hope growing inside her, but she must not let it flower. 'What of Miss Rolfe's reputation?'

'To marry my cousin, she was happy to be the one to cry off. Her reputation will only bear a slight tarnish. It will be forgotten in a fortnight.'

'But yours?' She was afraid to believe this. 'People are already talking of us.'

'Let them talk.' He held her again and brought her face close to his. 'I want you to be my wife. To be the mother of my children. Cal and—and—

Dory. And the babies we will have together. We will be a proper family.'

He was offering her everything she'd never dared to dream of. It meant she could share his bed every night, wake up beside him every morning, give Cal and Dory the love and security they deserved.

'What say you, Anna?' His brow creased in worry.

She broke into a smile. 'I say yes!'

He threw his arms around her and swung her around in joy. 'Come, Anna! Let us go home and tell our children the good news.'

* * * * *

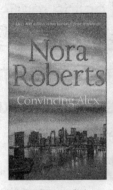